THE IMMORTAL SECRET

The Immortal Bound Series

EVERBOUND PRESS

THE
IMMORTAL
SECRET

CHRISTINA FARLEY

Published by Everbound Press

Library of Congress Control Number: 2024915649

www.ChristinaFarley.com

Cover and Interior Artwork: Trif Book Designs

Map Artwork: Veronika Wunder

ASIN: B0CP4FDCPM

ISBN (hardcover): 979-8-9864624-4-8

ISBN (paperback): 979-8-9864624-3-1

ALSO BY CHRISTINA FARLEY

The Immortal Bound Series

The Immortal Legend (Novella)

The Immortal Secret

The Immortal Heart

The Gilded Series

Gilded

Silvern

Brazen

The Dreamscape Series

The Dream Heist

The Dream Hunt

Adult Books

Fairy Tale Road

Middle Grade Books

The Princess and the Page

The Thief of Time

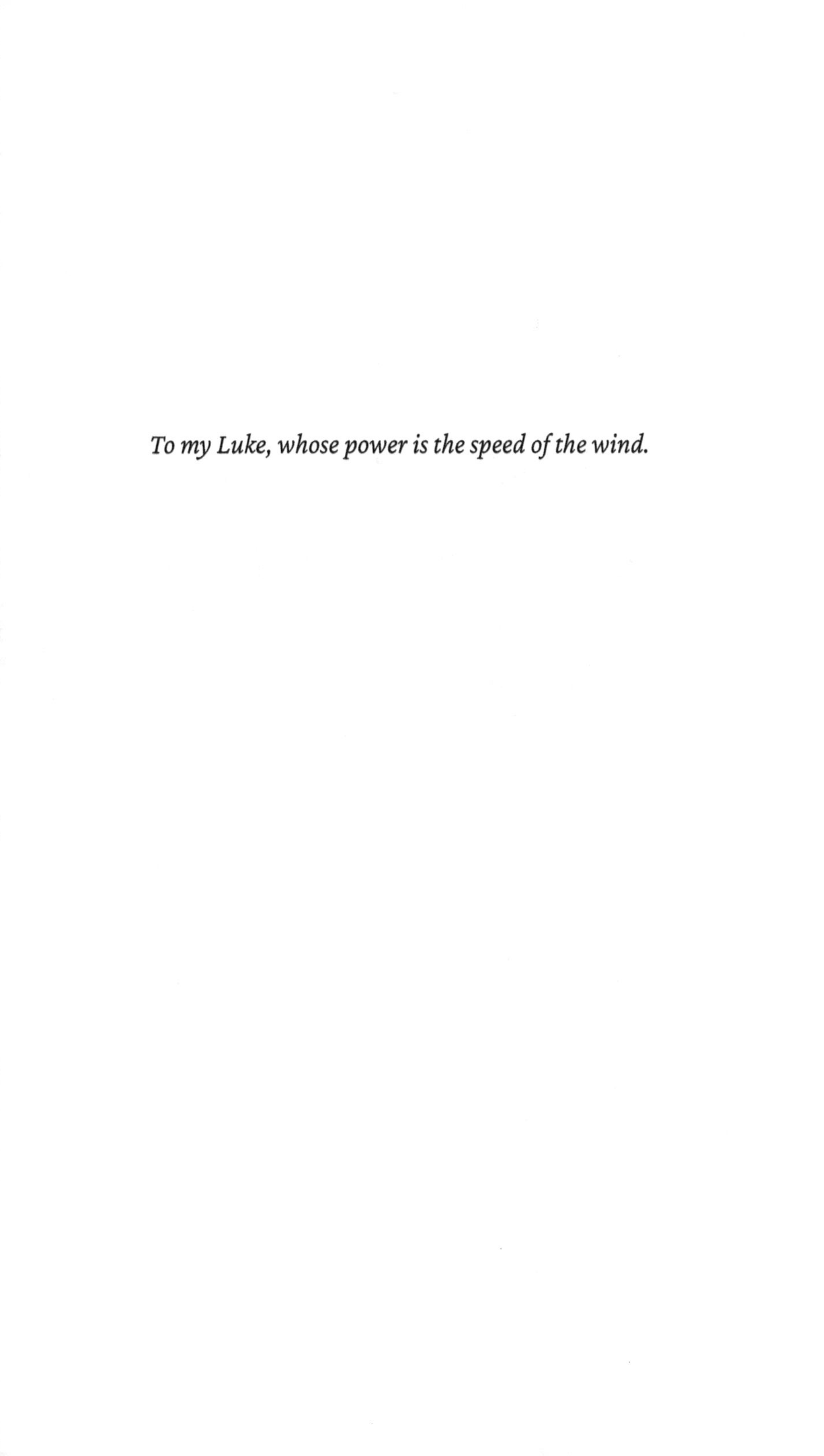

To my Luke, whose power is the speed of the wind.

The
The Northern
Landing
Hall of the Ring
Ic
West Dwelling
Wraith's
Spire
Recko
N
W
E
S

Kingdom
tica
Ice Garden
East Village
Ice Cave
Library
Ice Pillars
Midnight Academy

1
STARLIGHT, STARBRIGHT
ESTRELLA

The Midnight Kingdom, Antarctica

It is believed that starlight carries a heart's deepest wish.

And tonight, I'm desperate for mine to come true.

The midnight sun reflects off my gown, making the gossamer folds shimmer like snow as I hurry out of the palace's ice corridors and into the biting-cold night. A festive excitement hums throughout the Midnight Kingdom as lanterns are strung along the frosted trees, ice sculpture carvings are set out, and the scent of honey-baked bread wafts through the air.

A twist of anticipation courses through me, but also one of fear knowing all my people's hopes could be dashed if I fail them tonight. But the petals of the soft red rose encased in my palm soothe me as I hurry to find Dion. Even with the dome the Empress created to protect our lands and keep our existence among mortals a secret, flowers are rare here in the cold plains of Antarctica.

Which I suppose makes Dion's and my meetups even more special. When I found the rose, our secret message to meet, lying on my dresser, I was determined to see him.

Especially because late last night I finally managed to sneak into the forbidden section of the library. Buried deep in a bottom shelf, almost as if it was trying to be forgotten, I found a scroll that confirmed my suspicions. I've spent months searching for the truth, so the discovery was a sweet reward.

My feet hurry along the long row of tall ice pillars rising up on either side, leading up to the eastern gate. Since this section of our protective dome is poorly guarded, it's the perfect exit to slip out onto the snow-swept plains unnoticed.

Jagged ice-crusted mountains rise up in the distance sleeping under a midnight-blue sky as the last tendrils of sunlight cling to the land.

My heart skips. I don't have much time.

On the horizon, the outline of a mortal outpost cuts against the pale sky. According to our scouts, scientists work there, keeping themselves busy checking temperatures and digging about in the ice. Since our dome's magic keeps mortal eyes from seeing our kingdom, they have no idea we even exist.

I abandon all thoughts of mortals when my gaze lands on a lone silhouette standing beneath the icy-blue arch of a glacier. A midnight cloak billows out behind him, snapping against the arctic winds. His black, short-cut hair contrasts against the white of the world, and his dark eyes shift in my direction as if sensing my presence.

My pulse ratchets up as I close the distance between us. I duck into the icy cavern of the glacier, chills of excitement racing up my spine.

"Estrella," Dion whispers my name as if it's magic in itself. He reaches for me. "I wasn't sure if you'd have time to come."

"I'd conjure us extra time if that were my power," I say, taking his hands in mine.

Electricity pulses beneath his skin at my touch, and its power awakens inside of me. My channeling abilities may be strong, but are they strong enough to pass the test? I don't know.

And that's what terrifies me the most.

Because if I fail tonight, I'll die. My fears cut deep inside me once again and suddenly the air seems too thin to breathe.

"You're worried." Dion's brow furrows and he steps closer so he's a heartbeat away. "Don't be. I know your powers will be strong enough to pass the test."

Except I spy doubt in his eyes. He's worried, too.

"It's not just that." I gnaw at my lips. "Everyone is relying on me to be the Conduit. And if I'm not...?"

His expression softens. "Don't let the Empress get into your head. She's determined and devious enough, she'll find a solution. Just focus on what you do best: channeling. But are you *sure* you want to do this?"

"I have to." I close my eyes and clench the necklace tucked under my dress. My only remaining memento from my parents. Ever since the Sabians killed them, I've been training my whole life for this moment. "I won't fail."

And I say those words with as much conviction as I can gather.

His palms tenderly cup my face and his thumb runs along my lips, smoothing out the worry biting them. I shiver under his touch, the need to be with him coursing through me.

The winds kick up and snow flits about, snapping up my dress and hair. We have only moments left.

"There's something else," I say. "I found something in the forbidden section of the library."

This deepens his frown. "What did you find?"

A bell tolls, signaling my ceremony is about to begin.

"A secret that has either been forgotten or purposely hidden. Tonight after I pass my test, I'll show you."

I lift up on my toes until my lips find his. Our kiss is as perfect as it is every time our lips touch, hopeful and passionate like the hungry winds shifting and howling around us. My hands reach up and run through his hair as our kiss deepens, half-passion, half-desperation. He tastes like power and it sets my blood on fire.

I don't want to leave him.

Slowly, I skim my hands down his face and chest, memorizing every inch of him. Because what if things go wrong? From my studies, I know there are too many possibilities and ways to fail.

I pull away, wishing this ache in the pit of my stomach would vanish.

"Everything will be fine," he says as if reading my thoughts. "You'll be amazing."

Except what if it's not? What if *I'm* not?

"I've got to go," I say.

"Don't doubt yourself. You were born for this."

My words cling to the back of my throat, unable to escape so I just nod, desperate to believe him.

I step away, but our hands don't let go, our fingers clinging to one another for a final moment. Another step and then our hands fall away, allowing cold air to swoop between us. Leaving him is a sharp knife, cutting and painful.

And then I'm hurrying once again across the barren plain back to the safety of the ice kingdom. But when I slip back through the gates, I realize my hands are empty.

Somewhere along the way, I lost my rose.

2

I WISH I MAY, I WISH I MIGHT
ESTRELLA

The Midnight Kingdom, Antarctica

The Overlords enter the Hall of the Ring, filing in one by one, the silence as thick as the mist swirling across the stone pillars. I trail in their wake, my silver gown skimming across the ice floor. I lift my chin higher, determined no one sees the fear shuddering through my veins, threatening to send me buckling to my knees.

This is my moment. My one and only chance to prove my worth. And I will not fail.

The Overlords' faces are unreadable, veiled beneath silver robes as they circle the Ring of Eternity. The moon-colored stone is breathtaking, stretching nearly thirty feet high. In the torchlight, the surface glimmers as if it's been drenched in diamonds.

I've only seen pictures of it during my studies, but none come close to it in real life. The Ring of Eternity transports the Conduit into the World of Between. It is there that we immortals gain our power, our visik. Without it, we are nothing.

Nothing but human.

The only immortal with the ability to wield the Ring's power is the Conduit. In a few short moments, I'm about to find out if I am that person.

"We have waited many years to renew our powers," the Empress says, her sharp voice echoing against the stone. She's also wearing a silver robe, but her crystal crown signifies her rank above the rest of us. "Tonight, should we gain a new Conduit, it will be the beginning of a new era for the Nazco, and we will finally be able to crush those Sabian dogs into submission.

"Estrella," the Empress continues. "Are you prepared to take the test?"

"I am willing," I say.

"Chain her," the Empress says.

One of the Overlords snaps a chain around my ankle to ensure I don't get lost within the Ring. According to my instructor, many prospects over the centuries have found themselves lost in the World of Between.

"Now take your place on the dais," she says.

"Yes, Your Majesty." I bow and then mount the stone steps, the chain rattling in my wake. Except I hesitate at the last step and glance down at my hands, pale and trembling in the torchlight. I squeeze them into fists, reminding myself that I am a Nazco.

Maybe powerful enough to become our people's next Conduit.

I must always remember that.

The moment I step onto the dais, a rumble fills the hall. The ceiling splits open at its center and the sides slide down until the ceiling sinks into the ground, exposing the hall to the night sky with the glacial-white barren land spread out on all sides as if grasping for eternity. Chills slither down my arms as I gaze at its beauty.

Wind rushes over me, tasting of snow and ice, and snuffs out the torches with its breath. Starlight glitters across the Ring, illuminating it in a wintry glow.

The Ring glows brighter and brighter as if it were consuming the starlight. Then, as if pulled by a magnetic force, the intensity multiplies, and I suck in a gasp as the Ring begins to spin, sparkling. It's terrifying, and yet, thrilling to watch. My knees tremble as the Ring spins faster, a whirling and churning snowstorm, until a rainbow of color streaks through its center like a whirlpool.

My heart skitters because somewhere deep inside me I hear it whispering to me, tales of magic, old as time itself.

"It's beautiful," I whisper.

"It is time," the Empress announces. "Prepare yourself, Estrella."

Every fiber inside of me wants to turn and run from this test. If only my heart would stop pounding and my knees would unlock from their icy stance, I might have the courage to take the first step. Except without a Conduit, everyone's powers will wane while the Sabians only grow stronger through the power of their own Conduit.

Four years ago when my parents were murdered by the

Sabians, the headmistress of our academy told me she thought my channeling abilities might be strong enough to be our next Conduit.

That hope got me out of bed each morning.

That hope drove me to endure the grueling training.

Because if I were the Conduit, I'd have the power to avenge my parents' death.

Except fear still claws at my throat. There are stories of Ralco, who tested thirty years ago. He's never been seen again after he entered the Hall of the Ring.

And then there was Nefertari, who tested five years ago. The rumor was her body crumbled to ashes before she even entered the World of Between.

Quadril, the head Overlord, lifts the lute and begins playing a haunting song that harmonizes with the polar winds swirling around me.

Instantly, the pull of the Ring tugs at my chest. Gritting my teeth, I face its center and peer within its depths, a pool of water, swirling with a rainbow of colors.

"Touch the Ring of Eternity." The Empress's voice is soft but laced with steel.

There isn't one Nazco who hasn't experienced the Empress's power, and more importantly, the quickness of her anger when she nearly wiped out a human. It's fear mixed with hope that pushes me to stretch out my hand and slip my fingertips into the Ring's shimmering surface.

Fire pulses through my veins, hot and fierce, unlike anything I've experienced. It surges through my body with the viciousness of a raging animal. I scream in agony. My knees collapse beneath me, but the Ring's power holds me airborne. It's as if the Ring is searching my very being, deciding if I'm worthy.

Will this be my end? As quick as Ralco and Nefertari?

The pain morphs into a rushing thrill as the fire trails through every part of me down to my very core. Then it burns back out through my fingers, returning into the Ring.

I'm still alive! I think numbly, still airborne.

But the Ring is not finished with me yet. The fire meshes together with the Ring's colors, twisting and pulling until they form an image.

A forest.

I squint at the picture and then gasp. The wind is shifting through the pines. And that's when I understand. It's not an image. It's real.

The World of Between.

"A forest?" the Empress says, her tone eager, excited. "How curious."

The Empress and the Overloads all are seeing what I see. The thought is slightly unnerving, but there isn't time to consider this.

A force wraps itself around me once again, this time, grabbing hold so strongly, I can't even breathe. Then I'm sucked inside the Ring's core, my scream drowned by the wind.

Even though I received lessons over the last few years, nothing could possibly prepare me for this. My body flies through a rainbow of colors, and then with a thud, I'm dropped into a forest grove. The impact punches the air out of my lungs.

I roll across the ground, my gown tangling around my legs and arms. Finally, I manage to stand.

This place is unlike anything I've ever seen. Gnarled trees as tall as a bird could fly rise up around me while their roots tangle in a dance. Sunlight streams in through the branches, radiating a rich, warm glow through my body, so foreign from the bitter cold of home.

A gleam in the distance catches my attention and my hands burn to touch it, feel it. Is this the power source of our visik? Or is it a trick of this land, luring me into its folds so I'll forever be lost?

Doubt tickles in the back of my brain. Something isn't right, but I don't know what.

My training kicks in, reminding me to follow the pull of the Ring. I break into a run, the chain wrapped around my ankle feeling as light as a vine. I leap over logs and race into the foliage, the branches bending to allow me entrance. My feet fly across the ground at a speed faster than I've ever been able to run in real life.

In this place, I'm powerful.

Unstoppable.

I stumble upon a cliff edge, jutting out like a perch. Pink tendrils of clouds drift around me. When I look down, the valley falls below, a lifetime away. Across the valley, lies a mountain range, and tucked within snow-capped peaks, rises a castle.

A shadow materializes, blocking my path. "No!" it screams. "This is not your way."

Confused, I try to find a way around the shadow. Perhaps overcoming it is my test. But it only grows larger until the forest transforms from vibrant greens and rich browns to muted grays. Frantic, I spin around and take off running down another forest path, trying to focus on the tug of the Ring.

I don't know how much time the Empress will give me but running around this forest like I'm lost will hardly please her.

A voice calls out from behind me. "Come back, Estrella. Your place is with us!" It's the Empress.

I spin around, my eyes darting through the trees, searching for the Empress. Why does she want me to go back? Is it because I failed?

Sweat trickles down my back. I can't ignore the pull of the Ring. It's still tugging at me, calling me deeper into the forest. What am I supposed to do?

Go back or follow the Ring?

I can't fail.

I won't fail.

Suddenly a young man, not much older than me, emerges from the tree line and the forest around him brightens. I eye him. Could he be a lost Conduit? Or a vision? My instructor warned me of tales of Conduits who see dangerous and strange things within the Ring.

His light, wavy hair falls into his eyes, hanging almost to his shoulders. He's wearing a solid red cloak with a twisted golden clasp holding it in place and black pants tucked into riding boots.

He freezes mid-stride when he sees me, as if he has spotted a wild bear that's about to attack him.

His eyes darken and his palm moves to his hip, clasping the hilt of a sword as if ready to unsheathe it. "Who are you?"

"I—" my voice falters. "I followed the Ring. It took me here. To you?"

I wait, my palms tingling and pulse thundering, expecting him to attack. Which would be bad since I haven't come into my powers.

"What sort of magic is this?" he asks. His stance loosens and he releases his hand from his sword.

His body shimmers and he disappears as if he never was there in the first place.

In his place stands a pedestal where a ball of fire burns. I reach out and the flames hungrily leap into my palm.

My heart soars. I did it! I claimed the visik power source within the Ring.

Except, the flame is red. It should be blue, right?

Nazco blue.

The shadows scream and a cold darkness grips me, pulling on my ankle and yanking me backward. I cry out in surprise as the forest is ripped away from me.

My body drags across the ground, the chain rattling through the forest. In moments, I'm lying on the cold dais, back in the Hall of the Ring in the Midnight Kingdom. I gasp for air, choking and coughing while my mind reels, trying to figure out what just happened.

I look at my hands. The fire is no longer red, but a shimmering blue ball of fire.

Pride and joy rush through me, but also relief. I must have imagined the red fire. Or maybe it changed once I left the Ring.

The Empress remains stoic, cold as ice, and the Overloads keep hidden beneath the folds of their black robes.

I suppose I expected jubilation and excitement. But maybe it's just because my task is not completed.

Quickly, I climb to my feet and make my way down the stone steps toward the massive doors of the Ice Palace. They burst open, flooding me with lantern light.

The crowd cheers upon seeing me holding the visik. Ice sparklers are released and everyone begins hugging each other as I stride proudly into the ballroom, holding the fireball in my palms. The kingdom has waited for this moment a long time. Tonight there will be a celebration.

Icicles glisten from the ceiling, icy sculptures gleam around the room, and crystal glasses are raised in my honor. My pulse throbs with joy as I stride confidently up to the pedestal in the center of the room.

I place the fireball onto the pedestal. The stone bursts to life in sparkles and then, like a bolt of lightning, the fire sinks into the pedestal and splinters across the floor in streaks of blue.

Its power fills the room, seeping into each of our souls, fusing with the walls, and filling bodies with renewed power.

Dion pulls me into his arms, swirling me in a circle.

"I did it!" I say. "The Ring of Eternity accepted me."

"I'm so proud—" But his words are cut short as darkness swoops into the ballroom.

Everyone falls silent as the Wraiths enter. They surround the perimeter of the room, their black cloaks floating eerily in a breeze of their own creation. These creatures were created a long time ago to protect us. But sometimes, they feel more like they're keeping us in check.

Their wings are half-lifted as if ready to fly at something and strike. I've never seen so many of them at one time.

"How dare you!" Quadril growls, marching through the doors I had only moments ago triumphantly entered.

He slaps me across the face, so hard I fall to the ground.

"What are you doing?" Dion demands, shoving himself between Quadril and me.

"Move," Quadril growls at Dion. "Or pay for your insubordination."

The Empress glides to Quadril's side, her mouth pinched tight. Horrifyingly silent.

I gape at the two in shock and clamber to my feet, pushing Dion behind me. The power of the Ring still hums through my body, giving me the confidence to stand up to the two most powerful immortals in the Midnight Kingdom.

"I don't understand," I say. "The Ring accepted me."

I look about the room at my fellow Nazco. The ones who only moments ago cheered for me as I infused their bodies with power.

But no one moves. The celebration is forgotten.

"I did nothing wrong," I say.

"Nothing?" Quadril leers. "You must die for treason."

Three Wraiths descend upon me and I can see their hideous faces beneath their hoods. Beaks for noses. Streaks of red in their eyes.

A rock forms in the pit of my stomach. Somehow I've failed.

"No!" I scream as two Wraiths grab my arms. "This is a mistake. Just tell me what I did wrong. I'll fix it. Please give me a second chance!"

Undaunted, the third moves before me and raises a jagged dagger into the air. Fear screams through my mind. It's going to behead me! That's the only way to make sure an immortal dies.

Symbols writhe on its blade, promising death. Terror curdles, and I fight against the Wraiths' hold, kicking and screaming.

"Stop!" Dion kneels before the Empress. "This is wrong. She just saved us all from losing our powers."

"What is this?" The Empress's glittery eyebrows rise as she stares at Dion, holding her hand up. The Wraith's knife freezes.

"We saw it with our own eyes," Quadril says. "She *will* betray us. She must die."

"What?" My mind whirls. "No. That isn't true."

"If I hadn't pulled you back with the chain," the Empress says, "I don't know what choice you would've made."

"The red fire," Quadril spats. "It was Sabian fire."

My heart stutters. The fire I touched in the Ring had been red, hadn't it? But when I left the Ring, it turned blue. Does that make me a traitor?

"I cannot live if her soul is gone." Dion's words cut through my thoughts. "Perhaps there's another way."

"There is no other way," Quadril snaps. "She's already been given a second chance."

"Then make her mortal," Dion says.

I jerk my head up. "Mortal? No!"

My two best friends were excommunicated and made mortal by having their memories wiped. I promised to find them, but now my promise will mean nothing.

"What an idea." The Empress taps her lips thoughtfully.

"You do know, if she were to become a mortal, she wouldn't remember you."

"I'd rather that than her death."

My heart tears at his words. "No. There must be another way."

Nodding, the Empress lifts her hands into the air. "So be it."

Quadril steps between the Empress and me. "It's too risky," he whispers.

"Hardly. Once her memory is wiped, she'll be harmless." A smile creeps across her white lips. "I know the perfect place to send her."

"No!" I scream, thrashing against the Wraiths' hold. How can I avenge my parent's death? Everything I've worked for and found, everything I've been training for will be lost.

Dion leans in close. "I will find you," he says into my ear. "I promise."

"The secret I was telling you about," I whisper. "Go to—"

But he's dragged away before I can finish.

The Empress stretches out her scepter. A flash of blue light hits my forehead and piercing pain wracks through my mind.

The darkness sweeps over me, empty and colder than ice.

3

HAVE THE WISH I WISH TONIGHT

ESTRELLA

Florida

Five days. That's all I know. All I remember.

Ever since I woke up in the hospital bed, I have moments where a strong rage rattles against my bones. It's as if my mind is furious at me for forgetting my former life. And then there are other times where I just feel... nothing.

I can't decide which is worse.

I mean, it doesn't hurt to forget. I guess a part of me thinks I deserve to feel some sort of pain after the accident. It's not fair that both of my parents were killed while I escaped without a scratch.

I gaze out the window of the car, wishing I could ignore my caseworker, Ms. Blaire, and her constant, upbeat chatter.

Instead, I finger the patient wristband I refused to take off when we left the hospital an hour ago.

"I know this is hard for you, Estrella," Ms. Blaire says. "But don't worry. Where you're going will be a far better situation. New friends, plenty of food, and comfortable lodging. You're going to *love* your new life."

A lump forms in my stomach at the words, *new life*. What if I don't want a new life?

"I was hoping I could go back to my home. Maybe seeing it could jog some memories for me."

"I considered that, too, so I took some photos of your house for you." She releases the steering wheel with one hand and pulls a stack of photos from a folder resting between us. "But the place is a bit of a—"

She presses her lips together as she passes me the photos.

It's of a trailer home that once was white, but now the sides are charcoal black. The roof hugs the ground, caved in, while the bushes are scorched. Seriously, the whole place looks like a forgotten barbeque. I swallow hard at the destruction, but I can't stop myself from gazing hungrily at the images, craving for something to jog my memory.

Except there are none. I frown, jamming the photos back into the envelope. "I must have relatives somewhere," I press. We've already been over this at the hospital, but I refuse to give up. "Maybe if we wait a little longer, a long-lost aunt will show up."

"I'm sorry, but we couldn't find any living relatives." Her brown eyes soften with concern. "Are you sure you don't want to cut off that hospital bracelet? I've got scissors in my purse."

"No." I press my wrist against my chest.

I don't want to part with the ridiculous piece of plastic. There's something familiar about it in this unfamiliar life. Besides, it's the only possession I truly remember as mine.

I run my thumb across my fingernails, wondering if I like to wear nail polish and what color I'd choose. Do I have any friends who are missing me right now? What's my favorite food?

I shake my head because these questions are going to drive me crazy. I turn on the radio instead. Except, as soon as the music blares through the car, I'm back at the needing to know.

What kind of music do I like?

Did I even like music?

I flick through the different stations as if they will give me answers. Mrs. Blaire sighs beside me, gripping the steering wheel tighter. "Why not just pick one?"

She's obviously frustrated, but I'm betting not as much as I am.

And then soft, lilting music breaks through the chaos in my mind. My hand freezes on the radio nob. I know this song. A fuzzy image solidifies in my mind.

Two hands clasped. Laughter. And then warmth as I'm drawn into an embrace.

Lips brush across mine, full of promises. Full of...

Pain sears my head, sharp as a knife. I cry out, pressing my fingers to my temples.

Mrs. Blaire turns the music off.

"There, there," she soothes, patting me awkwardly on the shoulder. "Maybe no music for a while."

I lean against the back of the seat, breathing in and out

like the doctor taught me until the pain subsides and I'm finally able to open my eyes again.

"You took your medication before you left, right?"

I think about the pills tucked away in my bag and nod.

"Good. Just be sure to not miss a dose," she warns. "The headaches will get worse without it."

We must be getting closer to the ocean. The ground has flattened out and the deep-blue sky stretches out like it's getting ready for a long nap. Palms wave at us in greeting and the hot sun heats my skin even though it's late in the day.

Finally, Ms. Blaire turns off the main road, and we wind through a series of streets until she pulls onto a sand road. It dead-ends at a large iron gate planted in the middle of the Florida jungle. Moss dangles over the gate's spikes and thick brush threatens to climb up along the entrance's brick pillars.

I take in the forest of Spanish moss-covered cypresses, sycamores, and palms that rise up behind the entrance and shiver in apprehension.

My fingers hover over the door handle. I don't know why, but every part of me screams, "Jump out of the car! Run!"

But that's silly. It's not like this place is dangerous.

Sure, the tops of the pillars are a little creepy with the massive bird-man statues perched on top like they're guarding the premises. The creatures' beaks are stretched wide open, making them look almost alive.

Mrs. Blaire's fingers drum the steering wheel as she impatiently waits for the gate to open. But I'm frozen in place because it's as if the statue's stone eyes transform into pools of inky liquid. Boring into mine.

Spider chills skitter over my skin, and I throw open my car door, ready to escape.

"Estrella!" Mrs. Blaire grabs my arm, pulling me back into my seat. "What are you doing?"

I blink, and my illusions vanish.

Outside, the cicadas chirp and the stone statues are just that. Stone statues.

Great. I'm proving to myself by the second that I should've been admitted into the psychiatric ward.

I shut my car door and clasp my hands together, watching the gate finally creak open. Still, it's a relief when we pass through, away from the stone sentries.

Massive oak trees arch over us as we bump along down the narrow sand-packed lane, blocking out the last remaining light of the day.

"What kind of place is this?" I ask, trying to push down my apprehension.

"Nadia's Home for Girls is a place of refuge for girls just like you who have lost their memories," Ms. Blaire says. "You won't ever get your memories back, but this place will help you start a new life. The best part is even after you graduate from high school, you can stay here as long as you wish."

The words high school send another arrow of worry through me. According to Ms. Blaire, I'm a senior.

"I still don't know how I'm supposed to complete my classes since I've lost my memory."

"Don't stress yourself out, sweetie." Mrs. Blair pats my

hand. "That's what's so special about Nadia's. The home gives you a fresh start. No memories required."

We're interrupted when the road makes a soft turn, and I'm met with the full view of Nadia's home—or should I say complex?

The main building is a large three-story house with gables and tiny balconies jutting off randomly around the building. A wind-bitten porch runs its perimeter cluttered with rocking chairs and small tables. Wind chimes sway from the porch ceiling.

But I find the house's most striking element to be the seashell-white lighthouse that rises from its center. Even though it's still daytime, light glitters from inside its glass top.

It's a place the rest of the world forgot.

"Nadia is a lighthouse keeper?" I ask, intrigued.

"In a way." Mrs. Blaire shrugs. "She bought this old lighthouse a while back and renovated it. Come along and let's get you inside."

I'm not sure what I was expecting, but this wasn't it. Maybe living here won't be so bad. Maybe Ms. Blaire was right.

I slide out of the car. Instantly, I'm engulfed in the scent of sea and sand as a rush of wind swirls around me, snapping my long blonde hair against my cheeks. I lug my suitcase up the worn steps toward a blue door etched with strange-looking symbols.

There's something about the symbols that prickles the back of my mind. I reach out and swipe my fingers across them.

Ms. Blaire huffs up the steps and waves at the bell. "Go ahead. Do the honors."

The breeze kicks up again, sending the wind chimes swaying. They create a haunting melody, and for a brief moment, I almost forget what I'm doing.

My eyes drift to the sign by the door that reads, *Let go of your past and seize your future!*

I lick my lips and push the button.

The door swings open, revealing a woman with a lined face and graying hair tied up into a tight bun. She's wearing a flowered shirt, navy shorts, and sandals. Her face bursts into a smile the moment she sees me.

"Oh!" The lady clasps her hands together. "This must be Estrella. How exciting. We've all been waiting for you."

I shift uncomfortably. Who is 'we' and why are they waiting for me?

"Greetings, Nadia," Ms. Blaire says. "Good to see you again. And yes, this is Estrella. She's very excited to be here."

I am?

"How wonderful." Nadia opens the door wider, waving me inside. "Please come in and meet everyone. You came at the perfect time, really. You're just in time for tea!"

I nod, trying to smile.

Except I can't shake that deep sense of dread. As if going inside is a very bad idea.

But I clench my suitcase tighter and step inside.

4

MIRROR ON THE WALL, WHO'S THE FIERCEST OF US ALL?

DION

The Midnight Kingdom, Antarctica

I rub my eyes and crumble into my chair. The computers blink and shift before me, scanning image after image, but she's nowhere to be found. I've scoured every wretched transmitter, even snuck into the Deportment Office and ransacked their records, but there isn't a single notation or record of her whereabouts.

I stare at the map of South and North America where our Nazco strongholds are located. It's cluttered with pins that indicate the locations I've investigated. The only other option is to visit every Nazco facility. It would take a lifetime.

She's vanished.

I've lost her.

It's the first time I've acknowledged that thought. It already feels like an eternity since I last held her in my arms. Looked into her Arctic blue eyes. Kissed her soft lips. Panic rumbles through my chest and I can't hold back my fury anymore. I shove the papers, tablets, and frames off my desk. They tumble and crash to the floor, shattering. The sound brings me momentary comfort and I stalk the room, destroying everything within my grasp.

I will not give up. She still has time! I tell myself this over and over like a war cry.

A knock interrupts my furious thoughts and I stiffen.

"Have you not read the indicator?" I shout at the door. "It says do not disturb!"

In response, the thin frosty glass door's lock unclicks and whooshes open. In the Midnight Kingdom, there is only one person who has the power to enter an abode without permission. And considering the guards at my door would never let anyone through without the Empress's permission, I'm hardly in the mood to speak.

I snarl as Chandra strolls into the room, her long, shiny black hair swaying as she walks. She's wearing a black jumpsuit and her usual bright red lipstick.

"Hello, Dion." Her voice purrs despite my glare, but her smile falters just a little once she scans my quarters. Her eyebrows lift in shock at the carnage.

"Working for the Empress now?" I ask.

"We all work for the Empress." She rolls her eyes. "Don't act like you don't as well."

"Maybe things have changed." I cross my arms and

clench my jaw. "I can't live under the Empress's rule after what she did to Estrella."

"Be careful. Those words are blasphemous."

"I'm already imprisoned in my own quarters." And the Empress took away the only thing worth living for.

"Your obsession with that girl is going to get you killed," Chandra says, staring at my pinboard with a frown. "The Empress sent me to bring you to her."

I turn around and stare out through the window at the ice plain. My rooms are located above the kingdom's stone walls so I have a great view of the barren plain. Well, barren except for a group of tourists taking pictures of the penguin colony just outside of our kingdom's protective dome. "Tell her I'm very busy."

"You can't sit in here and mope forever."

"Mope?" I scoff. More like rage. Not that I'm going to let Chandra know. "I can do whatever I wish."

"You should just come with me peacefully, Dion. Why do you have to make everything so difficult?"

I clench my fists, electricity sizzling through them, eager to escape and find a mark.

Chandra huffs, rolling her eyes. "Fine. Have it your way then."

She snaps her fingers and three guards barrel their way into my quarters, sidestepping over the mess. They wear the white uniform of the Empress, shimmery pants overlaid with a purple tunic bearing the icy ruler's snowflake emblem.

The Royal Guard.

"Dion, the Empress requests your presence." It's Viamire, the head guard, with his ridiculous goatee and hair slicked back with too much grease. He clasps his hands behind his back and smiles triumphantly at me.

Blistering stars. He knows how to test me.

I summon my composure and lift my chin. But it's rather difficult to be unflustered and regal when my quarters indicate my unbridled rage. He nods to the two other guards who approach me warily. I don't blame them. I've got powers they could only dream of.

"Please refrain from resistance," Viamire says loftily.

"Such an honor," I quip as I hold out my wrists. "To grace her majesty's presence."

"Don't be ridiculous, Viamire," Chandra snaps. "There's no reason for security bracelets."

"Can never be too careful." Viamire grunts and his jaw ticks as he assesses me. The two guards flank my either side and slap bracelets onto my wrists. They glow icy blue, indicating their stun ability. Serenely, I fold my hands together before me.

"You may escort me now," I say, smirking.

Chandra chuckles under her breath while Viamire bristles.

"I am the one who decides when we leave your abode," Viamire says. "Not you."

"If you say so." I give a careless shrug.

Viamire spins on his heels and parades out, snapping his long purple robe as he walks. I chuckle and follow, stepping purposely on a broken vase and grinding the pottery shards against the marble floor with my boots. It helps ease the tension in my muscles.

We march down the silver-carpeted hallway. The lilting music meant to calm us only jabs at my nerves. Through the paned-glass windows, I watch snow flitting down, mounding onto the ground around the city like piles of diamonds. There once was a time when I'd stare at the Empress's beautiful creation in awe, wondering how one could be so powerful as to create this kingdom of ice, but those days are long gone.

Now it's just another reminder of the perfect cage she has built for us on the cold plains of Antarctica.

We are all held tightly in her stony, arctic grasp.

I'm not precisely sure why the Empress has called for me, but one thing I do know is it can't be good.

Soon, we exit the buildings and come to a long bridge where the Empress's ice palace stretches out before us. It's the startling epitome of pure magic along with a constant reminder of her power. The palace is built on a pinnacle of ice rock, completely surrounded on all sides by a plunge into a thousand-foot drop. Spires twist in silvers and blues, their tips spearing to the sky. Beams of light wash the palace in an iridescent glow, sparkling and glistening.

As we cross the ice bridge. I take measured steps. One slip would send me flying over the edge into the abyss below. Blue torches flicker on either side of us, leading toward two massive silver doors imprinted with the Nazco snowflake emblem.

The doors swing open and Viamire steps aside, jerking his head to the left as if to indicate for me to go without him.

Chandra falls in line with Viamire, apparently staying behind as well. "Good luck," she says. "You're going to need it."

"Too petrified to come along, are you?" I egg them on, even though I know they aren't allowed to enter. "Not to worry, I'll be sure to tell the Empress of your inadequacies."

Chandra glowers darkly at me while Viamire starts to stutter out a response, but I've already turned from them to focus on the long icy hall stretched out before me, more blue torches casting shadowy light. The ceiling arches above my head, engraved with battles of victories past, but otherwise, the palace is silent as a tomb.

Even with all my bravado, I'm terrified. After all, only a fool would leap happily into the Empress's lair. Viamire touches a button on his watch and a sharp prickling jabs me in the wrist before shooting through my entire core. I clench my fists and stiffen against the pain, making sure to glare at him over my shoulder.

Then girding up my courage, I stride down the ice hall, my fate at the mercy of my queen.

5

WE'RE ALL LOST HERE.
YOU'LL FIT RIGHT IN

ESTRELLA

Florida

"Come along into the tearoom," Nadia says, eagerly directing me into a tile-floored hall with a wood-paneled ceiling above. When we come to an arched doorway, Nadia announces, "She's here! The newest member of our group. Estrella, say hello to your new family."

Ten girls about my age sit in an assortment of white-painted chairs, a gold upholstered couch, and its matching loveseat. They're each holding a teacup on their laps. Most look friendly, giving me waves or smiles, some just stare off into space, while one with dark, short hair narrows her eyes at me as if I'm not welcome.

"Hi." I manage a tentative wave.

"Well, I'll be running along now," Ms. Blaire, my case-worker, tells me. "Estrella, I'll be calling in a few days, and then I'll see you in two weeks for a check-up."

"She'll be fine," Nadia said. "We always are."

"I do hope so." There's a touch of worry in Mrs. Blaire's tone. But then she turns to me, squeezes my hands, and leaves. I stare down the hall at the closing door, feeling more lost than I did when I left the hospital.

"I'm so pleased you arrived in time for tea." Nadia takes my suitcase and sets it by the wall. "Please find a seat. You must be parched."

My feet remain rooted in place. I don't remember anything about my past, but I know I've never seen a place quite like this.

Hanging from the ceiling are mini chandeliers, each a different color like a rainbow dripping from above, spilling colorful light across the room. A piano rests in the far corner of the room and a girl with long sandy-white hair and dark brown skin sits on its bench, not playing, just staring at the sheet music. In the center of the circle is a low table with a tea set and a platter of mini cakes dusted with sugar.

"Would you like some key lime cake?" one of the girls asks in a soft, wispy voice. She's got dark hair, twisted into tons of tiny braids. "It's so yummy."

"I'd like that," I say. "Thank you."

The girl scoops a slice onto a plate and brings it to me. "I'm Tiffany by the way."

"It's nice to meet you," I say.

As I take the plate, a flash of orange registers in my peripheral vision. It's a girl bouncing her way into the room with pumpkin-colored hair. She's wearing an army-green tank shirt and a frilly yellow skirt with black tights. One glance at her is equivalent to the energy level of a burst faucet. Her green eyes sparkle when she spots me.

"You must be the one Nadia's been telling us about," she says. "I'm Lexi." Then she turns to Nadia. "Sorry I'm late to tea. Homework is killing me this year."

Nadia presses on a smile as if she's slightly annoyed by Lexi's tardiness.

"Come, you can sit next to me." Lexi takes my free hand and drags me to the couch, forcing the blonde-haired girl sitting there to shift off to the side so I can sit between her and Lexi. The girl doesn't look my way, instead just fiddles with her spoon.

I settle my plate on my lap while Lexi helps herself to cake of her own. Meanwhile, Nadia comes over and pours two cups of tea, and hands them to Lexi and me.

"And now there are twelve," Nadia says with a cheerful sigh and settles into a wingback chair, draping her arms over its thick armrests. "Estrella, every evening after dinner, we meet here for teatime. During this hour, we discuss life skills to help each of you acclimate to your new lives."

"Like it ever helps," the dark-haired girl mutters, frowning.

"Now, Mara," Nadia says. "Let's focus on positivity. How are we supposed to grow in our new lives without that?" Mara shrugs, pulls out a book, and starts reading. Nadia clears her throat, focusing back on me. "How's the tea, Estrella?"

Quickly, I take a sip. It's sweet as honey. "Delicious."

"I'm glad you like it. Truly, I'm sorry about what happened with your parents, but our motto here is to let go of the past and live for your future. To have a bright future, you must put aside all thoughts of what was and focus on who you can become."

Honestly, I'm just trying to get through one day at a time, but I say, "That makes sense."

"Lovely." Nadia smiles. "Now perhaps we shall start with today's lesson?"

"Do we have a choice?" Mara mutters.

"I have an idea for today's lesson topic." Tiffany raises her hand. "At school, one of the girls in my class was talking about a sale at the mall. You could give us some tips."

"What exactly is a mall?" I have a vague image in my mind of what one is, but I can't really grab a hold of it.

"The mall?" Nadia brightens and looks about our group. "Who here can tell Estrella what the mall is?"

Lexi pipes up. "It's a place to shop for things like clothing or jewelry. We haven't been to one in ages."

"That might be a great option for our next field trip," Nadia says.

She begins explaining what we might see or expect at a mall. Meanwhile, the girl beside me takes the fork off my plate and quickly tucks it into her pocket. I'm about to ask her why she took my fork, but she smiles at me, pressing a finger to her lips with a "Shhh."

I look at Lexi to see if she noticed my fork stealer, but she's busy secretly pouring tea into the plant beside the couch. When she notices me watching, she winks and then focuses back on Nadia.

By the time our lesson on the mall is finished, I'm feeling even more overwhelmed than I did leaving the hospital. Too many people, too much information.

"Now girls," Nadia says. "Finish up your tea and then you have an hour before lights out. Those of you going to school, make sure you get a good night's rest."

Suddenly the girl at the piano plays a single note that clangs through the room, jarring all of us. I spill tea over my jeans. I take a napkin and blot at the spill, glad that no one seemed to notice my clumsiness.

Nadia presses a hand to her forehead, clearly flustered. "Thank you, Min, for that lovely song," she tells the piano girl. "Now let's clean up, ladies."

"I have a feeling we're going to be friends," Lexi tells me, taking my tea and setting it on the tray before I have the chance to finish it. "Very good friends."

"I'd like that." And oddly, it's true. There's something about her. It's as if she gets me even before I even get myself.

The girls start rising from their seats, pushing the chairs back against the wall. My fork snatcher darts her eyes about the room and tucks a few more utensils into her pockets. I find one spoon she missed and slip it secretly into her palm.

She tucks it into the back pocket of her jeans, a slight smile playing on her lips even though she doesn't look at me.

Sure, a part of me feels completely hollowed out, but in the last hour, another part feels connected to this place and these girls. They're dealing with the same memory issues I am and knowing that makes me feel a little less alone.

"Are you ready to see your room?" Nadia asks, coming over to me. Her face looks a little strained and I wonder if she worries about each of us.

The thought of a room of my own perks me up. "That would be great."

"See you in the morning," Lexi says. "You're going to school right?"

The thought of a new place, new people, new situations makes my stomach twist.

"You can wait a few days," Nadia says kindly. "I know you're still trying to acclimate."

True, but at the same time, I'm determined to start my new life. Nadia's right. To have a bright future, I need to focus on who I can become.

"No," I say. "I'd like to go to school. Just rip off the bandage and get it over with."

"That's the spirit!" Lexi holds up her hand as if waiting for me to do something. Then she says, "You're supposed to slap your hand against mine. It's called a high-five."

"Oh!" Quickly, I high-five her, but the whole thing is a little confusing and throws me off.

Sucking a deep breath, I pick up my suitcase and trail after Nadia down the long corridor, eager to find out what my new life will be like.

6

I'M COLD AS ICE. CROSS ME, YOU'LL PAY THE PRICE

DION

The Midnight Kingdom, Antarctica

The throne room is covered by a marble floor swirled with creams and blues, and walls studded with sapphires and diamonds. Above, chandeliers hang from the snowflake emblem on the ceiling, casting sparkling light across the room. Five twisted silver-white pillars circle a dais.

The throne room is disconcertedly empty.

Suddenly, the center of the snowflake opens, and a throne lowers down with the Empress sitting upon it. Her diamond-studded dress billows out as she floats down, the breeze catching hold of long swaths of iridescent violet material. She sits there on her ice throne, arms draped over the curved armrests in the shape of an ice wolf's head, a smirk on her face.

Her white hair glitters like it's filled with a thousand snowflakes and her glass crown has five points that spear up like knives ready to plunge into unsuspecting hearts. As the throne settles onto the dais, it takes every ounce of my willpower to appear calm and unaffected.

"Dion," she says smoothly. "How pleased I am that you have chosen to come out of your cave and reenter civilization."

"Your guards were so enticing," I reply dryly. "I couldn't resist the invitation."

This makes her laugh, a high burst that reminds me of the winds shuddering over the open ice plains. "Indeed. And I do hope your visit will not disappoint me."

She stands then, and slowly, gracefully, steps down from her dais and glides toward me.

"I have heard you've been looking for *her*," she says. Her voice is low, dreadful even. But I knew she would attempt to bait me at this game of hers and I'm ready to play.

"Your Highness." I cock my head to the side, lifting my eyebrows. "I know not what you speak of."

"Of course you don't." Her lips quirk. "But I'm concerned about you. You have such talent, such gifts. They aren't meant to be locked away, gathering dust."

My insides seethe. How can I possibly focus on anything else knowing that Estrella is out there alone, trying to live life as a mortal?

Suddenly the sound of shouting and commands erupts outside of the throne room. The ornately decorated doors burst open, revealing Quadril standing in the center with two Wraiths at either side. The Wraiths' bat-like wings are still unfurled, water dripping from them as if they just arrived through the Water Channels.

I stiffen when I see Quadril. Instantly, all the pain and anger inside me surges to the surface. It rushes to my fingertips, eager to be released. I could bring Quadril to the grave with me, but it would be a death sentence.

"Control yourself," the Empress whispers to me. "This is not the time."

I grimace, holding in my power. Unfortunately, the Empress is right. I must be smarter. My time for vengeance will come.

There's a fire and eagerness in Quadril's steps that makes me uneasy. The Wraiths join him, tucking their wings against their backs as they advance.

"Tell me only good news," the Empress says.

"Your majesty." Quadril bows before her and holds out a broken crown. "The princess is dead and now the Sabians have no Conduit."

The Empress's thin lips curl, her ice-blue eyes shining. "Excellent. You and your warriors did well. And your losses?"

Quadril swallows and looks wary for the first time. "Significant, but now the playing fields are even. The cost was worth the price."

He sets the tiara at her feet and then rises back to standing. He still hasn't acknowledged my existence. Probably a smart move.

"Yes," the Empress says. "And now we no longer need to worry about the Sabians renewing their power. A great victory."

Then she takes her ice heels and smashes her foot onto the jeweled crown, smashing it to nothing but golden dust.

"You're dismissed," she orders Quadril.

Finally, he glances my way, narrowing his eyes. Then he bows again, saying, "Yes, your Greatness."

He strides out of the throne room with his dark escorts. It isn't until the door slams shut that the Empress turns her pale face to me once again.

"Today will be a day of celebration," she says, eyes shining. "Finally, we have the upper hand for control. Now you must be wondering why I've called you here, Dion."

I nod, clenching my hands behind my back to keep myself in check.

"You've been locked away in your room for too long," she says. "You need purpose. Something to remind you of how vital you are to me. You will go on a secret mission for me. No one must know what you are doing."

I snort, finally unable to control myself. She thinks she's giving me a gift by choosing me to go on one of her secret missions? Hardly. "I'm not going anywhere until you tell me where Estrella is."

Her eyes widen and suddenly the room grows colder. Frost coats my clothing and skin.

"How dare you try to bargain with me!" she barks, her voice echoing across the room. "You will do my bidding because I am your queen. Cross me again and see what happens."

Right now, I don't care whether I live or die. But if I die, I will never have a chance of finding Estella. So I swallow down my anger and bow my head.

"As you wish, my queen."

Her eyes narrow, assessing me. "Chandra will serve as your assistant and has been briefed on all the details. No one must know of this mission, understood?"

Chandra? Sourness churns in my stomach at the thought of her joining me. "Yes." I bow again stiffly.

"Excellent." The Empress's mouth crooks into a smile. I would've considered her nearly happy if it weren't for that icy coldness in her eyes. "Do not fail me."

7
THE DEAD DO TELL TALES
TRISTAN

The Castle of Stará, Slovakia

The song of the dead echoes against the Grand Hall's cathedral ceiling, adding to the haunting chill that now seeps through the castle's corridors. The mourners hold a single candle, its light flickering against the tapestry-lined walls, as they trail up the steps of the Courtyard of Cleavers and into the hall.

But I don't offer them a glance. In fact, I wish they'd just leave so they wouldn't see me in this state, kneeling at the casket's side, sword gripped in my palms, anger pulsing through every muscle in my body. Pain wracks me in anguish.

But I can't leave my sister, even though it's been a full day since she took her last breath. I grit my teeth as I study her face through the glass coffin. Her lips have been painted a ruby red and her long blonde hair, the very color of mine, has been brushed in gentle curls, framing her face in a way that makes her still look alive.

She'd been visiting friends in Paris for her birthday. Her attackers snuck in during the dark hours of the night. At her first scream, guards rushed to meet the attack, but the Nazco were swifter. Even with her Conduit powers, she didn't have a chance.

I touch the coffin with the promise of revenge burning through my fingers.

Because her blood calls to me. It seeks vengeance.

"I promise," I whisper. "You will have it."

Someone clears their throat from above me. I glance up to see General Sage, his chest heaving in and out. Since his clothes are still dripping wet, I'm guessing he probably ran directly from the Traveling Pool to the castle. The magical traveling channels within the earth's springs are the fastest means of transportation for us immortals. They allow us to go from one side of the earth to the other side in moments.

And with our kingdom tucked away in the mountains, far from the mortals' eyes, they allow us freedom and accessibility should we wish to avoid the same transportation mortals use.

He's wearing his full armor, travel boots, and a weapons belt where his sword and battle ax hang from. He must have just arrived from battle only moments ago.

My father, King Julian, and his two advisors join us. Father's limp seems more pronounced today and dark circles ring his face as if he hasn't slept for ages. I haven't seen him since he locked himself up in his throne room after the coroner pronounced Ivana dead last night, beheaded by the Nazco scum.

"Your Highness." General Sage bows to my father. He opens his mouth to speak, only to clamp it shut again. Not a good sign.

"Speak," I snap, rising to stand before him. Whatever he has to say, the sooner it's voiced the better.

"We failed." He lowers his head. "The Northern coast of France is now under Nazco control."

"Casualties?" King Julian says wearily.

"Twenty. Their bodies are being sent home via plane. The Nazco now control Calais and its governing rotunda. They have posted sentries all around the city. The only good news is the mortals are still unaware and they had no casualties."

"That's hardly good news." My gaze hardens on the general. "I'm sick of us sitting around waiting and reacting. This is one more example of why our hands-off tactics aren't working. If we had been proactive, none of this would've happened."

My father stiffens.

"There is something else." The General's eyes dart between my father and me as if anxious to ease our pain. "We were able to infiltrate their communication logs. Their records indicate they excommunicated their next Conduit."

My father gasps.

"Why?" I ask. "That's utter stupidity. Though, coming from them, perhaps it should make sense."

"We don't know for sure, Your Highness," the General says to my father. "But whatever it was, I would guess that was the reason why they were so eager to..."

His eyes shift back to Ivana, and I can't stop the growl erupting from my throat. I turn, clenching my fists, and stare at my sister's coffin. Those Nazco filth will suffer. More than anything, I wish for them to feel the pain that's ripping at my insides.

"An interesting turn of events," Father says. "If they don't have a Conduit like us, it could keep the balance."

"Or this girl could be useful to us," the General adds. "If we could persuade her to join us."

"Or she could be a trap," I say.

"The Nazco are known to abandon their people and projects at the whim of the Empress," Father says, undaunted. "What if this girl could be trained? She was forsaken by her own. She may be willing to join us."

"I thought of that but her powers are likely already lost or perhaps she never had any in the first place, which is why they got rid of her." General Gage shrugs. "It's probably not worth our efforts when there are other pressing matters at hand. We've lost too many souls of late."

"Yet this is a great opportunity," Father says, turning to me. "You want to be proactive, Tristan. This is your chance."

"Wait." I lift up my hand, cocking my eyebrows. "Let me get this straight. You want me to waltz into Nazco territory, capture this girl, and convince her to side with us? This sounds exactly like what they'd want us to do. They know how desperate we are with Ivana's passing."

"True." Father's face cringes slightly at my words. "You wouldn't have to exactly *capture* her. If she truly was excommunicated, she might not even be on their radar.

"She may have insider information she could give us,"

General Gage admits. "But it would be risky. It could be a trap."

"You are forgetting their archaic ways." I cross my arms. "They've probably wiped her memory to make her mortal. There's no way the Empress would let a Conduit just waltz free from her clutches."

"Hmm." Father nods slowly, rubbing his thick beard. That's when I realize he's truly buying into this outrageous idea.

"You can't be serious, Father." My blood starts pumping.

"If this girl can be swayed to our side, it could make all the difference." Father rests his hand on my shoulder. "Go, my son. Find this girl and bring her back here. Do this for Ivana. This will avenge her death and give us a chance to survive."

The moment he says Ivana's name, my throat constricts. How can I say no to that?

"As you wish, my king." I duck into a curt bow and then storm off across the Grand Hall.

8

WHO AM I?

ESTRELLA

Florida

Nadia takes me on a tour of the home once our tea ceremony is finished. After visiting the library and kitchen, we enter a large dining room with a table that fills nearly the whole space.

"Everyone eats all meals together precisely at 6 a.m., 12 p.m., and 6 p.m.," she explains. "Family style is how we run things here. Because we're your new family now."

That word *family* rattles about in my brain, and I'm not sure what to do with it. If I knew who my family was, it would help ground me. I think about the photos of the destroyed trailer home Ms. Blaire showed me and wonder when I used to eat my meals and if I got along with my parents.

Nadia waves for me to follow her and points through the

doorway of what looks like a common room. There are couches and bean bags in front of a large TV. In the corner, I spot an easel and paint. My heart flutters at the sight.

There's something very familiar about that. Did I like to paint before the accident?

"This is where many of the girls like to hang out," Nadia explains. "They watch TV, read, or play board games."

"That sounds like fun," I say. "Is that an art easel?"

"Tiffany paints," Nadia says. "She's quite good. Maybe you two could paint together?"

My heart lifts at the thought.

"Your room is located in this main building," Nadia says, pulling me away and up the stairs. "Once you graduate high school, you have the option of living in one of the cottages on the property or finding a place of your own in town."

My fingers trail along the wooden banister as we climb the narrow stairwell to the third floor. The house smells of old wood and sea, and things that once were but are forgotten.

Nadia points out all the rooms on the second floor and then heads up another flight of stairs, ticking off the rules I'm expected to follow on her fingers.

"Make your bed each day, attend all meals, no boys in the house, and you must go to school unless you're sick."

These rules seem easy to remember.

"The room at the end of the hall is yours." Nadia marches down the corridor of faded white walls and opens the door.

I step inside and take in the sparse furnishings: a single bed, a desk with a chair situated under the window, and a dresser and mirror against the far wall.

My own room. The thought settles me somehow. Maybe it's that I can finally ground myself to something in this day of shifting people and places. I set my suitcase beside the bed and touch the quilted bedspread, soft from years of washing.

If all goes to plan, I won't be here long. Once I find out more about who I was and if I have any family members, I can get out of here. Until then, I could make this room mine.

"Since dinner hour has passed, I'll have some food brought to your room along with some fresh tea to help you sleep. If you feel up to it, you can start school first thing in the morning. The bus leaves at six forty-five, and the girls who attend school can show you what to do."

She waits a half-beat for me to say something. I feel a little dizzy, and more than anything, I just want to be alone and try to process everything.

"Sounds good," I manage.

"Well, then. Good." Nadia lets out a long breath. "Now start unpacking. The morning bell will wake you up at five."

I gasp. "Five in the morning?"

"That will give you plenty of time to eat breakfast and walk to the bus stop. And don't forget to take your medicine. The doctor said you'll get headaches if you don't take it."

Once she leaves, I shuffle to the window and peek outside. Darkness hovers over the thick foliage surrounding the house and outer buildings. I try to find the moon and stars, but clouds have moved in, blocking any hint of light.

My fingers skim across the window ledge until I find the latch. Once it's unlocked, I slide open the window and a gust of sea breeze washes over my face, carrying with it the roar of what I'm guessing are crashing waves. Despite all my misgivings about this place, my shoulders relax at the soothing sound.

Leaving the window open, I decide to tackle my few belongings. I snap open the suitcase's clasp and peek inside. Ms. Blaire filled it with my clothes she recovered after the explosion. I pull out a pair of faded jeans, wondering when I wore them last. Then I hold up a tank top, trying to picture where the rip on the hem came from.

There's a faint smell I can't quite place—mothballs?—and I scrunch up my nose.

"So much for finding something familiar here," I mutter.

I bite my fingernail, thinking about the girls and what this new life might be like. Why was Lexi pouring her tea into the plant? And what about my fork stealer? Was there something to her stealing utensils or is she just trying to hold onto familiar things like I am?

I rub my head, realizing I'm not one to judge. I was imagining the gargoyles on the gate were real just a few hours ago.

It takes me less than five minutes to unpack the rest of my clothes. Afterward, I shrug into a tank and cotton shorts and move to stand in front of the mirror to study the strange blonde-haired girl.

"Who are you?" I whisper, gripping the sides of the dresser.

But she only stares back, eyes full of questions and pain.

"What good are you anyway?" My voice is rough and harsh. "You don't know anything!"

I spin around in anger, my long hair whipping out.

And that's when I see the reflection in the mirror.

The mark on my body.

I freeze, then lift my shoulder back, twisting just right so I can see it better.

Even in the fading light, it's distinct. A tattoo about the length of my fingers. It's a twisting of cords that forms a knot just above my shoulder blade.

"Estrella," someone whispers into my ear, a breath of a memory from the past.

A rush of warmth flows through me. Finally, after everything I've gone through, I feel safe and protected. I know this voice, deep and thick as honey, and suddenly that moment I saw in the car while listening to music floods my mind once again.

It's a guy, holding my hand as snowflakes fall on our noses and eyelashes. He leans in closer. Hot lips trail along my shoulder, down to the tender skin of where my tattoo is. I shiver at the touch, aching for his arms to wrap around me, promising that everything would be okay. His mouth moves to mine and he brushes a kiss across my lips. It's not enough. I want more. I reach for him and–

Fire flashes through my mind and sears me with pain. I cry out, ducking my head into my hands. Slowly, the ache subsides, and I'm able to lift my head back up.

No one else is in the room.

I stare back at the tattoo, rubbing my hand over it. A rush of adrenaline surges through me because deep down I know this mark is a clue.

A clue to my past.

I just need to figure out what it means.

9
KEEP CALM AND PLOT YOUR REVENGE
TRISTAN

The Castle of Stará, Slovakia

Determined to make this mission of finding the excommunicated Nazco girl a success, I march down one of the narrow stone corridors to find Katka, our mission prep specialist.

I don't like General Sage's idea, but what other options do we have? Without Ivana as our Conduit to enter the World of Between and gather new power for us, our powers will soon weaken. And we haven't identified another with the ability yet.

Still, the odds of the Nazco having another Conduit at their fingertips is highly unlikely. This is why it makes no sense that they'd excommunicate their Conduit unless they were certain she couldn't access her powers.

Or maybe she just pissed off the Empress.

I rap my fist on the heavy wooden door of Katka's workroom as I consider the situation. Regardless of the Nazco's reasons, I don't like the plan. The whole situation reeks of Nazco typical foulness.

The tiny window in the center of the door slips open to reveal Tia, Katka's assistant.

"We are extremely busy, come back later," Tia says in her high pixie-like voice. But when she realizes it's me, her blue eyes widen. "Oh! Prince Tristan. I didn't know it was you. If I had—what can I do—?"

"Open the door." I cross my arms. "I need to speak to Katka."

"Um, that might be difficult…"

I glare at Tia because this seems to be the way our conversations always turn. Katka threatens Tia's life if she lets anyone through the door—especially me—while I threaten her excommunication if she doesn't. It isn't Tia's fault that Katka avoids people at all costs or that I'm unbearably stubborn.

"Katka!" I shout. "Tell your assistant to let me in or I'm going to have you transferred to the mechanics' division."

Instantly, the door swings open, revealing Katka, her hands on her hips and her long red hair twisted into a tangled braid. Dark green eyes glare at me and her freckles seem to pop out even more prominently as her face darkens. Her apron is smeared with grease and her pants are wrinkled and stained.

"Let's see." She taps her fingers against her arm, staring up at the ceiling as if she's counting the wooden beams. "You transfer me to mechanics only for you to realize there are exactly zero Sabians who could replace me and set up an entire mission. How do you think that would go over with your father?"

"It would go over quite poorly." A smile creeps on my face. "All of our missions would fail, the Nazco would destroy us in one final swoop, and everyone would blame me. Which is why you should let me in. Right now."

"You are incorrigible, isolable, and insolent," she snaps but widens the gap in the door so I can step through into her workroom. This section of the castle, which once hosted tapestries, looms, and polite conversions over shared tea, has now turned into what looks like a commoner's garage.

"Homey as ever," I say as I sidestep an opened trunk full of dresses and skirts around a spilled toolbox.

"Shut your trap," Katka barks, "and tell me why you're harassing and threatening me."

"Oh, dear." Tia wrings her hands, and I don't blame her. No one in the Sabian Kingdom would dare talk to their prince in such a manner. "Can I get you a drink, my lord? Or a chair to sit on?"

I scowl at my surroundings. "This room is a complete disaster."

One corner is lined with racks of clothing, but I'm not sure why she bothers with the racks since most of the clothes are piled up on the floor. A long table runs nearly the length of the back wall stacked with drills, saws, a sewing machine, random engines, and tools. A telescope is set up by the double glass doors that lead out to the balcony. And the far corner is filled with books, umbrellas, hats, and boxes full of shoes.

"It takes about ten seconds standing here before this place gives me a headache," I say.

"Here, my lord." Tia tosses off hats from one of the chairs and drags it over for me to sit on. "Sit here. It will ease your mind."

"I don't have time for your whining," Katka says. "What do you want?"

"It's an emergency, a last-minute mission." I sit in the chair Tia offers.

She snorts and marches over to the table in the center of the room and starts hacking away at her computer. "Aren't they all last-minute-hurry-Katka-and-rush missions?"

"Quite possibly. But this one is different."

She peeks her head over the computer screen, eyebrows lifted, and she's got an I-don't-believe-you smirk on her face.

"The Nazco excommunicated their Conduit," I begin.

"Really?" Katka says, and for the first time, she appears slightly interested. "I haven't received any news on that. Are you sure? Oh, wait. Here's the General's memo from his mission today. Ouch. Not such a good day."

"Not at all."

I run my hands over my face. We haven't had a death-free, successful mission in far too long. Not that it's any of the Sabian's fault. It's just that the Empress has grown bolder and more aggressive in the last few months. She has overstepped her bounds in ways no immortal has in over a thousand years.

"Father believes we can entice this girl to join us." I rise back to my feet, suddenly feeling restless. "So that's where I'm going. To find this potential Conduit."

"Really?" Katka crosses her arms, eyebrows lifted in disbelief. "If the Nazco think she's worthless, then I bet she is. Sounds like you're wasting your time."

"My thoughts exactly." I straighten one of her picture frames on the stone wall, dusting the edges off with my fingers. "But I have to try. It's better than staring at Ivana's face and doing nothing. And I certainly can't twiddle my thumbs while I wait around for their next attack. Ivana's death calls for revenge."

Katka presses her lips together and a flash of sympathy crosses her face at the mention of my sister. I don't want her sympathy, and I'm about to open my mouth and tell her just that, but then she claps her hands.

"Tia!" Katka says, her red braid swinging as she begins digging through one of her clothes piles. "Get the suitcases and fill this with clothes that would fit Prince Tristan."

Tia races to me with a measuring tape but pauses as if she's too scared to touch me. "May I take your measurements, my lord?"

"Quickly," I say.

Tia's hands shake as she wraps the tape measure around my chest and arms. She sways a little as if she might pass out.

"You okay?" I frown as Tia scurries away into the next room. "Katka, I think you're overworking your assistant."

"Oh, I'm sure she's just fine." Katka chuckles as she digs through a box full of mortal paraphernalia. "It's not every day a girl gets to touch those muscles of yours."

Finally, she tosses me a wallet and then moves to the only empty stone wall and touches it with the back of her knuckles. The wall blinks to life, a full-sized computer screen appearing. I move closer as she pulls up a map of the world and the Nazco deployment list our hackers found a few months back. It lists all of the locations where Nazco warriors have been stationed.

"It's hard to say where this girl was sent to." Katka rubs her knuckles thoughtfully. "Looking at the communication logs General Sage found for us there hasn't been any activity or transfers to the Removal Facilities—that's where they send all their excommunicated."

"But look." I point to the deployment list. "It appears as if the Nazco sent two of their high-level Wraiths to Florida this week."

"Huh. That's odd."

"Very." I tap Florida on the map and zoom in on the location on the coast. A sinking knot forms in my gut. "That's where I'll start."

"Are you sure you don't want to check the other Removal Facilities first?" Katka asks. "We haven't had any Nazco activity or run-ins *ever* in our historical records in that area."

"No, I'm sure."

She shrugs. "If you say so, your lordship. Let's see what Tia has inputted into your mission file so far."

She minimizes the map and pulls up the mission check-list Tia has begun. I scan through my sizes, profile, and housing.

"We don't have any preset housing in the area so I'm going to have to find you a furnished apartment, car, and such."

"I'll pick out my own car. And all my weapons go with me."

"Now you're being difficult *and* ridiculous. You know you can't go strolling around town with your sword."

"Of course, I know that," I say, miffed. "I visit mortal areas all the time."

I'm definitely bringing my sword.

She rolls her eyes as I start scrolling through the car listing. I opt for a red Corvette.

"Subtle." She huffs. "I'm sure no Nazco will notice you driving around in that. By the way, how long do you think this mission will take?"

"Three days tops."

She types in two weeks.

"Thanks for the vote of confidence," I say.

"No problem. Now we just need to get you registered at the local high school and book you a flight."

I laugh. "There's no way I'm going to attend a high school."

"Where do you expect to find a seventeen-year-old washed-up Conduit? According to mortal laws, she'd have to be sent to school."

"I'm going to kill Sage next time I see him for even mentioning this ex-Conduit." I massage my forehead. "Wacked-out idea."

"For once, we're in agreement," Katka says.

10

YOU NEVER KNOW WHAT A STORM WILL BRING

ESTRELLA

Florida

"School is such a drag," Lexi announces as the four of us girls take the sandy path toward the gate where the school bus apparently picks us up. "But it beats staying at the house."

Even though it's morning, the sunlight hasn't quite worked its way through the trees yet, leaving the forest in twisted shadows and cloaked in a misty veil. This morning as I sat down at breakfast, I was surprised to learn that out of twelve of us, only four were going to school.

"I'm thinking of dropping out," Tiffany says softly.

"What?" Lexi exclaims. "No! You can't do that. Girl, at least graduate. You're so close."

"It would give me more time to work on my paintings,"

she continues, and then turns to me, smiling. "I'd like to set up a gallery."

"A gallery sounds great," I say, but when I spy Lexi's dark frown, I add, "But why not finish high school first? What year are you?"

"Senior, just like you." Tiffany adjusts her backpack. "But it seems like such a waste of time, don't you think?"

"I vote no," Lexi announces and pushes open the gate. "What do you think, Mara?"

Mara sat beside me at breakfast and since I was trying to make friends, I asked her about school. Except she was too busy spreading jam on her toast to respond. Lexi brushed it off, proclaiming that Mara wasn't a morning person.

"Let Tiffany do whatever she wants." Mara blows out air so her brown bangs billow up. "You need to stop meddling, Lexi. It doesn't help anyone. Carla is proof enough."

Lexi's jaw tightens. She tugs at the ends of her orange hair, bright even in the darkness, and marches out to the road as if trying to create distance between us.

"Why did you have to go and mention Carla's name?" Tiffany asks as she pulls out her inhaler. "That was low. Even for you."

Mara rolls her eyes. "Because Lexi needs to be careful if she knows what's best for her and all of us."

"Who's Carla?" I dare ask, curious why just mentioning her name upsets them.

"She was a friend," Tiffany whispers, pushing her way through the iron gate and out onto the road.

Mara's body stiffens as my attention focuses on her. "She was a reminder of what can happen to any of us if we're not careful," she says.

"Why do I feel like there's some big secret no one's telling me?" I press, already tired of the mind games. And it's only 6:30 a.m.

"It's best for your safety." Mara stops me suddenly, her large brown eyes focused on mine, face shadowed with worry. "If you don't ask questions and follow the rules, you might survive. Carla didn't do any of those things and now she's gone. Got it?"

"No." I shake my head, my pulse kicking up. "Not at all. What do you mean *survive*?"

A big yellow bus barrels down the road, its lights swooping over us and swallowing the shadows of the forest. Mara huffs, letting me go, and heads to the curb.

The three girls climb onto the bus, but my feet are rooted in place. My thoughts spin at Mara's warning while I'm simultaneously trying to calm my first day of school nerves.

I yank my blue tank top over my jean shorts and twist my backpack strap as the driver yells, "You coming or not?"

I can do this. I want to start my new life. School is the closest ticket to freedom I have. Besides, I'm a senior so I've obviously been doing the school thing for a very long time, right?

Right.

I suck in a deep breath and somehow drag myself onto the bus. The driver takes off before I've made it halfway down the aisle. Lexi waves for me to sit beside her, so I stumble down the aisle and tuck into the seat next to her.

"You're nervous," Lexi says as if it's not a question. "Don't sweat it. You'll be amazing. My first day at Olympia High School was hell but stick close to me and you'll be just fine."

"Any survival tips?"

"Act like you own the place and just go with the flow."

I sink lower in my seat. "So basically it's going to be a complete nightmare."

"Relaaax." Lexi pats my knee. "Just blend in. Be normal. Oh, and don't tell anyone that you can't remember anything. They'll think you're weird. A lot of people think us girls from Nadia's are weird, but whatever."

My chest suddenly feels really tight. "Mara said I needed to be careful to survive. What did that mean?"

Lexi shifts in her seat, darting her eyes about as if someone might be watching us. "Are you sure you want to know?"

Now my curiosity is piqued to an all-time high. "Of course!"

"Let's talk after school, okay? This isn't a good place."

We pull into the bus lanes of Olympia High, and suddenly the ride comes to an end all too quickly. I hug my backpack against my chest.

Blend in, I tell myself. Be normal.

Palm trees surround the school's cream-colored buildings while sandy-white walkways lead to the school's gates. As I take it all in, it only reminds me of how much I don't remember anything from my last school.

The doctor said I had selective amnesia so only parts of my memory are gone. I definitely can't remember my family or past life, but at the hospital, I was able to recite historical facts and read and write.

Beyond that? I guess I'm about to find out.

I can't decide what I should do first—throw up or get off the bus.

Considering throwing up would defeat my goal of blending in, I scramble off. Mara and Tiffany are already standing on the sidewalk, waiting for Lexi and me to join them.

"You don't look so good," Mara says, studying me intently. I wonder if this girl can't resist telling the truth or if she's just rude.

"Leave Estrella alone." Lexi hooks her arm through mine. Her skin is warm like a cozy fire. "She'll be fine. I'll get her registered and all set up."

"Don't worry about anything." Tiffany flashes me a kind look and squeezes my arm. "I felt exactly the same way on my first day. You'll get through it with no problems."

I try to smile my thanks for her encouragement, but Lexi is already dragging me away toward the doors of the school.

"Stick close to me," Lexi says. "And everything will be fine."

A cool wind whips at my hair and a tingling sensation skitters at the back of my neck. I jerk to a stop and look around. Above, brooding clouds scuttle by as if carrying with them a sense of dread. And then it's like a whirlwind is churning around me. Palm fronds and wood chips fly about. The sky turns dark and the wind tugs at my hair and clothes.

I cry out and cover my eyes from the flying debris.

But then Lexi's hand rests on my arm and instantly the world is back to normal again.

Trembling, I lower my hands from my face and look around. The sky is back to a soft morning blue and the palms wave gently in the breeze. A couple of kids are glancing over at me like they're not so sure if I'm normal or not.

Great. Way to make a first-day impression. It's no wonder kids think us girls from Nadia's are strange.

"You okay?" Lexi asks.

"I just thought I saw…" My words drift off. Okay, Estrella. Pull yourself together. You don't need to alienate your only friend in the whole world by saying you've got voodoo vibes. I try laughing off my fear and with a shrug say, "I'm sure it's nothing."

Lexi bites her bottom lip, eying the sky. "Don't sweat it. I remember my first day of school after coming to Nadia's. It was really tough. That's why a lot of girls don't come back. They don't want to deal with it. Last month during lunch, Jamie suddenly jumped up like she was being attacked or something and started throwing utensils across the cafeteria."

"Wait, what?" I gape. "Which one is Jamie?"

"The tiny blonde. She has this thing for utensils, especially knives. But she really likes spoons, too. Just stay on her good side because she's got crazy-good aim when it comes to throwing them."

"She's the girl I sat next to yesterday during tea," I say. Sure, it was strange that she stole my fork, but she seemed really nice. Except, what if I made a similar scene in school, too? "It's too bad she won't come back, but I guess I don't blame her."

"Maybe you can convince her to return to school. She at least hasn't tried to stab you yet." She tugs me through the front doors of the school before I can change my mind about this school thing.

The beige concrete walls of the foyer are slashed with slogans like "Go Titans!" and images of Olympic torches and lightning bolts cover the walls. The air smells of a mix of body odor, heavy perfume, and bleach. Students swarm the halls, jostling me left and right as I shove my way to the office.

When we step inside, I pull out the folder Ms. Blaire gave me. Supposedly it holds my old school records as well as the details about why I was transferring to a new school. It's sealed shut. I eye the seal, tempted to open it.

"Hiya." Lexi leans over the receptionist's counter. "My friend, Estrella here, needs to register."

"Of course." The receptionist smiles brightly at me, waving. "Hello, Estrella. Let me see if we can get you all set up."

While they chat, I slip to the corner of the lobby and stare at the envelope. Could there be a clue inside that hints at my past?

I can't stop myself. I tear back the seal of the envelope. Inside, I discover a letter to Olympia High School's principal. It discusses my memory problems, the accident, and the investigation of the explosion as well as a printout of my last school grades.

Straight C's. Looks like I'm an average student. But other than that, I can't find any new pieces of information about myself. I frown, shuffling through the papers. There must be more here. Like my former address or even the name of my former school.

It's like these records are incomplete.

The receptionist calls my name, so I quickly stuff the papers back in the envelope.

"Your counselor is in a meeting right now," the receptionist explains. "But your sponsor already met with us so we already have your schedule and school ID number. All we were waiting on were your school records, which I assume are in that envelope. Lexi, can you assist Estrella today? She'll need help finding her first-period class."

"Rest assured, I'll be the perfect host." Lexi snatches up my schedule. "Oh! We have first period together. Fabulous."

"Here you go." I pass the envelope to the receptionist.

"Excellent," the receptionist says as a bell rings. "You should be all set."

"Could you spare two hall passes?" Lexi asks. "Because that was the first bell, and we've still got to find her locker."

"Oh yes, locker. I knew there was something else." The lady ruffles through her papers and pulls out a small slip of paper, handing it to me. Next, she scrawls out hall passes and before I realize it, Lexi is dragging me out of the office and down a much quieter hall.

"This is the main hall." Lexi's voice now sounds like a tour host. "The lockers date back to the Regency era, known for their rust and smell. Your place of honor," she glanced at my locker number, "is in the eastern wing. Just this way, if you will."

I chuckle. "I take it you've given this tour before."

"You've got that right. I'm a school ambassador so whenever a new person arrives, I'm often called to give tours. It's helpful too when new girls arrive at Nadia's. Then I can be the one to acclimate them to school life."

"That's really kind of you."

"It's nothing really." Lexi's face darkens and all the brightness spilling out of her seems to vanish. "I wish I could do more. Sometimes, I don't know if I'm helping or hurting, you know?"

Is she referring to what Mara said about Carla? "I'm sure you're helping. I'd be lost today without you."

Lexi is quiet for once as if lost in her thoughts. And then, she points to what I guess is my locker. "Ah! Here we are! Check and make sure your combo works. Sometimes the office gets lockers mixed up."

I spin the combination. The long metal door pops open, letting loose a rotting food scent.

"Eww!" we both cry, clamping our noses shut.

A moldy hamburger is the culprit. Toad-green foam spread over the bun with brown liquid oozing out of it.

"That is *so* repulsing," Lexi says.

"I'll deal with that grossness later." I happily slam the door shut and then start laughing. It loosens the tightness in my chest.

We head down the hall and enter room 152, British Lit. I have no idea how I'm going to manage school with my memory all screwy.

Do I like English?

What were my favorite subjects?

Who were my friends at my old school?

"Good morning, Lexi," a man in khakis and a white shirt says. "I'm looking forward to this morning's excuse."

"Actually," Lexi hands him our hall passes, "it's quite legitimate. This is Estrella Milton. I'm her personal tour guide today."

The teacher runs his hands across his forehead, muttering something about class sizes. Then he glances my way and hands me a thick textbook. "I'm Mr. Terring. Welcome to British Lit. Find a seat wherever you like."

Lexi bolts to the back of the classroom and pats a seat

next to hers. "It's best to avoid Mr. Terring," she whispers. "Especially before he's had his coffee."

I nod. "Warning noted. Thanks."

Mr. Terring doesn't bother taking roll but leaps right into a lecture on old British poets. I try to focus, but my eyes keep wandering to the window. What had been a sunrise-streaked sky when I got off the bus had transformed into an angry gray mass with winds cutting through the palms in the courtyard outside.

Chills run up my arms at its familiarity.

It's exactly like what I imagined before stepping into the building.

I turn to Lexi. "What's up with the weather? Is this normal?"

"It's Florida." She shrugs. "The weather changes here a lot."

My gaze slides back to the window and my heart sinks as a nagging feeling resurfaces. And that's when the alarm goes off, ringing and jerking all of us out of our seats. A voice comes on the intercom.

"This is Principal Clayton announcing a tornado warning," she says. "All students are to follow Code Red instructions."

Everyone scrambles under their desks. I follow along by pushing my chair back and squeezing underneath, tucking my knees to my chest. I suppose I should be more scared like the girl opposite me with big eyes, furiously biting her nails, but all I can think about is how I feel like I have experienced this storm already.

That thought freaks me out the most.

"Isn't this the best?" Lexi asks. "Girl, I've been needing some excitement in my life."

"Do you get these tornadoes often?"

"Not in the year since I've been here."

Mr. Terring pulls down the shades and turns off the lights while the students around me giggle or talk in hushed voices. I think about Lexi's words. I don't crave excitement, I crave memories.

The Code Red doesn't last more than ten minutes. When the principal comes back on the intercom, announcing the all-clear, Mr. Terring draws up the shades, letting harsh light flood the room. The tornado came and went within moments.

"That's it?" Lexi throws her hands up. "So much for excitement."

We slug our way back into our chairs, groaning over the shortness of the drill. To make things worse, Mr. Terring jumps right back into his discussion as if the Code Red never existed.

But instead of taking notes, I try to recreate the tattoo on my shoulder blade. The flow of the lines helps me think and process everything.

Why did I get that tattoo? What does it mean? And who is that boy I keep remembering? Before I know it, I've filled the paper with corded knots.

Lexi taps my shoulder, jerking me back to the class. Everyone is pairing up into groups.

"Why are you drawing those symbols?" she asks, glancing around nervously.

"I just—"

She closes my notebook and in a whisper says, "Better

not let anyone see those, okay? Especially Nadia. She'll freak."

"Why?" I close the notebook. "What's the big deal about this symbol?"

"Shhh. Pay attention. Mr. Terring turns into a monster when you show him you're not listening."

"We need to talk after school," I say because now I'm just a mix of annoyed and desperate. "No more secrets, got it?"

Lexi presses her lips together and sucks in a deep breath. "You're right. We'll talk. After school."

Except I don't plan on waiting until after school to get answers.

First opportunity I get, I'm heading to the computer lab to do some research.

11
THE NEW BOY AT SCHOOL
ESTRELLA

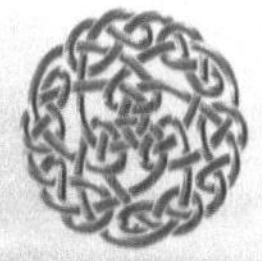

Florida

Lunch shouldn't be this difficult. But there are the lines, the choices, the showing of the student ID card, and then the deciding of where to sit.

Too much thinking. Too much information.

Thankfully, Lexi is easy to spot. Her bright hair beams like a beacon and her arms wave me to where she sits with Tiffany and Mara. I'm so relieved to have somewhere to sit that I almost drop my tray. I hurry to their table, setting my tray of fried fish and wilted vegetables in front of me as I plop onto the bench.

"So how's your first day going?" Lexi asks.

"I'm surviving," I say.

"Surviving high school can be intense," Lexi says.

"Don't let her worry you." Tiffany touches my hand

lightly, and instantly I feel relaxed and calm. "We all felt the same way on our first day. It's not easy to deal with memory loss."

"But you all seem to be adjusting well," I point out.

"Seriously?" Mara stabs at a carrot. "I wouldn't exactly call any of us well adjusted. They should've named the orphanage Nadia's Home for the Mindless. That would be so much more fitting."

"Mara!" Lexi glares at her. "That's awful to say."

But the truth is, I'm starting to like how blunt Mara is. Finally, I feel like someone is telling things how they really are.

"When the doctor told me I'd never get my memories back," I say, fiddling with my fork, "it was the worst feeling. And there are times when I feel…"

Wrong.

Incomplete.

Separated from the real me.

"Cuckoo?" Mara supplies, not caring how critical she sounds. "Yeah, we're all a little out there."

"Again, *mean*," Tiffany snaps.

"Whatever." Mara rolls her eyes. "It's the truth. If you're lucky, Estrella, you'll find a way to cope with it."

I stare down at my food, my appetite gone.

As if sensing my discomfort, Lexi changes the subject. "Did you girls hear the latest gossip?" She waves her arms excitedly to get our attention. "While you were all slaving away in third period, I was giving the most gorgeous guy *ever* a tour!"

"Life isn't fair." Mara pushes her tray of food away and

pulls out a textbook. "How do you always get first dibs on the hot new guys?"

"It all started after the Code Red," Lexi begins in a hushed voice as if she were about to dole out assignments for a covert mission. "I got called to the office to give two new students a tour. Apparently, the new boy—his name is Dion—and his sister—or maybe she's his girlfriend? I can't remember. But Ms. Reeds—she's the receptionist—said they marched through the front doors of the school, totally oblivious to the tornado outside. They're both new to Olympia High. Obviously. He was super nice plus he's got this hot Spanish accent."

"They came during the tornado?" I gasp. "It's that dangerous?"

"Ms. Reeds probably exaggerated," Mara says.

"They're from Argentina or Brazil." Lexi pauses, thinking. "I can't quite remember, but somewhere super sexy."

"He sounds dreamy," Tiffany says. "Did he ask you out?"

"Unfortunately no. But we can still name him."

"Name him?" I ask.

"It's what we do," Tiffany explains, tucking a loose strand of dark curl behind her ear. "Every boy at this school gets a nickname. Like Steve over there, his name is Jellyfish Shoes. You'll understand when you see him dance. And Andy, that cutie by the Coke machine, he's My Hunk."

"No." Lexi waves her pretzel in the air like a magic wand. "He's *MY* Hunk."

Tiffany lifts her eyebrows, smiling while Mara frowns, saying, "See? You always claim them."

"Whatever. You get the picture," Lexi says, and then her eyes widen after she glances at her watch. "Crapsticks! I've gotta scoot! The audition sign-ups are posted for the play. Estrella, want to come with?"

I push aside my half-eaten fish. "Actually, since we still have some time before fourth period, I'm going to head to the computer lab. There's something I need to check out."

When I enter the drop-in lab, a man with spiked black hair glances up from his desk piled with computer parts, random wires, and Frito bags.

"Need a computer?" he asks, twisting his screwdriver into the side of a monitor.

"Yes." I take in the long room where computers line all four walls. "Can I sit anywhere?"

Grunting, he sets aside his screwdriver and stands. "You're new, aren't you?" At my nod, he directs me to a station in the far corner. "Do you have a student number?"

I rifle around in my backpack until I find it listed on my schedule. He shows me how to log in and explains how to access the internet.

"Thanks," I say as he ambles back to his own computer.

I type in the words "knot symbols" for my search but frown in frustration. How stupid is it that I can use the computer but not remember a thing about my own family?

It doesn't make sense.

I take a deep breath and focus. That look of fear in Lexi's eyes when she saw the drawings of my tattoo bothered me all morning. What is so bad about drawing that?

My fingers reach over to where it's hidden beneath my

shirt. What would she think of my tattoo if I showed it to her?

As I search Google for answers, my frustration grows. From the images online, it looks very similar to the endless knot, which is basically a singular line that intertwines with itself with no beginning and no end.

I skim different articles but end up leaning back in my chair, overwhelmed and discouraged. Nothing here jumps out at me, other than the fact that it's an infinity symbol.

I sigh. I probably got the tattoo just because it was cool looking and now I'm making something out of nothing.

I'm about to Google my parents' names when the bell startles me, causing me to knock my mouse off the counter. Quickly, I snatch it back up, shaking my head.

I'm a complete mess. It's like I'm jumpy all the time.

Quickly, I gather up my backpack and exit the computer lab. Except there's something that suddenly feels different. I scan the hallway and stop when my eyes land on two teenagers. They're both dressed in black leather jackets and knee-high boots, strolling down the hall in my direction.

The moment my eyes land on them, I freeze.

The girl is modelesque, tall with smooth tan skin, sculpted features, and waist-length, shimmering black hair that sways as she walks. A couple of guys whistle as she sashays past. She responds with a coy smile as if she's soaking in every glance and whistle.

But my full attention is pulled to the guy at her side. He's even more breathtaking, with bronzed skin and short, dark hair. His body is lithe, and his walk is purposeful as if he holds the world in his palm. These two must be the ones

Lexi was talking about at lunch. She wasn't kidding about him being 'the most gorgeous ever.'

I can't seem to clamp my mouth as I stupidly gawk at them, but when the guy's gaze sweeps over me, a strange trickle of heat runs up my spine.

His perfect features twist into a mix of shock and anger. My heart starts beating, a hurricane stirring within me.

My head pounds. A flash of light and searing pain flares into my sight and I drop my backpack to the floor. I sag against the wall, trying to manage the pain.

Breathe in and out. In and out.

Instantly, the guy is at my side. Concern fills his eyes as he picks up my backpack. Even as my vision blurs from the pain, I can't ignore how his lips are just a breath away. So close, I could kiss him. Goosebumps erupt over my arms.

I blink. What is wrong with me? I must look like an absolute idiot.

"Are you okay?" he asks softly.

His voice. It's warm and yet cold.

I nod, blinking back the pain as I grab my backpack and hug it to my chest.

"Thanks. Must have been lunch," I say, trying to joke this moment off.

But he doesn't smile. There's a fierce intensity to his gaze, like just seeing me makes him angry. Really angry.

Which makes no sense whatsoever.

He rises and steps away, clenching his fists at his side. And then he's leaving like he can't get away from me fast enough. The beautiful girl hurries to join him. She glances over her shoulder and shoots me a glare before hurrying away.

Okay, that was weird.

Then the same piercing agony penetrates my brain once again and I press my hands over my eyes, biting back a scream. I wait until the pain leaves. When I finally open my eyes, they're gone.

The hall is empty.

And I'm late for class.

12
THE FAIRYTALE HAS ENDED
DION

Florida

I storm down the school hallway, my anger raging through my body. If I don't get out of this place soon, I'm going to kill a mortal. Or burn the building to ashes.

Students swarm around me, with their sweaty bodies and reeking of perfume. Their fragile lives push dangerously close to mine. I clench my fists, desperately keeping my powers in check.

The school is a warren of passages but I finally find an exit. I shove myself through the door and step out onto a path that leads out to some kind of field. My mind flicks through my mortal studies. This must be a soccer or football field.

As if I give a damn.

Because Estrella is lost.

Lost to me.

I slam my fist on the fence. Electricity rushes from my palm, eagerly seeking the metal as an outlet for my anger. The air sizzles and sparks fly along the railing.

I hang my head, breathing in and out as I grip the fence tighter.

"Dion," a voice says behind me.

Chandra. I roll my eyes. The last thing I need is for her to see me as weak or out of control and report that back to the Empress. I suck in a deep breath to collect myself and then stand back up, turning to face her.

"It was a surprise," I admit. "Here I thought this was some random mission. But in truth, it was a slap in the face."

"It was a shock for me as well," Chandra says, looking away.

"You didn't know?"

She swallows. "I knew, but seeing her as a mortal, it was...well, she's so fragile, so ordinary."

I nod. It shouldn't surprise me. As immortals, our bodies are not only stronger with many of us having powers, but we also possess an inherent beauty that mortals don't have. This is why we are careful when interacting with mortals as it can draw their attention.

So seeing her today, having already lost so much of the glow and power radiating from her, was a blow to the heart.

"It would've been helpful if the Empress had warned me," I say. "Then I could've been mentally prepared to see her again."

"The Empress has her reasons." She shrugs. "Still, I

would've expected you to be happy to see her again. Don't tell me you haven't been searching for her."

"You expect me to be happy?" I throw up my hands and start pacing along the field's fence. "Didn't you see her? She didn't even recognize me! And she's changed so much."

"And not for the good."

"I'm leaving. I'm going back to the Midnight Kingdom and giving the Empress a piece of my mind."

Chandra snorts. "And then what? Get yourself killed? Right. That will help Estrella out. Besides, what are you whining about? This is what *you* wanted. I heard you beg for her life at the party. *You* asked that she become a mortal."

I clench my jaw. "They would've killed her if I hadn't."

"Exactly. This is your chance to make sure she completes the mortalization process properly, and then you can return home knowing she can lead out the rest of her mortal life without Quadril and his Wraiths getting stab-happy."

Her words hit just where she obviously wanted. I stare at her, searching her face. "What's in this for you? I know how much you and Estrella didn't get along."

Chandra shrugs, now suddenly interested in her sharp, brightly-painted nails.

"The Empress promised you something, didn't she?" I press.

"Don't act like the Empress won't reward you should you complete this mission properly."

I glare at her, but a dark form catches my eyes. A hooded figure wearing a black cloak is standing on top of the bleacher. Watching us.

My heart sinks.

It's one of Quadril's Wraiths.

"Appears as if Quadril is keeping a close eye on Estrella's transformation process as well," I note.

Chandra follows my gaze, her face becoming pale. "This is an unexpected development."

"And not a good one." I groan.

Estrella's life is still obviously in danger. Why would Quadril send his Wraiths here?

This is going to be harder than I possibly could've imagined. But it doesn't matter. I'm going to be there for Estrella through all of this, I decide.

And do whatever it takes to keep her safe.

13

HAPPINESS IS A BEACH DAY. UNLESS YOU'RE BEING STALKED

ESTRELLA

Florida

I can't stop thinking about him. The boy in the hall. There was something that happened between us. I just know it. Did he feel it, too?

Dion. That's what Lexi called him.

For the rest of the school day, I search for him, and when I enter each class, I keep hoping he'll be in one of the same classes as me. What is it about him? Sure, the guy is hot, with those dark eyes that I can't seem to get out of my head. But there's this presence about him that seems to pull me to him.

It's like my whole body craves to be in his presence. It makes no sense, but my every thought is consumed by who he is and why he seems so familiar. That urgency to talk to him propels me to scour the rest of the building after school, making me nearly miss the bus.

It's not until I slip into my seat beside Lexi that I spot him. He's standing in the bus loop, reading a book. How had I missed him? I must have walked right past the guy. The bus begins to pull away, and at the last second, he lifts his eyes up from the book and they meet mine.

I gasp and duck away from the window, my heart racing. It's almost like he knew exactly where I was. That I had been watching him. Had he been avoiding me? Is that why I never saw him the rest of the day?

When we arrive back at Nadia's house, I know I need to get my mind off him and my head out of the clouds. The most important thing is to focus on getting my life back on track and find answers to all the questions tumbling about in my head.

Like who is Carla and why won't the girls talk about her?

Why must we be so careful to survive?

Instinctively, my fingers trace the area around my shoulder blade where my tattoo is, leading me to my final question. Why shouldn't I show Nadia the drawings of the symbol of my tattoo?

If there's anyone here who knows something, it's Lexi.

"Hey." I nudge her as we head into the kitchen to grab a snack. "You promised me a talk, remember?"

She picks up an apple and takes a bite out of it as if stalling for time. Finally, she says, "Let me change, and we'll go. Meet me out on the porch. And oh! Just don't mention that we're going off for a walk if Nadia asks, okay?"

"Sure," I say even though it feels like an odd request. "I'm going to change into something cooler as well."

After I grab a handful of nuts, I race up the stairs, huffing by the time I reach my room. Being on the third floor really is going to give me a calf workout every day. I switch out my school clothes for a tank and cotton shorts.

Once I've changed, I thread my way through the corridors, careful to walk as nonchalantly as possible past Nadia's office door where she's reviewing paperwork at her desk, Lexi's warning front on my mind.

But before I'm in the clear, I hear Nadia call my name.

"Estrella!" she says.

I freeze in the middle of the hall, my stomach churning about. Suddenly, I feel guilty like I'm about to do something wrong. Which is silly. I'm just going for a walk with a friend. There's nothing wrong with that, right?

I backtrack and slip into Nadia's office, practically hugging the door frame.

"So, how was your first day of school?" she asks, smiling over at me, her hands resting on a pile of paperwork. "I'm sure it was all a bit overwhelming."

"It was." I swallow, carefully choosing my next words. "Lexi was great. I'd have been lost without her. But my classes are going well."

"Excellent." Nadia's eyes flicker to her computer screen and a crease forms along her forehead. "Did you meet any new friends?"

My pulse kicks up as the memory of Dion rushes back to me. The sharp jawline. The curve of his lips. "Not yet. I'm sure I'll have a chance once I get more settled."

"Wonderful." Nadia's smile suddenly seems forced. "I'm

very impressed with you, Estrella. You seem to really want to embrace your new life with passion. This is going to make all the difference in your transition."

I nod, and even with Mara's warning to not ask too many questions, I still can't help myself. The emptiness in my chest just won't let up.

"If any of my family emails or calls," I say, "you'll let me know, right? I mean, it's only been a week since the accident. Maybe a relative will hear about it and come looking for me."

Nadia's brown eyes warm and she nods sympathetically. "Absolutely. You'll be the first to know."

The tension in my chest loosens a little at her words. Knowing that a family member could still find me gives me hope.

"But don't get caught up on your past," Nadia adds, rising from her seat and coming to stand beside me. "Over the years, I've found the girls who find the most success in their new lives can let go of the past..."

"I know." I roll my eyes. "And seize the future."

Nadia beams and gives me a hug. She smells like the antiseptic soap at the hospital. "Would you like some hot tea before you start working on your homework? I always find it soothing."

"No, thanks," I say. "I'm going to get started right away on my homework before dinner."

Nadia smiles, patting my arm. I give her an awkward wave before I hurry down the hall.

Almost as if I'm escaping.

The moment I step outside, I take a deep gulp of sea air. It's warm and thick, and though I recognize the scent, it still feels oddly foreign. I must not have visited the beach very often. Maybe my old trailer home wasn't close to the ocean.

The wind chimes clang over my head, relaxing me, and suddenly I'm wondering if a nap might be a better way to spend the afternoon than traipsing out to the beach. The reality is today has been exhausting.

Lexi half-bounces out of the house, her hair bobbing up and down along with her. She's changed into a spaghetti-strapped blue shirt and cut-off jean shorts. She looks so relaxed and carefree. She's got confidence that says she knows who she is and what her future holds.

I wish I had that confidence. Right now I'm just trying to get through each hour without stabbing headaches or figuring out how to deal with every situation I'm in.

"You okay?" Lexi's face switches to concern. She threads her arm through mine and tugs me down the steps of the porch.

"More like overwhelmed," I say, following the path as it winds its way through a thick mangrove patch. "I guess I have so many questions on top of just coping with this new life. I think if I had a clearer understanding of things, I'd be able to cope better, you know? Like what was up with Mara saying I shouldn't ask too many questions or I'd end up like Clara?"

Lexi presses her lips together as if she's trying to decide what to tell me or not.

"See?" I point to her face. "You've got that look that tells me you're not sure if you can trust me."

This makes Lexi laugh. "Wow. Am I really that transparent? But yeah, I mean, around here I've learned to be careful who I can confide in. It's hard to know who to trust. I trust Tiffany and Mara. But the others? I don't know."

The path dead ends at a set of wooden steps that lead up to a walkway. Lexi skips up them, but my feet balk at her words.

"Why can't you trust them?"

"Some girls will tell Nadia that you're asking questions and that's never a good thing. I know this sounds strange, but I've been here for a long time, and if you ask me, Nadia doesn't want us to remember our pasts. I've seen her get upset at girls who have tried."

"Like Clara?"

"Exactly like Clara." She leans against the wooden railing. "Clara was always asking questions that made Nadia uneasy. During one teatime, she demanded to see her records. When Nadia brought them out, Clara got really upset. She said things were missing and it wasn't complete."

My mind rushes back to my school records. How they were missing my former address and school name. I'd thought the very same thing Clara had.

"So what happened after Clara confronted Nadia?"

"At first, nothing." Lexi blows out a long breath and rubs her forehead. "But then one night, noises woke me up. I snuck downstairs and found Clara had broken into Nadia's office."

"Wow. That was bold."

"Right? But you should've seen the room. It was a complete disaster. All the drawers were opened, papers covered the floor, and books had been tossed off the shelves. The worst part was seeing Clara. She was sweating and her eyes were wild. She was running about the room, searching it, muttering, 'It's here. I know it's here.' When I went into the office to calm her down, Nadia, Mara, and two nurses showed up."

Lexi goes silent, staring down at the wooden walkway. The sea breeze kicks up her hair, the sun making the strands look like flames.

"What happened next?"

"The nurses tried to grab her, but she climbed out the window."

"So she ran away?"

"She's gone. Never saw her again." Lexi crosses her arms and nods, still unable to look at me. "Mara saw the whole thing, too. Clara and she were really close so I think that's why Mara is still bitter over it all."

Fear crawls into my chest and I press my hand over my mouth to hold in my shock. Would that happen to me as well? Would I lose my mind like Clara? The scariest part is it doesn't feel too far-fetched.

"Come on." Lexi takes my hand. "Enough of this depressing talk. You've got to see this view!"

She drags me up the steps and as soon as I leave the mangrove tunnel, bright sunlight beams on my shoulders and heat radiates on my skin. When I reach the top of the stairs, a short walkway leads out to a shell-white beach. And then beyond it stretches the ocean, all blue with frothy white-capped waves crashing onto the shore.

Wind whips my hair against my face, bringing with it the scent of sea and sand.

"It's gorgeous!" I exclaim.

"Right?" Lexi kicks off her shoes and runs out onto the beach.

I follow after her, and my feet sink into the hot sand. It hugs my toes and warms me up, and I decide I love the ocean. We race out to the water, laughing like we're little kids. We kick at the waves and then Lexi splashes me, the cold water waking me up as it hits me. The sea tastes like salt.

"Oh, no, you don't," I say, giggling, and then start splashing water back at her.

Finally, we stop and collapse onto the sandy beach. I push my wet hair out of my face and squint against the sun.

"You need a pair of sunglasses," Lexi decides. "Maybe this weekend we can get Nadia to give us permission to do an outing at the mall."

"Outing at the mall?"

"Yeah, it's so annoying." She groans dramatically. "Nadia doesn't let any of us go off on our own without permission. But every Saturday, the staff takes us out on the center's bus, and we go somewhere fun."

Tiny seashells are scattered around me, and I start collecting them. "Do you ever wonder what your life was like before Nadia's?" I finally ask.

"All the time." Lexi digs her toes into the sand. "But let's not talk about depressing stuff. Tell me what you think about your first day of school."

I laugh and start tossing the shells one by one into the surf. "Well, you're not going to believe it, but I'm pretty sure I met the guy you gave a tour to today."

"Oh!" She crosses her legs under her and turns to face me. "Yes! The hottie from Brazil."

"The very one." I grin, and it takes everything in me not to sigh over the memory of seeing him. His smooth, long gait. Those rich chocolaty eyes. "He was walking down the hall when I first saw him. He was with a girl who also was pretty gorgeous herself."

"Oh, her." Lexi makes a gagging noise. "I heard she's his girlfriend, not his sister, which is so sad."

My heart sinks. "His girlfriend? You sure?"

"I went to the office and asked. I'm nosy, what can I say? But I think we should still name him."

"Agreed." I nod. "Something about his eyes."

I kept thinking about him and that look he gave me. Am I crazy to think there had been a spark between us?

Although there's the fact he seemed really mad when he saw me and ran away. And he did avoid me at the bus loop. So yeah. I'm probably making something out of nothing.

"You've got the hots for him, don't you?" she asks.

"It's silly to be mooning over a boy who already has a girlfriend." I brush the sand off my hands. "Besides, I doubt he'd be interested in an orphan from a trailer home who can't even remember her own parents."

"Who cares about all of that? And if he thinks those things about you, he's not worth your time."

"To make matters worse, I practically fainted from a headache the first time I saw him. I'm definitely not throwing out sexy-girl vibes."

Lexi shoots me a sympathetic look. "I'm sorry."

"Well, he's got a girlfriend, so it doesn't matter anyway."

"Boys leave their girlfriends all the time. Don't let her stand in your way of victory."

"Lexi!" I punch her playfully in the arm. "You make it sound like you want me to break them up."

"Sometimes a girl has to live a little, right?" She chuckles and lies down so her face stares up at the sun. "There is something about him, isn't there? I almost felt a sense of déjà vu when I first saw him."

"Me, too! Maybe he just has a familiar face."

"Or he's secretly a movie star!"

We laugh, but then I notice a lone figure standing on the beach in the distance. The person is wearing a long black robe, the ends fluttering in the breeze in a ghostly flap. An oversized hood droops over the person's face, hiding their features.

Icy chills run down my spine because it feels like the person is staring right at me.

Searing pain hits my temples, and I cry out, clamping my eyes shut and ducking my head against the sudden harsh sunlight.

"Estrella?" Lexi grabs my shoulders. "You okay?"

Her voice fades as a buzzing rushes into my ears and images flash through my mind.

Jagged, silvery knives.

Hooded figures advancing.

Razor-sharp claws.

And then the vision fades and the buzzing retreats. Lexi is rubbing my arms, saying, "Just breathe. Just relax."

I blink open my eyes and scan the beach for the dark-clothed figure. But the beach is empty other than Lexi and me. Whoever that was has vanished.

Or perhaps the strange, cloaked person was a figment of my own imagination.

14

AN IMPOSSIBLE PLAN CAN REALLY RUIN A DAY

TRISTAN

Florida

I drum my fingers on the steering wheel, eyeing the humans entering Olympia High School. There are literally thousands of them, voluntarily subjecting themselves to torture. What kind of madness is this?

I shake my head, reminding myself to stay on task. Today's plan is simple. Find the girl and convince her to come with me. If all goes to plan, we can be at the Traveling Pool by lunch. Back at the castle by dinner.

I check the schedule Katka uploaded into my phone and take another sip of coffee, rubbing my forehead. I'd forgotten how killer jet lag is.

My schedule is a nightmare. Economics. British Literature.

Calculus?

I'm going to kill Katka.

I can't believe I agreed to go along with this idiotic plan. It's going to be a complete waste of my time. I can think of a million things to do other than chase after some mindless Nazco who's been ripped of her memories.

To make matters worse, we have no clue who this Conduit could be other than there are rumors that it's a female. Unbelievable. How am I to weed out this Nazco among all these high schoolers without knowing what she looks like?

I try to stretch out my legs, which is a hopeless cause in this ridiculous Kia Soul car, and I stare back at my dismal situation. My heart stops, and I suddenly realize this mission may be more difficult than I thought.

Because there, hunched on the edge of the roof, gazing down at every person entering the building, hover two Wraiths. At least the sick predators are cloaked in an invisibility enchantment to the human eye. Otherwise, I can only imagine the chaos those despicable things would create. Still, their presence tells me I've come to the right place. The difficult part will be getting past them without being noticed.

Another issue is my outfit. Katka has me dolled up in a tie, khakis, and button-down shirt. Between the damn car and ridiculous clothes, I could kill her. I rip off my tie and punch in her number on the cell phone.

"This better be an emergency, Tristan." Katka's voice is clipped in annoyance. "You are only allowed to call me if you're dying."

"This is an emergency. First off, these clothes you've got

me dressed in are nothing like what the students are wearing. I might blend in with the teachers perhaps, but otherwise, those Wraiths are going to spot me a kilometer away."

"There are Wraiths there?" And for a moment, I hear a tinge of worry in her voice. "Still, that does not qualify for an emergency."

"Second, where's my Corvette?"

"I sent you a car, dimwit."

"Really, Katka? This toy can hardly qualify for a car. I can barely sit in the seat. And there isn't a place for my weapons or jet propulsion. If things go sour, there's no way we'll be able to escape."

"Fine. I'll work on it."

"Finally, you didn't send me a picture of the girl." I know this last one is a stretch, but annoying Katka is one of my favorite pastimes.

"You're such a spoiled brat, you know that? No one knows who she is or what she looks like. Next time, don't call. Even if it's an emergency."

Then with a click, the line goes dead.

"Right." I sigh and pocket the phone. "As usual I'm the one sent to the front lines completely unprepared, completely undervalued."

I make quick work of my clothes. Using my knife, I cut my pants into makeshift shorts, untuck my shirt, roll up the sleeves, and unfasten the top two buttons. Then I stash the knife into the glove compartment and grab my backpack, where I've got all of my fake transfer information.

As I weave through the cars in the parking lot, I search for an unsuspecting student I can latch onto. If I'm paired with a human, the Wraiths will be less likely to notice me. I slip beside a girl that looks like she's been doused in pink. Pink shoes, pink skirt, and a pink shirt. It's a wonder her hair isn't pink.

"Hello." I sidle up beside her, smiling and fusing as much of my glamour her way as I can. The last thing I need is for her to freak out and alert the Wraiths. They wouldn't need much convincing to eat her for lunch.

She stares up at me, slightly startled. "Uh...hello there," she squeaks. "Do I know you?"

"I'm new here," I continue, glancing up briefly at the roof as we grow closer to the entrance. So far the Wraiths haven't indicated they've noticed me. "Could you point me to the office?"

"I'd love to." The girl flashes me a smile, giving me her full attention. "I'm Lexi. If you'd like, I could give you a tour of the school after you check in."

"That would be fantastic," I say, feeling slightly guilty about manipulating her emotions. But seeing as the Wraiths never noticed me and every student is still alive, I'll give the moment a win.

When we enter the main office with statues of Greek gods and images of ancient Titans, I can't resist a chuckle. If only these humans knew the real story behind their myths.

15
THIS ISN'T AMNESIA, THIS IS LUNACY
ESTRELLA

Florida

In the shuffle of exiting the buses, I lose my friends in the crowds as I head into school.

But I'm fine. *I can totally manage on my own*, I think, shoving down my fears.

Today's number one goal is to make it through the entire day without passing out or causing a scene. I can do this.

"Hello, Estrella."

Startled, I glance over my shoulder. When I see who it is, I stumble in surprise, nearly falling flat on my face. It's the hottie from yesterday.

Dion.

His long, lean body lounges on one of the benches in the school's courtyard with his well-defined arms stretched across the back and head tilted toward the sky as if he doesn't have a care in the world.

He levels his gaze at me, smiling. "Surprised you, huh?"

You have no idea.

I'm rooted to the ground, unable to move, speak, or even think properly.

What is wrong with me? *Pull yourself together!*

I shrug in a carefree manner. I bet I'm not the first girl who's fallen head-over-heels for him—literally—and I'm slightly embarrassed I joined the ranks.

"Sorry about that," he says, and in a way I believe him.

Honestly, with those melt-worthy eyes and thick, dark hair, I could forgive him for anything.

"How do you know my name?" I ask suspiciously and tilt my head to the side, pretending to be angry. "It's not really fair since I don't know yours."

Except I do, but he doesn't need to know that. Except then his deep, tanned complexion lights up and he jumps to his feet.

So much for being tough on him.

"True." He moves closer, focusing only on me. Suddenly I feel like I'm a lamb and he's a jaguar, sleek and swift. Sweat trickles down the nape of my neck.

"My name is Dion, and I have to confess, I asked around to get your name."

I don't know if I should be creeped out or flattered. Okay, I'm definitely flattered.

As if sensing my hesitancy, he says, "We met in the hall yesterday. Guess I didn't make much of an impression."

Other than obsessing with this crazy gut feeling we'd met before, no, not at all, I think sarcastically.

"Sure, I remember," I say, starting to walk again as he steps in stride alongside me. "You were the one that waltzed into school during a Code Red storm like it was a summer shower. Everyone's talking about it."

"I'm sure I'm old news by now. Look, after seeing you in the hall yesterday, I wanted to find you and apologize for my rude behavior."

"Rude?"

"You know, running away after you fell. I had some upsetting, and honestly quite shocking, news I needed to deal with. And I didn't want you to think poorly of me."

Oh. I think about his expression after he talked to me briefly in the hall. That mixture of pain, and was it disgust or shock? Here I'd thought I'd brought those emotions out of him, but maybe I was wrong. Or maybe he's just trying to make me feel better.

"Is everything okay?" I ask.

"Everything is great now." He smiles and pushes a dark strand out of his eyes. "I've just had a lot to adjust to recently."

As we stroll side by side, my stomach does these little flips like I hadn't eaten enough for breakfast or maybe I ate too much. I fight this irresistible urge to grab his fingers, which would be mortifying if I suddenly did, so I clamp my hands on my backpack straps. There's something strangely familiar about him like we've talked before.

Maybe the doctors were wrong. Maybe this isn't amnesia, but lunacy.

"Since I'm new here," Dion continues, "perhaps you might show me around town sometime?"

Is he asking me out on a date? Nope, don't let your imagination get out of control. "I'm new, too, so I might not be the best tour guide."

He laughs, a deep, rich-sounding laugh. "Perhaps we will have to find our way around together then."

The bell rings and I grimace. We were just getting to know each other. "Got to get to British Lit. According to my friend, Mr. Terring flips out when we're late."

"Maybe I'll see you at lunch."

"Yeah, that would be great."

We part ways at my hall, each heading to our own locker. I hum softly, ducking past football players shouting some pregame mantra until I find mine and spin the combination.

"Love that tune," Lexi says and leans herself against the locker next to mine. "What is it?"

She's sipping a Mountain Dew and looking more like a flamingo than a girl.

"That outfit looks even brighter under these fluorescent lights," I say, lifting my eyebrows. The mix of shiny pink boots, short pink skirt, and cheerleader-style pink top is so...pink.

"Don't get me started." Lexi rolls her eyes and takes a swig of her drink. "What can I say? I lost the bet. And now I've got to pay the price. The worst part is I met this beautiful boy before school and his first impression of me was pink."

I giggle. "Maybe he likes pink?"

"He seemed a little distracted by the pink if you ask me. Listen, I've got to stop by the drama teacher's room first to ask her a question about tryouts, but I'll see you in class.

Hey, could you hold this for me? Ms. Oates always makes a fuss when she sees me drinking caffeinated fun."

Lexi pushes the can into my hand and struts off. I'm staring after her, trying to process her words when Mara sidles up next to me.

"Isn't it the greatest?" Mara chuckles, staring at Lexi's disappearing form. "We made a bet. Whoever could come up with the most Shakespearean quotes won. The loser had to wear that."

"Remind me to never bet against you." I shake my head and pull out my textbooks.

"Yeah, you'd lose." Mara sighs as if this is pure truth.

But between Lexi's Mountain Dew, my piles of books, and talking with Dion, everything seems off-kilter, and within seconds, the books are sliding out of my hand. I try to catch them but end up dumping the rest of Lexi's soda over everything.

"Ouch." Mara grimaces at my mess. "Is that Lexi's soda? Why do you let her run all over you?"

"She's my friend, so I do nice things for her," I snap, suddenly super annoyed with Mara.

She lifts her thick, dark eyebrows. "Somebody's in a bad mood."

"I'm sorry. I shouldn't have snapped at you. It's just sometimes I feel so...wrong. You know? Like my brain can't think properly. I can't walk without tripping. I can't even hold things properly."

Mara's annoyed expression smooths out and a softness fills her eyes. "I'll grab some paper towels in the bathroom and get you cleaned up. Just a sec."

I'm trying to rescue as many of the books from the pool

of soda when someone snickers behind me. I turn to discover it's the girl I saw in the hallway yesterday, walking in with Dion.

AKA: Dion's girlfriend.

Dion's girlfriend is wearing a short leather skirt and a top that shows off her every curve. Silver hoop earrings dangle from her ears, a sharp contrast to her stylish long black hair. From the gleam in her eyes, she doesn't seem to approve of me.

"Oh my, this isn't your day, is it?" A chuckle erupts from her perfectly sculpted throat. She crosses her arms, showing off candy-apple red nails. "I saw you chatting with Dion."

"Excuse me?" Has she been spying on me?

She steps closer. I nearly choke on her perfume. "Stay clear of him. Trust me. It's for your own good."

"What's going on?" Mara steps to my side, a wad of paper towels in her hands.

"Lovely." The girl's eyes focus on the paper towels. "I see you're preparing for your new career by joining the janitor staff. I must say, it's a perfect fit for you, Estrella."

"How do you know my name?" I ask, but the girl spins on her red heels and clips off in the other direction. Then I mutter, "And why do you hate me so much?"

"Wow." Mara shakes her head. "You sure know how to make enemies fast."

"I think she's mad because I was talking to Dion."

"Jealous much?" Mara smirks at the girl's retreating back. "Forget her. She's just threatened by your spellbinding clumsiness. It's hard to compete with that."

We laugh and my muscles relax. I'm a little surprised Mara and I are getting along. I've always thought she disliked me. Between the two of us, we manage to sop up as much of the soda as we can.

"So the hottie talked to you, huh?" Mara tosses the dripping paper towels in the garbage. "You like him?"

"I know this sounds weird, but it's like we have this connection. Except, according to his girlfriend, I need to stay away from him. It's for my own good."

"She said that?" Mara's eyes darken. "She doesn't decide what's good for you. That's your job."

"You know what?" I shut my locker. "You're right."

Mara might be a little gruff and blunt, but she's not cruel, I decide as we head to class. Unfortunately, by the time I enter British Lit, I'm late.

"Good morning, Miss Milton," Mr. Terring drones as if today is anything but good. "Glad you decided to join us."

So much for making good impressions and meeting my goals about not making scenes. And first period hasn't even started!

"Where did my happy humming girl go?" Lexi asks as I drop into my chair, slamming my book bag on the desk. "And how did I get to class before you?"

"It's a tossup between my sticky soda-flavored books or Dion's girlfriend. I can't decide which is more disgusting. By the way, no soda for you. I dumped it over all my books."

"This girl has really got you all riled up. Now I'm desperate to meet her."

"Trust me," I say. "You don't want to."

Mr. Terring is eyeing me, so I shut up and flip open my notebook to last night's homework, determined to not let anything ruin my chances of putting my life back together.

Lexi groans as Mr. Terring pulls up portraits of Frost and photos of his house on the Smartboard.

"At least you did your homework," Lexi whispers. "But let's be honest. Who cares about homework when your hottie is here in your class?"

"What?" I hiss.

"Behind you, one row back to the left."

I raise my eyebrows, but Lexi's already nodding and bobbing her head encouragingly. How could I have missed seeing Dion as I came into class? And why hadn't he mentioned we were in the same class earlier?

I crane my neck back just a little so I don't look too desperate and peek over my shoulder. From where I'm sitting, I spot the top of his dark hair and his arms stretched over the desk.

My heart flutters. It's him, all right.

But there's something familiar about this moment. Something on the tip of my mind. The room blurs, and for a heartbeat, it's like I'm sitting at my desk, but in a different place altogether.

One with white walls and dark, wooden tables.

The room swirls. I suck in the air-conditioned air, forcing my eyes to focus. Lexi's hand clutches my arm, her eyes searching mine.

"You okay?" she whispers.

"Sure," I lie. What is wrong with me? The last thing I need is for her to think I'm swooning over some silly guy just because he's cute. Except that would be better than her knowing I can barely handle sitting here in class. "You're right. He's—" I can't think of the right word as my mind is still trying to process that vision I saw. Or...my heart stutters...was it a memory?

"Cute? Dreamy? Sexy?"

I smile. "All of the above."

Mr. Terring's voice jolts me from our conversation. "And now who would like to read today's opening for us?" he asks.

"I would be glad to," Dion calls out.

"Very good of you, Dion. Especially this being your first day of class. Proceed."

Dion stands up and strides confidently to the front of the classroom, sporting black jeans and a white T-shirt. Lexi sighs dramatically behind me.

"I know today's poem is "In Neglect," but I'd like to read "When We Two Parted" instead," Dion says and surprisingly, the teacher just bobs his head as if Dion could do whatever he wanted.

He reads the poem so beautifully, it almost sounds like singing. A couple of girls, including Lexi, sigh as he reads. But there's something about the way Dion recites the poem that makes me feel like there's truth in the words he's reading.

Once he finishes, he looks up and flashes me a mischievous smile.

My heart flips. Twice.

"Someone crank up the AC," Lexi murmurs.

He heads back to his seat, but this time, as he passes by me, he leans over my shoulder from behind and whispers, "Sorry about my friend Chandra. She's a real pain sometimes. I'll make it up by giving you a ride home today. Trust me, it'll be far more comfortable than that bumpy ride you get on the bus."

My ear tingles from his breath. Had I heard him right? He called Chandra his *friend*, not his girlfriend. He settles back at his desk and doesn't look at me again. For a moment, I wonder if I imagined it all.

But when I glance over at Lexi, I know it wasn't my imagination. She's bobbing her head up and down in a yes, her eyes wider than Nadia's pancakes.

My mind whirls back to Chandra's warning. She seems like the kind of girl who would follow through with a threat. But then Mara's words drown out my worries and I sit taller. Mara is right. This Chandra girl isn't going to make my decisions. That's my job.

I pick up my pen and scribble out, "I'd love a ride. See you after school." Then when Mr. Terring's back is turned, I pass it back to him.

And now I get to wait six hours for school to end.

16

HIGH SCHOOL. IS THIS SOME NEW METHOD OF TORTURE?

TRISTAN

Florida

"I can't find her anywhere in this wretched school," I bark into the phone. "Any updates on some kind of intel on her? A photo? Description?"

"Hello to you, your lordship," Katka says dryly. "You've now called me three times in the last hour. This is really unacceptable. I told you *not* to call me."

As annoyed as I am, I can't resist grinning. Both of us know she has to answer my every call and she can't say no to me. Which makes her cranky.

A bell rings, which I think means I'm late or nearly late for something. How do humans live like this?

"So is that a yes or no?" I press, joining the throngs of students outside.

I hold up a school map in one hand and cross the court-yard in search of the English building. Benches line the walkways shaded by waving palms. Above, the blue sky is lightly streaked with wispy clouds. If it weren't for the vulture Wraiths perched on the rooftops and the frantic rush from class to class, this place might actually be tolerable.

"That's a negative," she says, then sighs. "But being who she is, she's probably got light hair and startling blue eyes."

My heart twists in pain because I know this. Once again, I'm reminded of my sister's eyes, once bright and full of life. Laughing over my silly jokes and teasing me over my inability to best her at swordplay.

And now she's gone. Her heart no longer beats, and her last breath was one of pain. I grit my teeth and crush my schedule into a ball.

But I can't think about her now or the pain will rip me apart once again and I'll fall apart right here in the middle of my mission. I push those thoughts aside and put all my defenses back in place.

"So you're saying I need to start looking into all the eyes of every blonde girl here at the school?" I ask. "I'm sure that will go over well with the female population."

"You are impossible, you know that? And why are you talking to me during school hours? You did read the hand-book, correct? No cell phones at school."

"Absolutely, what kind of idiot do you take me for?" Which was only seventy percent a lie since I had skimmed through the manual on the flight over. "Stay on the line."

"In case you need me," Katka says, and I can imagine her rolling her eyes.

I'm ducking around the corner, trying to find my next class in this depressing concrete block corridor when I nearly plow over a lady wearing a flowered shirt and black pants with heels. Her dark hair is neatly tucked back into a shining ponytail. The ID dangling from the lanyard tells me she's a teacher. My heart sinks.

"Please accept my apologies," I say, and I'm about to skirt around her when she clears her throat and holds out her hand.

I stare at it blankly.

"You must be new here, Mr.—" the teacher says in a brisk tone.

"Tristan Longshire, at your service," I say.

"Then Mr. Longshire, you must have forgotten the rules about no cell phones used during school hours. Hand it over."

"My phone?" Oh, good lord, no.

"Most certainly."

"Right." Then into the phone, I tell Katka, "Err..., I've got to go." She's currently too busy laughing to respond. Numbly I click END CALL and relinquish the phone.

"You can pick it up today after your detention," she says.

"Detention?" My eyebrows rise. I don't remember reading about that in the manual.

"That's right." She makes a note on her tablet, a glimpse of a smile on her lips. "You'll be visiting Mr. Terring's class-room at 2:30 p.m. Better run along now and get to class. You have one minute until you're late."

This place is madness. Who subjects themselves to this sort of torture?

But I merely smile and bow my head to the lady, saying, "As you wish."

She lifts her eyebrows as if dumbfounded by my response.

I turn on my heels and run as fast as I can to class per her instructions. What seemed like a simple grab-and-go mission is starting to turn into a complete failure. The hallways have emptied out at an alarming speed. I turn a corner as a kid kicks their locker closed. A quick check at my wrinkled, half-torn map tells me I'm nearly at my next destination.

Art with Mrs. Cummings.

Except as I look back up, a black-cloaked figure slips into the hall, the shredded material floating about it as if caught in the wind. My sudden appearance must have startled it, and it turns to stare in my direction. It halts in place after seeing me.

My heart stops in fear. Though its hood drapes over most of its face, cloaking its features, there's no mistaking what this creature is.

A Wraith.

17
SOMETHING FOREIGN. SOMETHING DANGEROUS
ESTRELLA

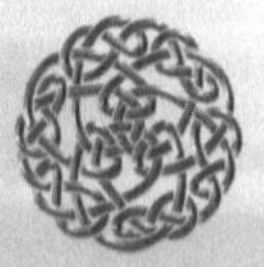

Florida

I can't believe I'm going to be late for class again. Lexi was showing me the school theater and backstage area when the first bell rang, which gave us exactly five minutes to haul it to the other side of the school.

Lexi and I race to art class, careening around the corner and entering the long art corridor. But there at the other end is a strange man with flowing black robes fluttering in the non-existent wind and a heavy hood draped over his face.

I stop, frozen-still.

It's the same Reaper-wanna-be as on the beach. Which definitely isn't cool.

Is he following us or something?

Lexi stops in her tracks and sucks her breath in, making

a choking sound, which tells me I'm not imagining this creepy man dressed up like Death himself. I clench her arm, waiting for the weird guy to do something, but he just remains as still as the walls around us.

My eyes drift to the one other person in the hall. A blonde-haired guy is leaning against the wall, reading from a book as if completely oblivious to the creepy dude staring at us.

"Greetings, ladies." The guy pushes off the wall.

I jerk at the sound of his voice, carefree with a distinct accent.

"Oh!" Lexi says, voice quivering. "It's you. New guy."

"That's me. The new guy." He ambles toward us, blocking my vision of the creepy guy at the other end of the hall. "Are you ladies attending class? Perhaps I can escort you?"

Lexi nods faster than a bobblehead. "Yes, yes, please. We're late."

"Yeah." I eye the weird guy warily, but as bizarre as he is, Lexi's freaking out has me even more worried. "You okay, Lex?"

"Yep! Great!"

I mean, that guy dressed up like Death is super creepy, especially since he seems to have really freaked her out, too. That can't be a good sign, right?

"Let me get the door for you," the guy says.

"Such a gentleman." Lexi giggles but it's forced as if she's acting for a play she hasn't rehearsed.

I flash the guy a grateful smile as I step into art class, trying to figure out what exactly is going on with Lexi and that strange guy out in the hall. And what's up with this new guy and why does he sound like he's from the seventeenth century?

When the door shuts firmly behind us, my muscles instantly relax. I'm not the only one because Lexi lets out a long breath and wipes away a bead of sweat from her forehead.

"You sure you're okay?" I ask her. "You don't look so good. And what was up with that guy out there dressed like the Grim Reaper?"

She swallows hard and her eyes grow big and wide. "Grim Reaper?" Suddenly the bell rings, signaling class is starting. "Oh, did you hear that? We're not late. That's great. No tardies for us!"

"Okay." I shake my head. "But something is definitely up with you. You're acting weird. And don't tell me you didn't see that creepster out there."

"Wait." New Guy steps closer to us, focusing on me intently. "You saw someone else in the hall?"

"How could I not?" I glance at the door and shiver. "So you saw him, too? I'm not losing my mind?"

The guy's sky-blue eyes light up, and he suddenly smiles as if I've somehow completely made his day. "I most certainly did," he whispers.

My breath catches at his intensity. There's definitely something different about him. Sure, he's tall with broad shoulders, and there's no doubt he must work out in the gym, but there's something *more*.

Something foreign.

Something dangerous.

He's wearing a black button-down shirt, the top buttons undone enough to reveal a leather necklace wrapped around his neck. I realize it's three cords twisted into a knot.

A knot just like my tattoo.

My whole body stills.

And then that same horrible, annoying pain pierces me. I cry out, ducking my head and shutting my eyes to stop the fire racing through my mind. Why does this piercing headache always show up at the most annoying times?

A strong hand supports me before I crumble to the floor. New Guy holds me up as I sway from the sudden impact of the searing pain.

"Estrella." Lexi's voice echoes through my agony, dragging me back to the moment. "It's going to be alright. Just stay calm and take deep breaths."

The room swims as New Guy half-carries, half-directs me to a chair, which I gladly sag into while Lexi trails alongside me.

"Class is starting!" Ms. Cummings calls out from somewhere across the room. "Today we're going to start our next unit, which will be painting. So everyone grab a smock and then find a seat at an easel."

Finally the room refocuses, and I realize that New Guy is hunched by my side as if ready to catch me if I fall out of my chair.

"I'm going to get you some water," Lexi says, her face pale under the fluorescent lights.

I feel terrible for making her worried and nearly causing a scene in class. I'm just glad I didn't pass out like I did in the hallway after seeing Dion.

"Can I get you anything?" New Guy asks, his eyes searching my face in worry.

I shake my head, trying to laugh off this very awkward moment. "Don't worry. I'm fine. I just get these weird headaches from time to time. It's a medical condition."

"A medical condition?" His brow knits up as if trying to process what I'm saying. "I'm sorry to hear that. My name is Tristan."

"Tristan." I say his name, hoping it would sound familiar on my tongue, but nothing comes to mind. "I'm Estrella, and I'm actually new here, too."

But all I want to do is ask why he is wearing that necklace, considering it matches my tattoo. What does the knot mean? Lexi appears, pushing an apron against my chest and a cup of water into my hand. "Here. Take a sip of water and then put on your apron."

"Yes, Mom," I tease, rolling my eyes, but I'm grateful for her kindness.

"And thank you, Tristan, for opening the door," Lexi tells him. "And for catching my friend."

Tristan chuckles and flashes her a smile. It's a mischievous one that she returns with a glare. And somehow it all feels like the two of them share a secret that I'm not a part of.

"I hope our paths will cross again." He leaves but his presence seems to fill the room, demanding my complete attention.

I want to reach out and tell him to stay. Ask him the questions battering around in my head, but I've already made an idiot of myself and I'm not about to add asking awkward personal questions to my growing repertoire.

I glance around to see if anyone else has noticed him, and yep, everyone else in the class is eyeing him as well.

So it's not just me.

But my biggest relief is that no one seems to have realized I nearly passed out. I lean back against my chair and take a sip of water, letting my mind clear as Ms. Cummings takes roll and gives us instructions, explaining that we'll be free painting today.

"That was eventful." Lexi settles into the easel beside mine, but her hands flutter about like she's still unsettled. "Are you feeling okay, or do you need to go home? I think we should go home. Like right now."

"What? No!" I laugh, picking up my paintbrush. There's something reassuring about holding the brush in my hand. "My headache is gone. In fact, I actually feel good now. It's like a fog has lifted from my mind. Also, I think I used to paint before my accident."

"Really?" Lexi's frown hasn't lifted.

"This feels familiar." I stare at my brush and the smooth white canvas before me. "And now I know what I need to do next."

Lexi pauses painting and blue paint drips from her brush onto her pink skirt. "And what's that?"

I peek around my easel and scan the room until my eyes land on the new guy across the room, painting on his own canvas. "I need to talk to Tristan."

Lexi swallows. "I think that's a bad idea."

"Why?"

"Because he saw that guy out in the hall," Lexi whispers.

"But I thought you didn't see anyone in the hall?" I press, my heart speeding up.

"I may have seen someone."

From the other side of the room, Mrs. Cummings clears

her throat, interrupting us. "Today our focus will be connecting with our emotions. As you choose your color palette, think about colors that represent your feelings."

"I'm confused," I tell Lexi. "Now you're saying you did see that creepy guy?"

She grimaces. "Yeah."

"What does Tristan seeing that creepster have anything to do with me talking to him?" I ask. "That doesn't make sense."

She bites her bottom lip and a shadow passes across her face.

I touch her arm, suddenly feeling bad for pushing her. I've always thought of Lexi as the strong one at Nadia's, but it's in moments like this that I see she's struggling just as much as the rest of us.

"Don't let him get to you," I say softly. "I'm sure he's just some kid dressed up going around trying to scare kids."

Mrs. Cummings strolls past us like a dancer, her long brown skirt swishing gracefully around her ankles. "Pay attention, girls. Save the chit-chat for lunch. Right now I want you to think about something special." She pauses, staring at the two of us. "Do you have it pictured in your mind?"

As much as I can't wait to paint, it's hard to focus after everything that has happened today. But I nod, and she moves on. My mind whirls as I try to process everything that has happened. Dion offering to give me a drive home, Chandra threatening me and seeming to hate the very air I breathe, and even that strange Grim Reaper guy out in the hall who shook Lexi to her very core.

My eyes drift to Tristan across the room.

As if sensing my gaze, he lifts his eyes to meet mine. I suck in a deep breath because it's like he *knows* me, or at least something about me. The air between us crackles full of questions. I grip the sides of my chair, my emotions tumbling over each other.

Maybe Lexi will avoid answering my questions, but somehow I get the feeling he won't.

I need to talk to him.

"Estrella," Mrs. Cummings interjects. "You haven't started painting yet. I want to see some progress next time I come by."

"Of course." I clear my throat and stare at the white canvas on my easel.

Everyone's already sketching or blending colors. I should at least act busy, so I pull out some paints and line them up in a neat row. I close my eyes, trying to think of something to paint. But all I can think about is the corded necklace hanging against Tristan's chest.

The knot.

A twisting cord, endlessly moving, never-ending.

I groan, knowing there's no way I'm going to paint that. Not until I find out why Tristan's wearing that symbol around his neck and why I've got it tattooed on my body.

Mrs. Cummings is headed back this way, so I pick up the paintbrush and plunge it into the inky liquid. I swathe the white easel with streaks of black.

Behind me, Mrs. Cummings's rose perfume fills my nostrils. I turn to find her studying my painting, brow furrowed. She tilts her head to the side, tapping her glasses against her lips.

"Is this what you see?" she asks finally.

"Yes." Or at least this is how I feel inside, I think numbly.

"Look deeper inside. I think there's something there, emerging from the dark."

She moves on, but her words vibrate through my brain. I stare intently at the painting until my vision blurs. My hand aches to do just what she told me to. To paint my feelings and frustrations.

I dip my brush into the snow-white paint, splashing the brush across the emptiness because there's something in what she said.

Something hidden, a secret tucked away, deep in the darkness.

A spark crystallizes in my mind. I add purple and then swirl in blue through the white.

More white.

Colors whirl and spin in my mind and then on my canvas like a chest of gems. Sweat beads on my forehead and the tendrils of my hair cling to my cheeks. This stroke of the brush and the emotions spilling out onto the canvas are familiar.

Somehow I know that I've not only done this before, but I'm good at it.

And now that I've started painting, I can't seem to stop. It's like all the pain, the worries, the questions are spilling out from my brush.

Until it's complete.

I set down my paintbrush, suddenly feeling like I've poured a part of me out onto the canvas.

"It's finished," I murmur.

Lexi leans over to see. "Wow. It's so pretty."

Mrs. Cummings stands on my other side. "Inspiring!"

she pronounces. "The colors and the use of light bring it to life."

"It looks like a disco ball," Lexi says.

"Perhaps," Mrs. Cummings says thoughtfully. "Or something precious?"

"A diamond? Oh! I know. A star." Lexi crosses her arms, decided. "That's what it is."

My chest constricts and I turn my eyes away. I don't know where I saw this object or even what it is, and suddenly that thought makes me want to rip the painting to shreds.

A murmuring pounds in my mind, growing louder and louder. "*Shalik, shalik, shalalik!*" the voices say.

It's like one of those visions I had except this time I can hear the voices and they're terrifying.

I pick up the jar of black paint and fling it at the painting, streaking it with globs of black. It drips down the canvas like tears, pooling up on the edge of my easel.

The voices cease.

"Estrella!" Mrs. Cummings cries out in shock. "What are you doing?"

A few students stop painting to look over at what I've done. Great. Everyone is staring at me. I press my palms over my eyes, wishing I could just vanish from the room. Why did I do that? I'm such an idiot. But those voices...

"Ah!" Tristan's distinct voice says from behind me. "A Jackson Pollock imitator. Quite the creative painter in his splashing paint techniques."

Slowly, I lower my shaking hands.

"Well." Mrs. Cummings's eyes take in the paint dripping

onto the floor. "That may be true, but now I've got black paint on my beautiful floor."

"I'll clean it up," I say quickly. "Don't worry."

"There are cleaning supplies in the closet," she says tightly before clipping away.

I glance over my shoulder to find Tristan stepping up to my side. "You're a talented artist," he says. "You shouldn't hide your work behind black paint."

"I think you should go," Lexi tells Tristan and then shifts closer as if she's protecting me, which is comical considering she's like half his size and he's got muscles for days.

"Lexi," I whisper. "Why are you being mean?"

"I'm not being mean," she says, loud enough for Tristan to hear. "I'm just looking out for you."

Something flashes across Tristan's face. Guilt? Worry? I'm not sure, but whatever is going on, I'm definitely going to get to the bottom of this.

"You're lucky to have a good friend," Tristan says. "Maybe I'll see you around."

"Or maybe you should transfer back to your old school," Lexi snaps, eyes flashing.

Tristan presses his lips together and takes a deep breath.

I rise to my feet, tugging Lexi to join me. "Why don't you help me find the cleaning supplies?"

"Works for me," she says.

But as I brush past Tristan, he presses a small piece of paper into my palm, and then without a word to anyone else in the class, he strides out the door.

18

FORTUNE FAVORS THE BOLD
ESTRELLA

Florida

Lexi lets out a breath of relief. "So glad he's gone."

"Why are you so mean to Tristan? He was being nice."

"Was he?"

I drag her into the supply closet and turn her to face me. "Okay, what's going on? No lies. No vague, weird answers. I want to know why you pretended you didn't see that Reaper guy when you actually did and why you're acting so weird around Tristan."

"Girl, that's a lot of questions. And the answers aren't easy or quick or even small. They're big and..." She glances out into the classroom as if expecting someone is watching us. "And if I tell you, it could mess things up for you. Big time."

"You're not helping. I thought we were friends."

"We are." She squeezes my hands. "And I could be

wrong, but I think…I think we've been friends for a long time."

I frown. "What do you mean? I only met you a few days ago."

"See? Big answers. Complicated answers. And this isn't the place to talk about it with guys like Tristan, and as you call it, the Grim Reaper, hanging about."

Mrs. Cummings pops her head into the doorway. "How's the cleaning coming along?"

"Great!" I grab a mop resting against the wall and smile brightly. "We're just gathering up supplies."

Mrs. Cummings lifts her eyebrows. "The bell is about to ring so you'll need to hurry."

"Absolutely." Lexi snatches up a bottle of paint cleaner. When our teacher leaves, Lexi's voice switches to a whisper. "Listen. I don't know much, but I do know more than most of the girls at the home because unlike everyone else, I stopped drinking the tea."

My mind flashes back to each night when she watered the plant with her drink. "You think the tea keeps us from remembering?"

"Or it's some sort of blocker. When I stopped drinking the tea, I got those terrible headaches like you did, but I also started remembering pieces of my old life, too. Not everything, but moments."

"That must have been really hard."

"It was. I don't exactly remember you, but when I saw you the first day you came to Nadia's, I recognized you right away."

I rub my head, unsure of what to think about everything she said. Could we have known each other before? And if this tea keeps us from remembering, what does that make Nadia?

My heart stills as I try to process this information. Meanwhile, Lexi opens the door and is about to step out of the closet, but I hold her back.

"I think I saw that Reaper guy while we were at the beach," I admit. "Do you think he's stalking us?"

Lexi's eyes widen. "You did?" She peeks out of the closet and then drags me over to the sink and starts filling up a bucket of water. She leans in closer to me. "When I stopped drinking that tea, I also started seeing those Reaper guys hanging out around Nadia's home. I totally flipped out and I think... well... I don't even remember, honestly. But I think one attacked me."

"It attacked you? Oh my god!"

"Shh!" She furtively glances around the room as if she's worried that one might appear before us. "I'm fine. Obviously. But one moment that creepy guy was looming in front of me and the next moment, I was in the sick bay at the house, and everything was fuzzy and weird. Just like I'd felt when I first arrived at the home. I told Nadia what happened, and she got really upset. Said it was all in my head and that I needed to start taking some medicine."

"I'm so sorry, Lexi."

"So now I just pretend to not see them." She shrugs and fiddles with a sponge. "That's why you can't tell anyone what you saw."

"Have you ever seen one at school before?"

"Nope. Only at Nadia's. Knowing that they're here at school is honestly freaking me out."

She turns off the water and the two of us lug the bucket

over to my mess and start cleaning it up. My mind whirls with this new information, but I also have new questions that demand answers.

"I don't think anyone here at school can see them," she continues. "I mean, if they could, people would say something, right?"

"So what does it mean that we can?"

"It means definitely don't tell Nadia. She'll freak."

"Don't forget about Tristan." I plunge a paint-soaked sponge into the water and resume scrubbing. "He definitely saw that one in the hall."

"The fact that Tristan could see the Grim Reaper thing worries me the most. Other than you, no one else I've known can see them. Sure, he has a great European accent, and he's super hot, but I get the feeling he's not a good guy."

"Not a good guy?" I roll my eyes. "He was nothing but kind and helpful to us. You can't just base something off of feelings."

Guilt tugs at me. Of course, who am I to be lecturing her on feelings when that's exactly what I'm doing?

"My gut tells me he's dangerous, Estrella." Lexi soaks up more paint with her rag until it's black as pitch. "And it's my gut that has kept me from losing my mind when all the others at the home have lost theirs."

A lump forms in my throat. She has a point.

"Still. That's a big jump, don't you think?" I ask. "Maybe he knows something about these Grim Reapers that we don't. Maybe we can get some answers."

"I don't trust him," she says firmly. "And if you're smart, you shouldn't either."

The bell rings and the room bursts to life as students

pack up their materials and grab their backpacks. Meanwhile, Lexi heads over to the sink with the blackened washcloths.

My mind goes back to the coiled knot hanging against Tristan's neck. He knows something. I'm sure of it. His words vibrate through my head, "Maybe our paths will cross again."

Once Lexi's back is turned, I dig into my pocket where I jammed Tristan's note. Guilt slices through me that I'm not telling her everything, but right now, I don't know who to trust or what to believe.

I peek at the flowing handwriting and read his note.

Meet me in the media center during lunch. Come alone.

Tristan

19
LISTEN TO YOUR HEART. IT WON'T STEER YOU WRONG
ESTRELLA

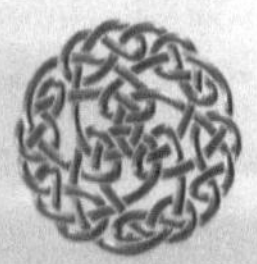

Florida

The media center entrance looms before me. I get the feeling that if I step through those doors, everything will change.

Or not.

I told Lexi I had to check on some work for history, and I'd meet her at lunch. That way I could come alone.

I fiddle with the straps of my backpack, take a deep breath, and step through the doors. The media center is warm and cozy with shelves of books filling nearly every free space. Couches paired with reading lights are tucked into corners and dozens of paper cranes hang from the ceiling, their rainbow of colors a bright contrast to the rich browns of the shelving.

The air smells familiar. I recognize the scent of aged paper and bound leather. Books, I realize. My heart skips a beat. I must have spent a lot of time at my old school's library because this smell feels comforting and inviting.

A quick scan of the place tells me Tristan isn't here; only a group of students whispering at a table by the entrance and a couple of kids checking out books. A sliver of disappointment cuts through me. But then what should I expect?

After all, how could some random stranger at school give me all the answers to my past? It's a silly hope. With my need to try to remember something before the accident, I'm obviously getting pretty desperate.

But even if Tristan isn't here, this place is packed full of knowledge. Maybe it can help me find a clue. I rub my shoulder, thinking about my tattoo and the research I did on it in the computer lab.

"Excuse me." I step up to the lady behind the desk whom I'm assuming is the media specialist. She blinks up at me through blue-framed glasses. Her brown, wavy hair is neatly pinned back. I read her name off the ID clipped to her flowered shirt. "Hello, Mrs. Thompson. I'm looking for books on symbols. Do you have any of those?"

She taps her finger to her lips in thought. "I believe so. Check out the non-fiction section. I think we have some books there on the second row at the bottom that might interest you."

"Thanks."

Once I find the location, I start combing the shelves until my fingers land on a few books that might be a starting point. Quickly, I stack them up against my chest and hurry back to the checkout desk.

"Oh, look at you," Mrs. Thompson says, taking my student ID that I finally got today and scanning it. "Appears as if you found what you're looking for."

"Yes, thank—" I begin, but my words die from my lips.

Because sitting in the corner of the room, lounging in one of the chairs and reading a book, is Tristan. Tousled hair, untucked shirt, hints of stubble on his face as if he doesn't have a care in the world.

Mrs. Thompson's scanner beeps, jerking me back to the task at hand. But as she scans each book, my mind tosses in debate. Should I walk across the room and talk to him or not?

It's a simple enough thing, right?

I mean, it's why I came here in the first place.

Except there's an undercurrent of danger surrounding him. I get what Lexi was talking about. I can't quite put my finger on it because it's not just that he's built. It's the underlying presence that hints he could face off against that Reaper in the hall and walk away unscathed.

A warning that there's more to him than he's letting on.

Maybe I should trust Lexi's gut more.

Suddenly, his eyes lift up from his book to meet mine. Bright, beautiful, and blue as a cloudless sky. There's a sharp energy in them, warning me that he's wild.

Untamable.

I suck in a deep breath. A spark ripples along my skin, igniting a part of me that deep down I know should be kept hidden. I don't know if it's my imagination or not, but it's like there's a connection that snaps into place between the two of us.

A puzzle that wasn't meant to be, and yet is.

I rub my forehead because I don't understand what is happening or why. As if sensing the same thing, he tilts his head, eyes squinting as if he too is confused. Or maybe he just feels frustrated that I haven't gone to talk to him. Ugh. I wish I knew.

Get your act together! I scream at myself.

Because the only way to find out is to walk across the room and ask, right?

Yet instinctively, I know if I do that everything will change for me because of *him.*

And that is terrifying.

He doesn't get up to meet me or even move an inch. Instead, his mouth turns up at the corner, his eyebrows lifting as if to say, *Won't you hear what I have to say?*

What do I have to lose talking to him? Nothing. And he probably—

"Estrella," a deep voice calls my name from behind me.

I spin around to find Dion striding my way, determined and confident as if he owns the world. His hair is brushed back, and his clothes hug his perfectly sculpted form. Just seeing him makes my heart skip. Instantly my muscles relax with him here.

"Hey," I say in surprise. "What are you up to?"

"I was headed to lunch and saw your friend in the hall. She said I could find you here."

I gather up my books, careful to make sure Dion doesn't see their titles, and slip them into my backpack. The last thing I need is for him to ask me questions about them only to find out I'm a freaky, brainless nobody who sees Grim Reaper look-alikes walking around school.

"Thanks for your help," I tell Mrs. Thompson and flash

her a grateful smile. Then I turn to Dion. "So lunch?"

"Rumor has it they have excellent meatloaf," he says, grinning.

I laugh. "I'll believe that when I see you eat it. The food is—to put it mildly—lacking."

"Is that a dare? Because if it is, I need to know what's in it for me."

"Nutritional value?"

He scoffs. "There's probably more salt than beef in their meatloaf. Nope. You must do better than that." Then he gives me a smile that's like hot chocolate warming me all the way to my toes.

"What's that smile for?"

"Just glad to be here. With you."

We head out into the hall, debating over what a proper reward would be, and it isn't until I'm halfway to the cafeteria that I realize I completely ditched Tristan. And he saw me do it right in front of him. My face burns with embarrassment. He must think I'm the worst person. That's the power that Dion has over me. The whole world seems to fade when he's in the room.

I think about Lexi's warning to not trust Tristan. I probably dodged a bullet avoiding him.

The two of us step into line and it's obvious by everyone's glances that they are checking Dion out. I mean, can you blame them? The guy is gorgeous and confident. It's a little unnerving that he's even talking to me.

"What's wrong?" Dion asks, picking up a tray and passing it to me.

I shrug. "Everyone is staring at you. It must feel a little awkward. Or maybe you're used to it."

Dion glances around as if he hasn't noticed anyone else in the room other than me. "Must be the new guy in school thing. They'll get used to me soon."

"Your girlfriend might not be so happy about seeing you with me." I pick up a banana and yogurt, adding them to my tray.

"My girlfriend?"

"Yeah, the girl I saw you with yesterday. Chan—something."

"Chandra?"

"Yeah, Chandra. She met me at my locker and basically threatened me to stay away from you." I say this in a joking manner, but as soon as I say the words, his face darkens.

"Did she now?"

I cringe, and my heart sinks a little. So he's not denying that she's his girlfriend. Which makes sense. She's the kind of girl I'd imagine him being with. Beautiful. Quick-witted. Confident. Quickly, I scan my ID to pay for my food and then search the cafeteria for my friends, eager to get as far away from Dion as possible. I'm already an emotional basket case thanks to my brain that refuses to work properly. I don't need a guy to further derail me.

Being with Dion seems to only make things worse because when I'm with him it's like I block out everything else in the world so it's just him and me. Oddly, things seem to make more sense when we're together, which is why adding Chandra into the mix is definitely not a good thing.

"I guess I'll see you around," I tell Dion and then go to take off, but his hand lightly presses on my elbow.

"Wait," he says.

Instantly, my skin tingles where he touched me. The

room shifts, brightening everything as if his touch heightened the colors of the room. I blink and he jerks his hand away as if what he did was wrong.

He gives me a weak smile that doesn't quite match his eyes. "I'd love to eat lunch with you if you'll have me."

My eyes drift across the cafeteria until they land on Chandra, arms crossed, a smirk on her face as if she's waiting for me to mess up. "Maybe another time."

I dart away before I change my mind. Lexi, Mara, and Tiffany are laughing over something when I slide into my seat, joining them.

"What's so funny?" I ask, desperately trying to not look over my shoulder to see if Dion joins Chandra at her table.

"We were talking about the stupid play." Mara rolls her eyes. "And how I should never have let Lexi talk me into auditioning."

"Congratulate Mara," Lexi orders. "She nailed a role in the play."

"Wow! That's great. Congratulations!"

Mara glowers.

"As a dog." Tiffany giggles. "I asked her how many hours she's planning on practicing her rolling and trotting."

"But that's better than getting cut," I offer, taking a bite of food. "You were worried about that, right?"

"It's still up for debate," Mara grumbles. "I'm not a fan of losing my dignity."

"What about you, Lexi?" I ask.

She dances in her seat, waving her hands about. "You're looking at the girl who landed the lead role."

"What?" I drop my fork. "That's amazing!"

"Thank you very much." She beams. "I wish you had moved here earlier so you could have auditioned, too."

"And play catch on the stage as a dog?" I say. "No thanks."

I laugh when Mara shoots me an evil glare.

We continue chatting about the performance and deadlines, except I'm unable to stop myself. My eyes drift across the cafeteria. Dion is sitting at Chandra's table. As if sensing my gaze, she looks over at me, and a slow, winning smile spreads over her face.

My skin burns in anger, and I clench my fork tightly.

Wow. I really don't like that girl. I hardly know her, but she definitely has a way of getting under my skin. I shake my head. What I need is to focus on other things besides Dion and Chandra. Because sitting here obsessing over a guy who already has a girlfriend is obviously not helping with my mental state.

"Do you think you all need any help with the sets?" I ask the girls. Hanging out with them doing play-related stuff would be the perfect distraction. "I could help paint them. You could join me too, Tiffany."

Tiffany shrugs. "That might be fun."

"Oh, that's a fabulous idea." Lexi claps her hands together. "Then we could all be a part of the play together."

And I will be too busy having fun with my friends to have a moment to think about Dion.

Or Tristan.

For the first time, I feel like maybe I'm finally making progress in this new life and taking a step in the right direction.

Except a niggling worry tugs at the corner of my mind as

I remember Tristan's necklace and cryptic note. What if he really can give me the answers I'm so desperate for?

20
HOUSTON, WE HAVE A PROBLEM
TRISTAN

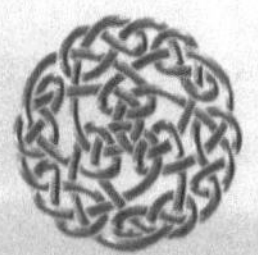

Florida

"We have a problem," I tell Katka, leaning against the concrete hallway wall outside the cafeteria.

I thought I had everything under control, but then that Nazco went and showed up at the media center, completely distracting Estrella. The worst of it was I recognized the guy right away.

He's Dion Cabral, one of the most promising, powerful, and upcoming immortals. And our families hate each other with a passion born from centuries of feuds.

The question is did he recognize me? We've never actually met. I've just seen footage and pictures of him that our scouts send back from time to time of immortals we should keep an eye out for. I can only hope he wouldn't think that the prince of the Sabians would be hanging out in a high school library.

"What kind of problem?" Katka interrupts my worries. "Like the I-should-be-worried kind or the hang-up-on-you kind?"

"This place is crawling with Nazco scum."

"You're in their territory. What did you expect? Did you find the girl?"

I rub my forehead. "Yes."

"So what's the issue? Grab her and get out of that place. If you work quickly, the Nazco won't even suspect it."

"It's not that simple."

She's silent for a moment. "You're not making any sense."

My mind flashes to the desperation in Estrella's eyes. She wants to remember her past, I'm sure of it. Except then that Nazco vermin showed up and she completely ditched me. Not that I should care, but he does pose a problem here. The guy practically hovers over her like he's her guardian or something.

Maybe he is. What do I know about the Nazco other than that they're rotten to the core?

How can I explain the dynamics to Katka? That this mission isn't your typical grab-and-go?

When Estrella painted in class, there was a fire in her quick strokes of the brush, a brightness in her eyes as if she were coming back to life. I touch the endless knot cord hanging around my neck. There's no doubt she recognized this symbol or at least felt a connection to it.

It doesn't take an idiot to see she's been through so much already. Once she realizes who I am and what I'll be asking of her, will she actually help my people?

Not to mention that this Nazco being here poses an even bigger problem because our families have a brutal history.

"Tristan?" Katka's voice hits me through the phone. "You still there?"

"Yeah." I sigh and rub my forehead. "I think this mission is going to take longer than I expected."

"You're acting weird."

"Since when did you become an expert on me? Also, you're not here. You don't know the full situation."

"This girl hasn't put some spell on you, has she?"

"What? No!" I roll my eyes. Katka has the wildest imagination. "But there was a Wraith outside her classroom door. And she was able to see it."

"So that's a good thing, right? You aren't too late."

"Maybe." I groan and hit the back of my head against the hallway wall. "I don't know anymore."

"There's something else, isn't there?"

"I get the feeling that if I just kidnap Estrella, it will alienate her from us and keep her from giving us what we need of her. I mean, she wouldn't even walk across the library to talk to me, so she's definitely not going to just jump into my car. This is going to be a more delicate situation than I first thought."

"Listen," Katka says. "Time is ticking, and we don't have much left. You need to act quickly. Who cares if she trusts you, likes you, or even wants to be in the same room as you? That's not important."

"But..."

"Tristan, you can't let this Nazco girl get into your head. Stay focused on the purpose of this mission. Grab her and get back her pronto."

I press my lips together, remembering how Estrella crumpled to the floor in pain. How she reached for me.

"Tristan? Hello? Oh my god. I need to get Conrad involved before you screw this mission up, don't I?"

"Don't you dare call him." I snap back to the moment. "I've got everything under control."

"Now that's funny." Katka mumbles something under her breath. "Fine. But if you don't get that girl to the portal in three days, I'm calling Conrad no matter what."

"Three days is plenty of time."

I end the call and blow out a frustrated breath. I can't believe she brought up Conrad. If he gets involved, it's going to mess everything up. Screwing up my life is his specialty. Okay, so he might be my best friend, but he also thinks he knows more than me, which makes me want to punch him sometimes.

I pull out a picture of my twin sister and trace my fingers across her face. Once again my heart shatters and the only thing shoving the pieces together so I'm able to breathe is anger.

Anger at what the Nazco did.

Anger at who they are and all they represent.

Katka is right. I need to remember my purpose and stay focused on the task. Grab and go. It's simple.

I stroll back down the hall to the cafeteria entrance and lean against the doorframe, trying to figure out my next steps. Across the room, Estrella is sitting with three other girls, laughing. She looks happy. Maybe even content.

But that will all change once she learns the truth of who she is.

And who I am.

21
PARANOIA KEEPS YOU ALIVE
DION

Florida

"Since when are you so keen to break the rules?" Chandra asks, marching over to join me at the front of the school. "You know, the usual fare: befriending her, asking to have lunch with her, driving her home. And the worst, letting her *touch* you! Really, Dion, are you that stupid? Yes, actually, I think you are. So why stop there? Why not just become mortal and start your own happily ever after with her?"

"Don't tempt me." If only I had the power to freeze Chandra's vocal cords. Why I ever dated her is beyond me. "Do you realize how terribly irritating your voice sounds when you whine?"

"I am not whining!" Her eyes narrow. "How dare you speak to me like that?"

Then she breaks into a full tirade on the dire consequences of disobeying the Empress and disrupting the order of the Nazco nation. Inwardly, I groan, wishing I had ignored the little witch in the first place. The Empress is most likely laughing hysterically with glee knowing she teamed the two of us together.

Instead, I try to mute Chandra's nasal voice from my mind and focus on the students swarming out of the building like inmates escaping a penitentiary. Estrella should be coming out at any moment.

"Oh, joy," Chandra says dryly. "Here she comes."

I smile, watching Estrella shuffle out of the front doors, wisps of blonde hair falling over her eyes and waving about in the breeze. Perhaps her face is rather thin, her cheeks slightly gaunt, and her skin too pale, but I don't care.

She's my Estrella and we were meant for each other.

She scans the crowd, chewing at her bottom lip. Seeing her like this charges an ache through my chest, a longing for what we had before—what she had before. But I chase those feelings away. She may never be that confident, strong girl I once knew, but she's alive and that's all that matters.

"Estrella!" I call out, waving.

Her face brightens and she takes a few tentative steps in my direction. That is until a burly schoolboy bumps into her. Her frail body wobbles and the pile of books she's got stacked in her arms goes flying.

"What a brainless wit she's become." Chandra shakes her head mournfully. "It's rather disturbing. Especially to think she could've been our Conduit."

I grit my teeth to keep myself from throttling Chandra

and instead dash over to help Estrella, gathering up the remaining books.

"Thanks," Estrella says timidly. "I guess I shouldn't have checked out so many books."

I lift up one of the books, reading its title, "*Enlightening Symbols*. Fascinating literature. Homework?"

She takes the book from my hand and shoves it back onto her already full backpack. "Yeah, I'm doing some extra credit for math class."

"And this one." I lift the other book up. "*Signs and Symbols of Infinity*. Sounds kind of boring if you ask me."

"No, it's all very interesting," she says.

And disturbing. If she were to start remembering, things could go poorly very fast.

"What's interesting?" Chandra asks, strolling up to join us.

Estrella visibly cringes as Chandra looms over her. I inch closer to Estrella, careful to not touch her while making sure to keep the titles of the books hidden in my other hand. I can't have Chandra snooping around, realizing what Estrella's reading during her free time.

"Come on, Estrella," I say. "My car is just over there. Chandra, I'll see you around."

"How am I supposed to get home?" Chandra pouts, throwing up her hands.

I chuckle. "I'm sure you'll figure something out."

When we reach my car, I open the door for Estrella, but she hesitates.

"We can't just leave your girlfriend here at school without a ride," she says, her beautiful eyes widening.

"Girlfriend?" I scoff. "She's not my girlfriend. And

honestly, not much of a friend. Don't worry about Chandra. She's a big girl. She'll figure something out."

The wind swirls around us, whipping Estrella's hair across her face. I glance over at Chandra standing on the sidewalk. Her arms are crossed, and a fierce glare is planted firmly on her face.

Don't do it, I mouth, shooting her a warning look.

"Come on, Estrella," I say. "Let's get you home."

But as I'm slipping into the car, a thread of unease curls through my mind. I pause, realizing I'm being watched. By an enemy.

I swear under my breath, and panic shoves me into action. I scramble back out of the car and scan the parking lot, but the only thing out of the ordinary from the humans is Chandra's furious scowl and the Wraiths eying me from the rooftop.

I shrug off the unease. This is all Chandra's fault, making me paranoid.

Except even as I peel out of the parking lot, lightly tapping my hands on the steering wheel to the beat of the music, I can't get over my initial sense that something is off.

"So." I side-glance at Estrella. She's practically hugging the door with a slightly terrified expression.

I decide to discover how deeply the mortalization process has progressed within her mind. Once she's mortal and loses her powers, only then will it be safe for us to be together. But if Quadril or his Wraiths discover the mortalization process isn't working, they will kill her instantly.

"Have you always lived here in Florida?" I ask.

"I recently moved from Orlando. You?"

"Brazil. My dad was contracted to work here for a year."

"Wow. You must be going through culture shock."

I chuckle. "Yeah, you could say that. Being new at school isn't easy, that's for sure. But I guess that's why I'm glad our paths crossed."

Her shoulders relax, and she allows herself to lean her head against the seat. "I have to admit, I was hoping you'd say you were from Orlando."

"Really? Why's that?"

"You're going to think I'm crazy," she says, then bites her lips as if to hold back her words.

"I would never."

"I lost my memories in an accident. My parents were…" She swallows and stares out the window. "Anyway, now I'm in the foster system. I keep hoping I'll meet someone I used to know, or something will spark a memory, you know?"

So that's the lie they fed her. I grip the steering wheel tight as I focus back on the road. To think about all she's lost. All we've lost. Every memory the two of us ever had together, wiped away.

My stomach twists with bitterness.

But this was the only way to keep her alive, I remind myself.

"The weird thing is you look incredibly familiar," Estrella says, startling my thoughts. "But that couldn't be, obviously, since you're from Brazil. I guess it was just wishful thinking."

I snap straight in my seat, head spinning at her confession. I look familiar? Does that mean there's a hint of what we had still there, embers waiting to be sparked?

Suddenly hope burns in my chest, and I'm grinning like

the fool I am. What am I even thinking? I can't have her remember me or know who I really am.

"Well, I'm glad we've met now," I offer, securing the lie that we've never met.

Her face brightens and she shifts her body away from the door, settling against the seat comfortably as if her confession has relieved whatever worries she had.

And that's when the guilt washes over me. Guilt for the thrill racing through my veins, giving fresh life to my body that once felt dead. For my selfishness. That I'm even here, putting her very life in jeopardy.

Guilt for the lies I'm spinning and the ones to come. I hate myself for perpetuating the Empress's agenda, but this isn't about me. This is the only way to make sure she lives. I will sacrifice whatever it takes to keep her alive, even my own happiness.

"Maybe it's a sign," I finally say. "Like we were supposed to meet."

"Yeah." She glances at me shyly and smiles.

It takes all my willpower to not lean over and kiss those soft lips. To pull her closer to me and take in her sweet smell. To run my hands through her hair and whisper in her ear that I would fight to the death for her.

Instead, I busy myself with checking the street signs. "Which street did you say you lived on?"

"Osprey Way. It's coming up here on the left. There. This is it."

She points to the thicket of palm trees on our left and a heavy gate that opens to a long, sandy road. Spider chills race up my spine. Two Wraiths are perched on top of either side of the gate, guarding the premises. Sharp claws clench the iron, their dark gazes sweeping across the car as if debating whether to rip it apart or ignore it.

The security is higher than I expected.

I suppose I should've expected that with Estrella now living here, but it's still concerning. One slip-up would send them slicing their jagged knives across her neck. Beheading her is the only way to ensure her death.

"Don't attempt the driveway," Estrella says, interrupting my thoughts. "You don't want your car to suffer. Also, it might be better if you don't go any further. Nadia has this weird rule. No boys allowed."

"Does she now?" Of course, she does. I should've expected as much.

I let the car idle at the entrance, and as Estrella shoves open her door, I peer through the brush and spy a sign that reads *Nadia's Home for Girls*. I'm about to jump out and help Estrella with the stack of teetering books when one of the Wraiths on the gate stirs.

It blinks down at us, its sharp nose reminding me of a beak, and yet its face is all too human. It beats its bat-like wings in a warning as if sensing my intentions.

I hold my breath, waiting for Estrella to see the Wraith and run screaming in terror. But instead, she pops her head through the car door, saying, "Thanks for the ride."

Is it wrong that it saddens me that she doesn't see them?

"Wait!" Once again I resist touching her. After the last time in the hallway, it proved too dangerous. Especially now that we're under the Wraith's watchful eyes. But it's pure agony and once again that selfishness rears its ugly head, tempting me. "Would you like to go out sometime?"

"Like on a—"

"Dinner? Friday?"

Sunshine strands of hair curtain her face so I can't read her expression, but then she says, "Sure. That'd be nice."

I lean against my seat, watching her wander up the pine needle path while the Wraiths leer down at her from above. One mistake, one glance, and they would pounce on her without a second thought. My whole body aches just to hold her tight once again. To kiss her passionately like I used to.

"Hang in there, my little star," I say. "Once you're fully mortal, we can be together again."

22

CHOOSING YOUR DESTINY IS HARDER THAN IT LOOKS

ESTRELLA

Florida

Oh my gosh! Dion just asked me out on a date. And Chandra isn't his girlfriend! My heart skips to a happy beat. The sky is a little brighter, the trees greener, and the air sweeter.

I turn around to give Dion a final wave, but the moment I face the gate of Nadia's Home for Girls, my heart slams in terror against my ribcage.

Two of those horrible Reaper things are there. Sitting on top of the iron gate, claw-like feet clamped around the rusted bars like giant vultures, poised for attack. In the shifting shadows of the trees above, I can make out the outlines of sharp beaks jutting out from their hoods.

My vision blurs and the books tumble out from my arms,

thudding onto the sand-packed road. The sound jerks me back to reality. The hooded creatures have shifted, and their full attention is now zoomed in on me.

Crap.

Dion's car skids to a halt, sand flying from the sharp motion. His car door flings open and he practically leaps out of the car.

"Estrella!" he calls and takes off toward me, racing through the gate and up the road.

He's at my side within seconds. Is it me or did he get here at an insanely fast speed? "Is everything alright?"

It's silly, but I want him to wrap his strong arms around me, tell me everything will be okay and that these creatures aren't real. But I hardly know the guy so that would be weird, right?

I crouch down, quickly gathering up the sand-covered books, my face burning, half from the embarrassment that he has to help me again, and half in terror from the creatures. Dion calmly helps me collect my books.

"I'm fine," I say, trying to evoke a light laugh. "I'm a complete klutz today!"

The fact that he didn't give those creatures a second glance, even as one of the dregs of their coats fluttered just above his head when he passed under the gate, tells me I need to be careful what I say around Dion.

He can't know I'm seeing things.

This is a guy who actually likes me. I won't have my hallucinations or whatever they are interfere with the only good thing going for me.

"I should've helped you carry these to the door," he says softly.

"Really, I'm fine," I say, but then the tree boughs shudder above, and from the corner of my eye, I see that one of those creatures just landed above me. Goosebumps shiver across my skin.

Do not look at it! I scream at myself.

"I tripped over a root." I stack another book on top while Dion grabs the last three. My hands are trembling, putting me in danger of dropping the whole stupid pile again. "I need to pay better attention."

"I'm glad I hadn't left then." Dion gently sets the last books onto my pile and then pushes the strands of hair out of my eyes. His fingers are electric on my skin. Sizzling and tantalizing me to come closer.

His touch makes me shiver all over again, but this time in a good way. I lean in until the only thing separating us are the books and the danger breathing down our necks.

He smells of spice and something else that I can't quite place. Something familiar. Something that feels safe and right. The last thing I want to do is leave his side, but I need to protect him and get him out of here, far from these strange creatures leering down at us from above. Lexi said one attacked her, which is why I need to stay in control. I can't let it attack Dion.

"Thanks for your help *again*." I plant a wide smile, trying to not focus on Dion's lips. "I promise I'm not always a bumbling idiot."

"That was the last thing on this planet I would think of you."

My heart skips.

Play it cool, Estrella.

Don't put Dion's life in jeopardy.

"See you tomorrow at school?" I offer, backing away. "You should sit with us at lunch."

"I'd like that." He moves to follow me. "Maybe I should walk you to the door."

I swallow down the yearning that's desperate to toss aside these stupid books and drag him into my arms.

"That's not a great idea," I say, which darkens his warm eyes in worry. "Nadia is super strict when it comes to boys."

My words seem to relieve him because his shoulders relax and he flashes me a smile. "That sounds like a challenge I'm willing to accept."

"You're funny," I say, and as I smile back, I practically run the rest of the way up the road, worry gnawing at the back of my mind.

Could these creatures be the reason Clara tried to escape? I think about Lexi's story. Clara had been searching through Nadia's office the night she died. Why? What was she trying to find? Why didn't she just leave?

The questions are unsettling.

It isn't until I'm on the first step of the porch that I dare glance over my shoulder. The path lies in silence save for a light sea breeze shifting through the Spanish moss hanging from the trees. Dion and the creatures are gone, leaving me alone with my tortured thoughts.

Sweat drips down my back and my hair clings to the back of my neck as I desperately fumble with the door handle. My eyes land on the sign by the door.

Let go of your past and seize your future!

Reading those words confuses me even more. A part of

me yearns to move on, but another part wonders if my past can answer my questions.

I duck inside, slamming the door behind me. As I press my back against its wooden frame, I take in deep gulps of air.

I'm safe. I made it.

Who needs Halloween decorations when you've got those horrible things hanging about?

"Estrella?" Nadia steps into the hallway, forehead pinched.

I practically jump out of my skin and nearly drop my pile of books all over again. It's like she came out of thin air.

"Nadia," I say breathlessly. "You scared me."

"What are you doing home so early?" she presses, and then looks about the hall. "Where are the other girls?"

Nadia's rules on boys and dating warn me to be careful of my next words. According to her, relationships can mess up our ability to settle into our new life.

"A friend gave me a ride home," I say.

Nadia steps closer, eyes narrowing on my books. "What is all this? So many books."

Crap. Something tells me that I can't let her know these are about the tattoo on my shoulder. Maybe I'm being paranoid, but after Lexi's warning in the art closet, I know I need to be careful.

"Just a history project. I'm really struggling in school, so I decided to buckle down and dig deep into the research."

I edge closer to the stairs, keeping her at a distance.

Nadia lifts her eyebrows but doesn't move to investigate them further. "From now on, I need you to ride the bus with the other girls. We don't know if this new friend is trustworthy, and one can never be too safe. We must be careful."

"You're right. We must be careful," I parrot her words, desperately keeping my face as unflustered as I can.

I don't want her to know how upsetting her demands are. If she knew I told Dion yes to a date on Friday, she would flip. Which also makes me wonder how I'm going to manage to go on that date at all.

"Unfortunately, I have an appointment so we'll have to skip our tea time today," Nadia says. "I'll be sure to have Cook whip up a pot though for dinner."

My head spins, thinking about Lexi's warning about the tea. But I merely lift up my books, saying, "Okay! I'm going to start on my homework now."

"Excellent." Nadia smiles but it's a crooked one, tipped up at the end like a knife. "It is good to have you here with us, Estella."

"Thanks." I back away toward the stairs, my hands slick as they grip the spines, and then race up to the third floor as fast as my legs can take me.

Ever since leaving Dion's car, my nerves have kicked up a notch with every step I've taken. Even the air of this old lighthouse laced with worn wood and the sea can't calm me.

I'm out of breath by the time I reach the top floor's landing, but that doesn't stop me from practically running to my room.

It's not until I've closed my door and deposited my books on my bed that I finally allow myself to relax. I stare at the pile of research I'd taken from the school library. Will any of that give me answers to my past?

Do I even want those answers?

Besides Nadia and her stupid rules, my life has definitely taken a turn for the better. I think about the pictures Ms. Blaire showed me of my trailer home and my old school records. I was never a stellar student, and my old home was nothing to brag about. Maybe I'm chasing after something that's not me.

Except there's that Tristan guy and those visions—memories?—that keep haunting me.

My hand moves to my neckline and I reach for something to grasp a hold of. Except nothing is there.

I frown in confusion. Why would I do that? Was that an automatic habit I'd forgotten? I think I'd been reaching for something that once gave me reassurance.

Something I used to wear around my neck.

Suddenly the last dredges of giddiness I felt with Dion drain away as the hopelessness of the situation threatens to undo me. No, I think, clenching my fists. I'm not going to let myself get down. I'm going to find answers as best as I can.

Determined to gain some sort of control over my life, I settle onto the floor and begin sorting through the books one by one. There's so much information here that I decide to chart up my findings.

Meaning of the infinity symbol
Locations found
Stories connected to the symbol

I'm deep in my research when my door flies open, and I jerk in surprise. Quickly, I snap my hand up and hold out my palm as if to protect myself.

But it's just Lexi flying into the room, red strands of hair whipping about like flames. "Woah, girl." She giggles. "What's up with the hand?"

Frowning, I stare at my palm and quickly drop it, stuffing it behind my back. Why did I do that? My stomach twists because once again I realize it was instinctual, just like me reaching for my neckline.

I grimace. "Um... you just surprised me, that's all. Anyway, what's up?"

"What's up?" Lexi flops onto my bed. "That's all you have to say after ditching us bus riders? I didn't know where you were after school. I went into complete panic mode and looked everywhere for you."

"I got a ride from Dion."

"Yeah, I saw you get in his car." She rolls her eyes. "It's the only reason I didn't call Nadia and 911 and the whole police department."

"I'm sorry. I should've told you."

"Yes, you should've. We girls have to look out for each other. You can't trust just anyone." She sits up and points at me. "Promise you'll be more careful."

"I promise. But I thought you liked Dion."

She nods thoughtfully, biting her bottom lip. "So I know this is silly, but we don't know much about Dion either, do we? I just think you should be careful. Take things slowly."

I think about how I'd been tempted to reach out to Dion and take his hand. That urge to kiss him as if my life depended on it overwhelmed me.

"But he's better than that Tristan guy," Lexi continues, yanking me from my thoughts of Dion's lips. "To be honest, that's why at first I went all mama-hen at school. I thought you went and ran off with him."

"Ran off with Tristan?" I laugh, but it's more of a choke. "I barely know the guy."

"Exactly. But you two were looking at each other so intensely in art class. Like you had a…"

Secret? Connection?

Yes. We did.

Still do?

I don't even know. My eyes trail to the books scattered across the bed, and suddenly I want to hide them. Hide them from everyone because there's something deep inside me that warns me that I shouldn't trust a single person.

Maybe not even Lexi.

"Just whatever you do," she says with a sigh, "stay away from Tristan. I have a bad feeling about him."

"He was just trying to be nice." I try to laugh it all off. "You act like he's going to kidnap or torture me or something. If anything we should worry about those Grim Reaper things." I switch my voice to a whisper, "I saw them outside on the gate. One flew up over my head when I was walking back to the house."

She jerks back as if my words slammed into her.

"I'm glad you're okay." She grabs my hands and squeezes them. "Those things scare me."

Sparks skitter over my skin, snapping my senses into place. The room grows brighter. The air tastes of ashes and flames.

I jerk my hands free and rub my palms.

"What was that?" I ask. "What just happened?

"I don't know." She scrutinizes me. "I didn't mean to upset you. You okay? You're acting weird."

"It's just..." I swallow, wondering if that sensation meant something or if it was merely an electric shock. A part of me wants to reach out and touch her again to see what would happen.

"It's just what?" Lexi prompts.

I stack my books onto my desk, spines facing the wall. "Let's forget about all this weird stuff for right now. I don't know about you, but I need something normal. Something fun."

She nods and the wariness in her face transforms like a warm summer day. "I am all for fun."

"Tell me about your play. Maybe I can help you memorize your lines."

She clasps her hands. "Oh! You'd do that for me? That would be amazing!"

23
OFF WITH HER HEAD!
ESTRELLA

Florida

Clang. Clang.

"The dinner bell calls," Lexi sings, putting aside the script she had been practicing with me.

Over the last two hours, I'd been helping her with her lines and laughing so hard over her different voices that time seemed to fall away. I'd almost forgotten about the strange things happening to me.

My stomach growls as we hurry downstairs and into the dining room. Tiffany waves us over to two chairs on one side of the table near herself and Mara.

As we all settle into our seats at the table, I count all twelve of us at dinner. Since I've been at Nadia's for less than a week, I'm still adjusting to these strange meals. Lexi,

Mara, Tiffany, and I clutter at one end while the Quiet Ones —as Lexi calls them—fill up the other seats.

Nadia sits at the head of the table like a queen ruling over her subjects. She never says much, instead studying each of us like we're a puzzle she's trying to take apart piece by piece.

A cup of tea is set in front of each of our place settings, steam curling up from the liquid. After Lexi's warning, all I can imagine is that it's as poisonous as a witch's brew.

I dart a glance over at Nadia. Her lips are pressed together and she's stabbing at her phone distractedly as if she's dealing with some sort of emergency. The turtleneck black shirt she's wearing is so tight around her neck, I'm surprised she can even breathe.

Why would she want to give us tea that kept us from remembering? It makes no sense.

Unless Lexi is lying to me. Or maybe she's confused herself? Except Mara and Tiffany haven't touched their tea either. Lexi pushes hers away and instead scoops up a large helping of mashed potatoes.

Nadia sighs from the other end of the table and sets her phone down, focusing back on our group.

"Shall we make a toast?" Nadia asks, and lifts up her teacup.

Lexi's gaze snaps to mine and then meaningfully at the teacup. Mara shifts uncomfortably in her seat while Tiffany pales a little. They must know about the tea, too. I pick up my cup along with the others.

"Let us toast to Estrella," Nadia continues. "Our newest member of the house. To Estrella."

"To Estrella," a mumble choruses around the table.

Well, nearly everyone.

Jamie picks up her spoon and starts stirring her tea while another girl, Izzy, simply ignores Nadia and begins ripping apart her roll and placing each chunk into a neat line in front of her.

"Thank you," I say, smiling at the group, and then make a show of placing the teacup to my lips.

It's a little unnerving because Nadia is watching me, eyes sharper than a hawk. It takes all my concentration to try to look like I'm drinking tea when I'm not.

"Mara and I are going to be in the school play," Lexi announces suddenly.

Thankfully her announcement rips Nadia's gaze from me. "The school play? Isn't that lovely?" Nadia sets her teacup down with a clank. The lines around her mouth dip as if she's actually not finding Lexi's announcement lovely in the slightest.

"I might quit," Mara adds darkly. "It's still up for debate."

"You wouldn't want it to get in the way of your school-work." Nadia nods at Mara as if quitting was a great idea.

Mara's fork freezes mid-bite. "Although," she considers, lowering her fork. "It could be fun. Maybe I'll stick it out."

"Truly." Lexi nods eagerly, pleased to have Mara fully onboard. But something tells me Mara's sudden enthusiasm for the play has more to do with Nadia's disapproval than the play actually being fun.

Lexi then launches into the entire saga of every moment of her audition, including rising to her feet and pronouncing the last line of her speech.

"Lexi!" Nadia snaps. "Do sit down. This isn't drama class."

Lexi sighs but plops back into her seat.

Mara snickers while Tiffany nods rapturously, saying, "That was amazing, Lexi."

A quick glance at the Quiet Ones tells me that none of them are really listening. Jamie's spoon still clatters against the edges of her teacup, dark liquid splashing onto the white tablecloth.

And a girl I've decided to nickname Sneaky is secretly stealing food from the oblivious girls on either side of her.

"Tiffany and I are going to help with the sets," I pipe up and then look to the Quiet Ones, adding, "If any of you would like to join us, you're more than welcome."

One of the girls, Flora, looks up from her plate, tilting her head to the side slightly. "Are you new here?" she asks.

Flora's brown hair is braided into a crown on top of her head. I've seen her every once in a while picking flowers outside in the garden. Tonight she's got them all tucked into her hair.

"Yeah." I fidget with my napkin. I mean, I know we all have memory issues, but for Flora to not remember me even after Nadia just offered a toast is a little worrisome. "I arrived a few days ago. I'm Estrella. I really like your hair."

"Estrella." Flora whispers my name like it's sacred.

"You have weird eyes," Izzy suddenly announces.

"I like her eyes," Jamie snaps. The clanging of her spoon falls silent.

"Oh, great," Mara grumbles beside me. "Now you've done it, Estrella."

"Done what?" I ask.

"They're weird!" Izzy smashes her fist onto the table.

"Quiet now, girls," Nadia soothes. "No need to argue. Take a sip of your tea. It will relax you."

"They're not weird," Jamie shouts back, holding up her spoon and pointing it at Izzy like a weapon. "How dare you say that."

"It's fine." I rise to my feet. "I'm honestly not offen—"

But before I can finish, Jamie picks up her chicken leg and throws it across the table at Izzy, a perfect aim to the face.

"Ow!" Izzy yells, holding her face.

"Jamie!" Nadia grips the side of the table. "Throwing food is unacceptable. We do not tolerate—"

But Nadia's words turn into a scream as she shouts, "No!" to Izzy who is picking up her soup bowl.

She's going to throw it, I realize. I scramble out of my chair, running to stop her, but I'm not fast enough. She tosses it across the table at Jamie. But Jamie is incredibly fast. She ducks and the bowl smashes against the wall, shattering. Soup splashes everywhere, staining the wall orange, and pooling on the floor.

"You got soup all over my outfit," Flora wails, fluttering her hands about in distress. "It got in my hair!"

"Don't worry." I grab a napkin and try to clean it off her. "It's just soup. It will wash off."

"Who took my phone?" Nadia demands, looking about. She jerks to her feet and searches under her chair.

I glance at Sneaky. Sure enough, the girl's got a devious grin on her face. She notices me studying her and winks.

I wink back as if to tell her secret is safe with me.

"Orderlies!" Nadia screams, and getting no response,

throws her hands into the air in a huff and storms out of the room, calling, "Sondra! Tasha!"

The moment Nadia leaves, Jamie pops back up from under the table and growls at Izzy, "Take back your words," before snatching every spoon and fork she can muster.

Bread Girl squeaks and ducks under the table. Sneaky slips out of the room. Piano Girl starts humming.

"Don't let Jamie get the forks!" Lexi yells, jumping to her feet.

My eyes widen as I realize what Lexi is insinuating. *Yikes.* And that's when I realize things are about to get wild.

I eye the door, glad Nadia has left the room. I need to get things under control. Something in my gut tells me if things didn't, these girls could get into big trouble. If I'm guessing correctly, Jamie is the most dangerous girl in the room, which makes the tips of those forks suddenly look danger-ously sharp.

"Hey, Jamie." I abandon Flora and edge closer to Jamie, warily eyeing her collection of silver utensils. "I think we should all calm down and just relax. Why don't you give everyone their forks back?"

"Weird eyes, weird eyes," Izzy taunts, pointing her finger at me.

"Stop calling her that!" Jamie demands, fisting the spoons and forks and waving them through the air.

She's about to launch at Izzy, but Lexi and Mara latch onto Jamie's arms, trying to hold her back.

"You ruined my outfit!" Flora screams from my other side.

"Hey, it's okay." I whip back around to Flora and take her hand to comfort her. "We'll get that cleaned—"

But my words slip away as a tingling sensation skitters across my fingers from where I touched her skin. The air changes, and it's like I'm breathing in springtime, sweet and bright.

Startled, I jerk my hand back, a shudder rippling through me.

What was that?

Then right before my eyes, the flowers in Flora's hair start changing. The petals grow jagged and sharp thorns spike out from the stems. She leaps up on her chair and crawls across the table, eyes glued on Izzy as if intent to rip her to pieces.

Flora's action seems to inspire Jamie because she tears herself out of Lexi and Mara's grasp and hurdles across the table, utensils raised in the air like daggers.

I scramble after Flora, managing to hold her back by her shoes. Meanwhile, Lexi and Mara race to intercept Jamie.

But Jamie is too fast. She stabs Izzy in the arm with a fork.

A vine trails out of Flora's hair and slithers across the table toward Izzy.

"Something is happening here!" I warn the others as I use all my energy to hold Flora back.

Mara swears, ducking as Jamie swipes a fork through the air. She aims for Izzy's mouth. The vine snakes around Izzy's ankle.

"Tiffany!" Lexi cries out. "Do something to calm them down!"

Tiffany hedges closer, wringing her hands as if she's terrified to get too close.

I don't know why Lexi thinks Tiffany can help. She's the last person I'd want to put into the path of these two girls.

Suddenly Nadia and two women in navy scrubs burst into the room. They grab Izzy and Jamie, who are kicking and screaming at each other, and plunge a syringe into their arms. Instantly, the girls fall silent, heads lolled to their chin as if they've been put to sleep. Then they do the same thing to Flora and as they do, the flowers in her hair sag and the vine shrivels up and dies.

Horrified, I stagger backward, taking in huge breaths to calm myself.

What kind of place is this?

Who *are* these girls?

And then I look down at my palms, the memory of the tingling raging through me.

Who am *I*?

Everyone in the dining hall is silent except for Piano Girl, who is rocking back and forth into her chair, still humming. The nurses drag the three girls out of the room and Nadia settles back to her seat.

"Oh dear," Nadia breathes out. She picks up a napkin and wipes the sweat from her brow. "Estrella, perhaps you should retire to your room early tonight."

"Me?" I lift my eyebrows. "But...but I had nothing to do with what just happened."

I stare at the wreckage. Pieces of food and broken plates scattered across the table. Chairs overturned. Shattered plates, cups, and food splattered on the walls and floor.

How could she think I was responsible for this?"

Lexi and Mara look away, and I get the strange sense

that they too believe this whole incident had everything to do with me.

Nadia doesn't even look at me, instead she claps twice. "Run along now, Estrella."

The clapping sound vibrates through my body, and it's like someone snaps the bones of my ribcage tightly into place with each clap. The tingling sensation lingering from when I touched Flora vanishes.

I jerk straight, shocked. Did Nadia do that to me or am I losing my mind?

And yet, I can't process what is happening. I look at my three friends. Tiffany is biting her nails. Mara is shooting a glaring look at Nadia, her fingers twitching next to a fork that had fallen out of Jamie's hands. Lexi is clenching her fists. I'm not sure if it's the light in the room or my imagination, but her red hair shimmers like its strands are on fire.

"Why does Estrella have to leave?" Lexi asks. "She didn't do anything. It's not her fault Izzy and Jamie lost their cool."

"I said *leave*," Nadia commands, her voice lower, stronger.

A thickness weighs on my chest, heavy as a blanket. It's hard to even take a single breath.

Something inside the pit of my stomach rises up, ready to resist Nadia's words, ready to shove back the blanket and let all my emotions explode from me.

Except, how can I do that? I'm not strong enough to overcome whatever has a hold on me.

And that's when I realize I need to be smarter about my next words and steps. Otherwise, I'll never escape this place.

So I plant a smile and look around at the girls. "Yes, I

think that would be a good idea. I have so much homework to tackle."

I scurry out of the room as if I'm fleeing. The worst part is the moment I exit, the heaviness pressing on my chest vanishes. And that confirms my deepest fear.

Nadia's Home for Girls is not a home.

It's a prison.

And we are more than just girls.

24
HOW GREATLY YOU UNDERESTIMATE ME
DION

Florida

I slam the car door shut and lean against its side. I should feel victorious knowing I finally have connected with Estrella. We have a date in just a few days. She's interested in me. There hasn't been any sign of the Sabians. If things go to plan, she'll have completed the mortalization process in record time. No immortal or Wraith will give her a second glance and we can be together.

She'll be safe.

She'll live.

So why do I feel this growing wariness? Why did my skin crawl as I walked Estrella to the car, and why did the Wraiths guarding Nadia's home hover over her like they were about to slice their daggers across her neck?

I shake these thoughts from my mind and start up the walkway to the villa Chandra and I share. But I stop mid-stride and frown when I notice a parked car on the roadside. This villa is a Nazco safe house, which allows for many of the extra amenities we normally wouldn't get when on assignment. Unfortunately, every Nazco leader knows of its existence, too.

"It appears we have company," I mutter.

Chandra is waiting for me at the front door, arms crossed and a grimace on her face. Her long, sharp nails tap against the doorframe, a tick she has when she's nervous or having trouble keeping herself in check.

Another bad sign.

Her leopard print leotard, halter top, and matching platform heels emanate her typical I'm-in-control look, but her tousled hair warns me otherwise. Something is up.

"Chandra." I nod curtly, pretending it's normal for her to be at the door waiting for me. "If we're to live under the same roof for the next few weeks, I think it best we avoid each other's company as much as possible."

"Quadril is in the great room," she says without preamble. "Appears as if you blundered this operation already. He's seething. If you don't hurry, he'll probably turn the entire house into an icicle."

I clench my eyes shut and force myself to resist attacking her. Quadril is probably here because of her and her meddling. If only the Empress hadn't sent her along, everything would be so much easier.

But I won't let Chandra ruin my plans.

I storm into the living room to find Quadril standing utterly still beside the white bookshelves. Books, lamps, and antique sets are arranged in neat rows on the shelf. He stands out like a red rose growing in the Antarctic plains.

And yet I can't help but notice how altered he looks, standing there without his usual silver Overlord robes. He's wearing a gray pinstriped suit jacket that hangs to his mid-thigh. Beneath, he sports a white crew neck shirt and black shoes. His white hair is slicked back to perfection, giving the air of a successful businessman.

Even though I know he's nearly four hundred years old, he appears like all fully matured immortals. Not a day older than thirty human years. When I enter the room, he cocks his head slightly, his brow furrowing in disapproval.

"Why have you not alerted us as of yet, Dion?" Quadril asks.

"Good afternoon." I move to the kitchen and withdraw two tumblers. "Would you care for a glass of orange juice? The juice here in Florida is intoxicating."

Quadril's eyes narrow. "I am not here for trivialities. What are you? Nineteen? Twenty? And yet, look how arrogant you are. Just because you were born with high powers doesn't mean you can flitter about and do whatever you wish."

"Quadril." I pour two glasses and take a sip from one. "I have no idea what you're talking about."

"A Sabian was spotted today at Estrella's school. Right outside her classroom. If a Wraith hadn't been there, she could've been taken."

I calmly take another sip, swallowing my shock that I hadn't seen the Sabian myself. How had I been so blind? To know that Estrella had nearly been kidnapped under my watch makes my insides chill.

"Why didn't the Wraith take care of the Sabian?" I ask. "That is their job, correct?"

"You act as if this is no concern." Quadril steps closer to me. "This is exactly what I was worried about. Why I would never have approved any of this nonsense. And of all people for the Empress to send, you are by far the least appropriate or qualified."

Hmm.... Quadril avoided my question, which means that the Sabian somehow outsmarted the Wraith. Not good.

Meanwhile, Chandra slips into the room, hovering by the doorframe. She keeps her mouth shut for once, likely hungry for me to take the blame for this.

"This Sabian is incredibly concerning," I say with a deliberate shrug as if I don't care. "Especially as it appears this one has outsmarted one of your Wraiths. But it is the Empress's wish for me to oversee Estrella's progress, and I intend to see it through."

"The Empress is too soft when it comes to you." Quadril settles on the leather couch, lounging back as if he were here for a night of drinks. "And blind to the dangers that Estrella poses."

"It is difficult to follow my orders when your Wraiths don't communicate with me on matters of importance. Why didn't they alert me of the Sabian immediately?"

"The Wraiths work for me and no one else." Quadril waves his hand as if he's stating the obvious. "I'm not sure why the Empress sent you here to muddy the waters, but my advice to you is to stay out of the way. The Empress may have a hard time letting go of the immortal Estrella once was. But I, on the other hand, don't share her sentiments."

"What are you implying?" My hand clutches the glass, webs splintering across the side beneath my palm.

"That you are incapable of doing your job correctly. Obviously. I have ordered the Wraiths to kill Estrella instantly should she speak or interact with any Sabian. You and Chandra are under these same kill orders. The safety of the Nazco is far more important than one of the Empress's ridiculous notions."

"Of course, Your Worship," Chandra says smoothly, dipping to bow her head.

I don't answer, but merely grit my teeth as Quadril exits the house at a startlingly fast speed. The moment the door slams shut, I hurl my glass toward the wall. But before it hits the stucco surface, the juice explodes from electricity bolts. The tiny pieces slam into the wall like hundreds of knives.

"Oh," Chandra coos. "Look who's throwing a temper tantrum now."

Electric rage crackles across my skin and along my palms, spiking temptingly across my fingers, ready to weaponize. I glare at her so fiercely that she whimpers and scurries away, slipping and sliding in her spikey heels on the now juice-coated floor.

"You think you've won, Quadril, you little devil," I say with a growl. "But you do not realize how greatly you underestimate me."

25
CHRISTMAS SECRETS
ESTRELLA

Florida

I race up the stairs, away from the madness of whatever happened between Jamie, Flora, and Izzy at dinner tonight. But the trek to the third floor is nearly unbearable as a deep pain throbs inside my skull, my insides stiff and cold as if they've been frozen into ice.

I pause on the second landing of the stairwell to rest and lean against the wall.

Nadia did something to me, I'm sure of it. And what was that sensation inside me? It was like something had been rising up, eager to... take control?

I shake my head.

Whatever happened at dinner tonight made no sense. I take a deep breath and attempt the third flight of steps. My thoughts skitter about in my head as I process everything.

Had thorns and vines really grown out from sweet Flora's flowers? Where did Jamie get those deathly throwing skills? And why did Lexi think that Tiffany could calm them all down?

Nadia blamed me for what had happened at dinner.

And that made the least sense of all.

Once I reach the top floor, I sag, pressing my palms on my knees. I take deep breaths and slowly whatever tightening had happened in my body in the dining room loosens. Soon I'm able to stand back up straight. I roll my shoulders, easing out the tension and thankfully, my mind begins working clearly once again.

Right away, my thoughts go to Sneaky. She'd run off with Nadia's phone without anyone realizing it. That girl is clever. I wish I could remember her name, but I get the feeling none of the girls here are going to judge the other for memory issues.

The important thing is she has Nadia's phone. If I can get hold of it, it might give me some answers to this madness I just experienced.

Her room is on the other side of the hallway as mine. I take a deep breath and knock on her door. When she doesn't answer, I turn the nob and peek inside.

The room is empty. It mirrors mine except it appears as if no one actually lives here. It's oddly void of anything other than a bed and dresser. Frowning, I step back into the hall, wondering where she must be hiding.

And that's when I spy another door at the far end of the hall. I've never noticed it before because the light at that end is out. But tonight the door isn't completely shut, as if someone had slipped inside in a hurry and didn't pull it closed enough.

A quick glance down the stairway tells me that everyone must still be in the dining room, probably getting a lecture from Nadia. I have ten minutes max to investigate.

I tiptoe across the hall, grimacing at every groan and creak from the worn wooden floor. I grasp hold of the rusty latch and pull back on it. The door moans as if it's resisting. Musty air tinged with a hint of cinnamon washes over my face. Inside, I discover another stairwell, this one even narrower than the first.

My heartbeat kicks up a notch.

What is this place?

I slip through the doorway and tuck the door carefully back, leaving it cracked so a sliver of light illuminates the stairwell. Then I take the stairs, cringing as the old wood grunts under my feet.

When I get to the top of the stairs, my head hits the ceiling. Confused, I lean back so the frail light from the hallway lightens the area.

It's a trap door, I realize. Reaching up, I shove it open. Eagerly, I push myself up through the hole in the floor and slide on my bottom onto the dusty floor above. Blinking, I stare at my new surroundings.

It's a square room, about half the size of the bedrooms in the house. The walls are brick, worn smooth. In the center, a metal staircase spirals up to another smaller door that I'm guessing leads to the top of the lighthouse. Two narrow windows are placed on either side of the room, revealing flickering light from the lighthouse glowing against the darkness of the night.

But what really captures my attention is what this room holds. It's cluttered with an assortment of furniture shoved against one wall while another wall hoists a bookshelf filled with objects. Twinkle lights merrily hang along the shelf as if creating a light show. A beat-up plastic pine tree with even more objects dangling from its boughs is stuffed in the corner of the room by the window.

Slowly, I rise to my feet and creep over to the edge to study the objects on the shelves.

Dolls, chipped mugs, blankets, keys, jewelry, books.

My fingers reach for an icicle on the plastic tree, trailing over the smooth plastic surface. There's something intrinsically familiar about it.

"Christmas," a soft voice says from behind me.

I spin around to find Sneaky. Her light brown hair curtains her face like she's trying to hide behind it. She's sitting on the floor under a sagging desk, holding—no, dissecting—Nadia's phone. Pieces of it are lined on the floor before her like sentries going out to battle. I hope she hasn't destroyed the phone because I'd been eager to see if it held information that could help me understand what exactly this place is.

"Hello," I say, my voice breaking the silence.

"My Christmas." She points to the frayed tree that I'd just been touching and flashes me a crooked smile as if she'd been expecting me all along.

"I'm Estrella," I begin. "And you are…?"

"Zayla, Zayla, Zayla."

"Zayla," I repeat. "Is this your place?"

She doesn't answer, instead focusing on the phone. I

creep closer and she scoots further beneath the table. I swallow down my eagerness.

"That's Nadia's phone, isn't it?" Carefully, I settle cross-legged onto the dusty floor before her. I'm desperate for a quick peek. "Would you mind if I took a look at it?"

She eyes me carefully and finally passes me the casing protecting the phone, which is totally useless. Then I spot a tablet behind her.

What is she doing?

"This is a great place you've got up here," I say, needing to gain her trust. "You've got quite a collection."

Are these things she's stolen?

"Secrets," Zayla whispers.

I point to a spoon on the shelf. "Jamie sure would like that spoon."

She grins as if she knows exactly what I'm talking about and nods. "Jamie's secret."

"And now you're trying to find out Nadia's secrets?" I nod to the phone. "That's clever."

She grins as if she's pleased that I've figured out what she's doing. I find myself relaxing knowing that she's not going to run off. Carefully, she plugs a cord into the phone and then attaches it to the tablet. Intrigued, I watch her tap on the tablet until something pops up.

She turns the device to face me. It's like looking at the front of a phone, but Nadia's phone at Zayla's side is still locked.

"Wow, you got around her password," I say, impressed. Zayla may be quiet, but she's got some tricks up her sleeve. "You've got skills."

She winks as if she's happy that I noticed.

"Are we able to look at Nadia's messages?" I ask.

Zayla nods and I lean forward as she pulls up a stream of text messages. Eagerly, I reach for the tablet and start scrolling through the messages. Most are about maintenance issues while some are complaints about funding. But I stop mid-scroll when my eyes catch my name.

> Nadia: Bringing Estrella here was a bad idea.

> NV: It's not open for debate.

I glance over at Zayla. She's reading this along with me and her eyes widen in understanding.

"That was a few days ago," I say.

I keep scrolling. There were complaints about the gardener and the lack of AC and then another message seemingly about me.

> Nadia: Things are getting out of hand. Requesting her extraction.

> NV: I will forward your request.

My heart stills and I glance over at Sneaky. "Do you think she's talking about extracting me? What does that mean?"

Sneaky presses her lips together, shaking her head.

Quickly, I scan down to the last series of texts, which based on the timestamp, was right about dinner time.

NV: A team has already been working on the case. Maintain order until further notification.

Nadia: You don't know what you ask.

NV: This is a Level 1. Be advised to stay on guard. Patient is highly dangerous and volatile.

My heart stills. "That doesn't sound good, does it?"

Zayla studies my face as if she's trying to understand me better. Then she crawls out from under the table and slips behind a wicker rocker. She yanks up a loose board and pulls out a shoebox from its depths.

She lifts up a necklace, a silver locket dangling from its end. Tentatively, like she's not sure if I'll burn her, she takes my hand and presses the cold metal into my palm.

"Estrella's secret?" she asks.

I study its surface, illuminated by the dancing lights of the room. My name is scripted across the top. I snap it open and find a picture of a man and woman inside. They look strange.

The man has dark hair, cut tightly against his scalp. His long, straight nose is a lot like mine. And the woman has long, pale blonde hair, the same color as mine. Hers is twisted into an intricate braid and woven into what looks like a crown on top of her head.

"Where did you find this?" I ask, my voice trembling.

"Nadia's secret place," Zayla says, and then presses her finger to her lips. "Shhh."

"Don't worry. I won't tell her about this or that you gave it to me."

Zayla grins. "Christmas secrets."

"Christmas secrets." I hug her, and though she stiffens, she doesn't run away. "Thank you, Zayla. To have something that must have once been mine means everything to me."

These people must have been important to me. Could they be my parents? That might be the worst part. That I don't even remember who they are. I came here searching for answers, but seem to have found more questions.

Suddenly, Zayla is pushing a spoon into my hand. "Jamie's secret."

"That's right." I grin down at it, remembering how Jamie was throwing the spoons like they were knives. "Her secret weapon."

I smile at Zayla as I tuck the spoon and locket into my jeans pocket. A spoon isn't going to keep me safe. After everything that happened tonight, I know I'm going to need something more than that.

26

WHEN YOUR ONLY DEFENSE IS A SPOON

ESTRELLA

Florida

I slip out of Zayla's hidden room upstairs and hurry down the hall, hoping to get into my room before Nadia notices I'm missing. Is she still lecturing the girls about the events from dinner? Will she be checking in on me?

The ache in my head is still intense, and I'm pretty sure it's the result of not drinking the tea for the last few days. As I turn the doorknob and step into my room, the room tilts a little and I'm forced to steady myself against the doorframe.

Am I strong enough to deal with this?

Lexi and the other girls did it, right? I should be able to do it as well.

"Estrella?" A voice calls my name from the lower stairwell. Nadia is coming up the stairs, a frown on her face. "I thought I told you to go to your room."

The memory of her clapping her hands and my body snapping into place shudders back to me. I don't know what she did, but I can't bear that happening again.

"I just had to go to the bathroom," I lie. There's no way I'm going to tell her I'd been sneaking off upstairs and reading texts from her phone with Zayla.

"Dinner got out of hand tonight," she continues. "Don't you think?"

I feel like this is a trick question. "Is everyone okay? Jamie, Izzy, and Flora...they're not hurt, are they?"

"They're fine." Nadia pushes back a loose strand from her bun and tucks it behind her ear. "They're resting now. I feel like your presence unsettled them. Because of that, I think it's best if you take all of your meals in your room until things calm down."

The hallway sways as my headache pounds against my skull like the waves crashing outside. I press my back against the doorframe for support.

"Are you alright?" Nadia frowns and presses her thin lips tight.

"I'm great. Just feeling a little overwhelmed between what happened tonight at dinner and trying to catch up on schooling."

She nods slowly, her eyes trailing down to my pocket. I dart a glance, suddenly worried that my locket might be dangling out, but it's just Jamie's spoon traitorously sticking out.

"Why are you carrying a spoon?" Nadia asks, her voice turning very low.

I laugh it off, patting it to make sure it remains in place. "This was Jamie's. I'd taken it from her but forgot to put it back."

Nadia sighs and runs a hand over her forehead as if just mentioning a spoon has stressed her out. She holds out her palm. "Pass it over. Cook will be concerned if she finds she's missing another spoon. This is getting a bit out of hand."

Carefully, I withdraw it and hold my breath as Nadia snaps it out of my hand and marches back downstairs. I think I'm clear from her when she pauses and glances back at me. "You haven't seen my phone anywhere, have you?"

I shake my head. "Sorry." And then I hurry into my room, shutting the door firmly shut. I stumble to the bed and press my pillow over my head, taking deep breaths to calm the pain.

As I lay there, I find myself thinking about Dion. His slow smile and the way his eyes stare at me as if I'm the most important girl in the universe. As if he knows my worst and my best and both are equally beautiful.

And then a flash of a memory bursts into my mind.

His hand is reaching for mine and we're strolling through a winter wonderland. It's just the two of us with glacial-blue mountains rising up in the distance and the valley glistening under a pale sun. Powder-soft snowflakes dance around our bodies, tickling my nose and caking my lashes. He's laughing, and it's deep and rich and my heart swells from it.

The pain in my head subsides and for the first time in the last hour, I find relief.

I throw the pillow off my head and jerk to a sitting position. What was that? A dream? A memory? I frown, lightly touching my nose and eyelashes. It felt...real. Like it was a moment in time.

A moment from before.

But that's impossible, isn't it?

He's from a completely different country, and I'm just an orphan from a trailer park. With the pain in my head easing up, I stand and start pacing the room, trying to think through everything that has happened.

My mind goes to Tristan. He said he could see the Grim Reaper guy just like Lexi and me. I bite my lip, wishing I'd stayed and talked to him in the library. He might have some clue as to what is going on.

Unlike everyone else in my life, he's the only one who seems to want to give me answers. First thing tomorrow, I'm going to look for him.

Darkness presses over me and an aching cold snakes through my veins. I swipe the air but find only emptiness. A pale beam of light radiates from above and centers on three black-cloaked figures, their tattered garments fluttering in the chilled breeze. They stand in a line, still as statues. A low hum mounts, vibrating around me.

Run! But my knees lock. Fear courses through me like ice and I sink onto a marble floor. In unison, they advance, so smoothly it's as if they are gliding.

"Please!" I shove my hand out. "Give me a second chance. I promise it was a mistake."

Still, they come.

They are so close, my fingertips could touch the hems of their black cloaks.

"Shalik, shalik, shalalik!" they chant over and over.

One cackles. His body shakes so hard that his hood slides back, exposing a crooked nose pointed like a beak, crimson eyes, and skin so pale it crawls with blue veins. He lifts his arm, revealing a toothed knife. Wings spread out from his back, and they engulf me like a prison.

The dagger lifts into the air. Ice slithers through my body. My throat freezes and my tears icicle.

I scream.

I wake up, sitting in bed. I'm still screaming, and it echoes across my room.

I heave in deep breaths, all the while clutching my blanket over my heart. With that loud of a cry, I must have woken everyone in the house. Still, after that dream, screaming is a relief.

As if on cue, the door flies open. Nadia, wearing a long white nightgown, stumbles inside, holding a thin metal bar. Her eyes are wild, frantic even, as if she's preparing for something perhaps as horrible as my dream.

But as her gaze takes in the room, she lowers the metal bar, and her shoulders relax. Meanwhile, Lexi, Tiffany, and Mara race in behind her.

"Are you alright, Estrella?" Nadia finally asks.

"We heard you screaming," Tiffany says. She hugs the door, luminous eyes scanning the floor as if there might be monsters creeping beneath the bed.

Lexi hurries to my bedside and pulls me into a hug, rubbing my back. "You just had a bad dream, right?"

I try to wipe away the tears, but my face is wet. My hair is drenched as if I'd been running through a rainstorm. "Yes. A bad dream." I swallow away the lump in my throat. "Just a dream."

Or was it a memory?

"Of course." Nadia lets out a long breath, before hurrying to slam my window shut, locking it with a firm snap. "You shouldn't keep your window open. It's not safe."

I'm not sure how keeping my window open on the third floor out in the middle of nowhere is not safe, but I'm too traumatized to argue with her.

Mara, who had left, returns with a glass of water, a deep frown filling her face. She passes the glass to me. I drink from it, gulping it down as if that would take away the bitter taste in my mouth. The horror tearing at my insides.

"You gave us such a scare," Nadia says. "I'll call the doctor in the morning."

"No, please don't," I say. "I'll be fine."

A nurse rushes into the room, her cap skewed slightly. She's holding a tray with a cup of steaming tea.

Nadia frowns at her. "Took you long enough," she barks.

The nurse bobs her head, splashing the tea over the edge. "I'm so sorry. Got here as soon as I could." Then she holds out the teacup to me. "Take this. It will help you sleep."

"Are you sure you need it?" Lexi asks, squeezing my hand.

I know Lexi is telling me not to drink the tea, but she

didn't have that dream of mine. She didn't see the knife, hear the screams, or feel the pain.

If remembering my old life means remembering that horrible dream, then I don't want any of that. And the thought of that nightmare recurring propels me to gulp down the tea as quickly as possible, swallowing it as if to chase away the memories.

Evil memories.

Nadia nods in approval while Tiffany blows me a kiss. Lexi squeezes my hand one more time while Mara lays an additional blanket over me.

"I'm not coming in here every night to tuck you in," Mara warns. "So don't get used to this."

"Do you want me to stay with you?" Lexi asks.

"No." I fall back against my pillow. "I'll be fine."

They all trudge out, but Lexi hovers by the door as if to say something. She opens her mouth and then shuts it. Finally, she leaves, too. Once I'm back alone, the dream still replays, lingering in my mind.

I shiver under the blanket.

"It was only a dream," I whisper into the dark. "Only a dream."

27
ESCAPING SURE SOUNDS LIKE A GOOD IDEA
ESTRELLA

Florida

I open my eyes, blinking into the aching light of dawn. I drink in the air. The bedroom churns around me, so I wait until it slowly eases and stills. When I sit up, I realize I'm lying on the floor. A rock tumbles out of my palm. There are grooves and indents in my skin from where I had clutched it so tightly. Books are strewn all around me.

I lick my dry lips, trying to figure out why I'm on the floor while panic rushes over me like ice-cold water.

I must have stayed up late studying. But no, I remember going to sleep.

My stomach twists. I lurch for the trash can, barely making it in time before I throw up. I linger over the bin's lid, my hands shaking and my headache pounding so forcefully that my vision spins once again.

Something happened last night. But what? I press my fingertips against my forehead, hoping their coolness pushes my mind into focus and I'll remember. But it only spears prickling pain through me.

There's a haze about my brain as if all the previous days are jumbled together. A teacup is sitting on my bedside table. I slide across the bed to find it nearly empty. Wait. I took the tea because of some bad memory.

Terror strikes me. I've come so far. I can't lose what I've gained with my memories.

My legs shake as I shuffle to my dresser. A quick glance in the mirror shows me a girl with hollow cheeks and eyes scared of what they may find. Someone knocks. I swivel around to find the door jammed shut by the back of my chair. I frown.

"Estrella!" It's Lexi's voice. "You okay? Did you sleep alright? It's almost time to catch the bus. Are you awake yet?" The doorknob twists and turns, but the chair keeps it clamped firmly into place. "Why doesn't your door open?"

I have no clue why my chair is pushed against the door. It would really make it easier to think if my head would stop pounding like a jackhammer. I grab the chair and slide it away just as I read the words scratched into the white paint on the back of it.

Remember. Escape.

It's as if someone doused a bucket of icy water over my chest. Who wrote those words? And why? Suddenly, the door flies open and Lexi barges inside, bouncing up and down in a red baby doll dress and yellow leggings. I grip the chair and push the back against me to cover up the words.

"Hey." Lexi's face is pulled tight with worry and her eyes drift to the chair I'm clutching. "You okay? After last night, I've been so worried about you.

"What happened last night?

"You had a bad dream. Woke up screaming and then Nadia came and brought you some tea. Don't you remember that?"

"No." And that's not good.

"You sure you're okay?"

"I'm fine." I try to smile. It's as stiff as dried toast.

Don't let her see the words.

"Good. I'm glad," she says, but a wariness settles over her. "Do you need help picking out something to wear? Maybe something fun and..."

Her eyes drift to the floor and she gasps.

"What?" I follow her gaze.

The books I checked out the other day are strewn about on the floor, pages torn and scattered about. But what made me gasp are the symbols scratched into the wood. One symbol specifically repeats itself over and over across the floorboards. The endless knot—an infinity symbol.

"What..." Lexi presses her hands over her mouth as if she doesn't know what to say. "What is this? Why did you draw all over the floor?"

Unconsciously, I touch my shoulder where the symbol is hidden beneath and my eyes drift to the rock I'd been holding when I woke up.

"I don't remember," I say and then cringe. "Please. Promise you won't tell Nadia."

"Trust. Not a word." Lexi lifts her hand up as if she's solemnly swearing to a judge. "You have the mark too, don't you? Is that what this is about?"

"You know about the mark?"

She nods solemnly and then turns around and pulls down the edge of her shirt far enough for me to see the faint outline of a symbol that looks just like mine. I gasp.

"I'm not one hundred percent sure," she continues. "But I think all of us have it. I've seen it on the other girls. No one at school has it from what I can tell."

This information rattles in my brain. "So not only have we all lost our memories, but we also all have a mark. Why? What does that mean? Do you think someone put it on us before we came here?"

"That is one of the questions I've been trying to find out since I got here." She darts over to the door, and yells down the hall, "Mara! Hold the bus for us!"

"As if!" Mara shouts back.

"Ugh." Lexi rolls her eyes. "She's so annoying. Come on, we need to hide this until I can figure out what to do about this mess you've...engraved."

I run my fingers across the groove on the chair of the two words hidden beneath my palms.

Remember. Escape.

I place it against the wall instead of tucking it under the desk where it belongs. Lexi hurriedly begins collecting the books and papers as if cleaning up the evidence will make everything right once again. Grimly, I stare at the carvings on the floor. Nothing will take those away.

"Thanks, Lex." I stack the books on the desk. "I honestly don't remember doing this. It's kind of embarrassing."

"You have nothing to be embarrassed over." She flashes me a wide grin, and for a moment I think her hair is on fire. But it must be the way the morning light hits her head. "This symbol. There's probably a reason why you're drawing it. Did you find any answers in these books?"

"Not yet. What do you think it means?"

"Honestly," she shrugs, "I don't know other than it's an infinity symbol. But if you figure it out, will you tell me? I'm curious about it as well."

"It will be our secret," I say.

Mara pops her head into the room. "Bus should be here soon." But then her eyes land instantly on my etchings on the floor. "Ohhh," she breathes. "Someone's getting into so much trouble."

"Shut up and come help us move this bed," Lexi orders.

I grab Mara and yank her into the room, shutting the door. "Please. Promise you won't tell Nadia."

"I knew you were trouble the first moment I laid eyes on you," Mara mutters. "Fine. But only because I like you fifty percent of the time."

Together, we drag the bed, so it covers the carvings.

"It's not great." I grimace. It's obvious the bed shouldn't be there.

"One glance at the bed's location," Mara says, "and Nadia will be suspicious."

"Come on." Lexi throws a pair of jeans and a blue tank top at me. "Put these on as we walk."

I run to the bathroom to brush my teeth and wash my face. Somehow I manage to pull on my jeans as I hop down the stairs and slip the tank over my head as I pass through the kitchen.

"You don't look so good, Estrella," Nadia says as she steps into the doorway, blocking my exit. "I don't think you should go to school today. We'll get some medicine for that headache of yours, too."

She has no idea how tempting it sounds to avoid school, but the words of the chair burn into my mind. I need to get away from this place and figure out a way to escape. But with no money, driver's license, degree...I don't know how that's going to happen.

Tristan's name niggles at the back of my brain. I need to talk to him.

"I appreciate your thoughtfulness, but I'm really trying to live out our motto here, *Your future begins today!*" I point to the sign.

Suddenly, a car honks from the driveway. Nadia frowns and spins around. Meanwhile, outside, I hear Lexi say, "Well, look. Pretty boy just arrived."

"We still need to name him," Tiffany says with a sigh.

"*Or* maybe Pretty Boy is his name," Lexi says with a wide grin.

"What's this?" Nadia marches outside and down the steps. "What is *he* doing here? Interfering is what."

I hurry to join them and find Dion pulling up a candy-red sports car. Sand and dust kick up in the wake of the tires as he skids to park. Then he hops out like he drank espresso for breakfast, smiling with self-importance.

He's wearing dark jeans and a white shirt that shows off his perfect skin and dark hair. Pretty isn't quite the right word, I think as he opens the passenger door. No, he's beautiful as the night sky, scattered with a thousand stars.

"Good morning," he greets us while we all just gape at him. "I was here to give Estrella a ride to school this morning."

Tiffany clasps her hands together. "Oh! How fancy."

"Don't say no to Pretty Boy," Lexi tells me.

"Dion," I finally manage, trying to get a handle on my emotions. "That's sweet of you, but..."

His face falls and I glance over at my friends. The events of last night are fuzzy, but I know that the girls were there for me then and this morning.

"I'll only take your offer if you agree to take my friends to school, too," I say.

"Whatever you wish," he says, "it's yours."

My heart does a million backflips. He's so romantic. So perfect. Is it too good to be true? The girls squeal and rush to the car, cramming into the back seat.

"Wow." I grin. "Maybe next time I need to ask for something bigger. Like a car of my own."

He laughs and reaches for my hand. The moment our fingers meet sparks flutter across my skin. Our touch is electric.

"If Lexi keeps hogging up all the space," Mara is saying as she squeezes into the backseat, "public transportation might be the better option."

Meanwhile, Nadia is wringing her hands, trailing after us to the side of the car, "Do you have authorization for this?"

I squeeze inside, confused by Nadia's words. "Why does she need authorization?" I ask my friends in the backseat.

"He's just a kid from school."

"She's so weird," Lexi says.

"More like controlling," Mara adds.

"I think he's sweet," Tiffany says.

A memory flickers in the back of my mind.

Her clapping. Harsh, sharp, snapping my spine into a frozen block. I shiver as the moment holds, latching onto me like a warning.

"How about you do your job," Dion tells Nadia firmly, "and I do mine?"

I expect Nadia to do or say something, but instead, she backs up a little and presses her lips together as if she's afraid of Dion.

"That was super weird," I whisper to my friends.

Their eyes are all as wide in shock as mine.

"No kidding," Lexi says. "Maybe she's got the hots for him, too."

Tiffany giggles and Mara smirks, but a strange feeling slithers through me. Jealousy?

Dion and Nadia continue talking but their voices have lowered enough that I can't hear them. A sense of dread settles over me. Something isn't adding up.

"Why is he acting like he knows her?" I press. "He's not from this area."

"Maybe Pretty Boy is more than he lets on," Mara says, narrowing her eyes on him suspiciously as he leaves Nadia and rounds the car to the driver's door.

"But I like Pretty Boy," Tiffany whispers. "Let's keep him around. At least for the rides."

Slowly the fog in my brain lifts a little more and I remember being huddled beside Zayla under the table, reading Nadia's texts.

A team has already been working on the case. Maintain order until further notification.

Could he be a part of that team? There's no way. He's a teenager at school just like me.

Dion eases into his seat and flashes us all a smile as he turns on the car. "Shall we head to school?" he asks.

I snap on my seatbelt, pushing down my worries. Instead, I focus on how today I'm going to get some answers.

"You can't drive away from here fast enough," I say.

28
WE MIGHT BE ATTENDING ESTRELLA'S FUNERAL
ESTRELLA

Florida

Dion walks beside me as we head across the parking lot toward school. Lexi, Mara, and Tiffany stroll just ahead of us, giggling and probably plotting out new things to tease me about.

"I just need to check on a few things before class," Dion says, glancing around distractedly.

"Sure." I'm not going to lie. I'm slightly disappointed he's not going to walk with me to class. "I'll see you in first period though, right?"

He slips on dark sunglasses, which somehow makes him look even more gorgeous. "Absolutely."

And even though he smiles down at me, I feel his attention is being pulled elsewhere. He goes to reach for me and then stops suddenly. I flinch at the slight. He doesn't seem to notice because he's already hurrying across the parking lot, scanning the area as if he's looking for someone.

My eyes land on Chandra, who's standing still as a statue except for the breeze kicking up the edges of her skirt and sleeves. Even though her gaze is focused on Dion, I realize she must have been watching Dion and me.

Is she the reason why Dion was so distracted? I shake my head and hurry to catch up with my friends as they step inside the school's entrance.

"So what's up with you and Pretty Boy?" Lexi asks as I slip in beside them.

"He asked me out on a date yesterday," I say, unable to hide my grin. "This Friday."

Lexi pauses mid-stride. "Nadia's going to allow that?"

"The better question," Mara says, opening her locker, "is if his girlfriend will allow it."

I scrunch up my nose, remembering Chandra's threats yesterday. "He said Chandra isn't his girlfriend."

"That doesn't stop her from being super scary," Tiffany adds, adjusting her backpack. "You should be careful."

"Bummer." Lexi pouts. "I was hoping we could do something fun together."

"Well, we might be attending Estrella's funeral," Mara mutters. "You know. Once Chandra murders her."

"So dramatic." Lexi rolls her eyes and groans. "Estrella isn't going to die. Now go away and stop sucking away my positive energy."

Mara chuckles.

Tiffany is about to leave but pauses and touches me

lightly on the arm. A rush of warmth and calm runs through me like warm sunshine.

"Are you okay after last night?" she asks softly. "I've been worried about you."

"Worried?" I ask. "Why?"

Did Lexi and Mara tell her about the mess I made in my room?

"Well, between the fight with Izzy, Jamie, and Flora," she says, "and then your nightmare...I just wanted to make sure you're okay."

"What fight?" Fear creeps along my skin like spider legs. I didn't remember a fight. "What are you talking about?"

"You drank the tea," Lexi says. "Last night might be fuzzy for you."

Which could be why I can't remember desecrating my floor.

Mara eyes me, lips pressed together as she slips a book into her backpack and shuts her locker. "Listen," she finally says. "I know it's hard to push through the pain, but if you want to keep your head about you, don't drink the tea. It's not something we talk about because Clara is the one who made a big stink about it and now...she's gone."

"Do you think that's really a good idea?" Tiffany asks.

"Well, it makes sense." I lick my lips. "I threw up this morning. Maybe that's why."

"That's good." Lexi hugs me. "It means your body rejected it. So maybe the tea won't take full effect."

"You're going to have to tell me all about this fight," I say.

"It was pretty epic." Mara shrugs. "Jamie tried to stab

Izzy with the utensils and Flora was crawling across the table."

My eyes bug out. "Wow."

"Listen," Tiffany says. "I've got to run to first period. See you all at lunch? We can catch you up on the details then."

Tiffany and Mara wave goodbye. As I watch them leave, a need to protect our group of four surges through me. These three girls know my deepest secrets, and they've stayed and helped me through it all.

"Lexi," I say as we head to English. "You're going to have to tell me exactly what happened last night."

Lexi starts rehashing last night's details. By the time we make it to first period, I'm shocked by what she says, not to mention that Nadia apparently blamed me for everything. Now the words on the back of my chair make more sense. That was why I wanted to escape.

"It's such a wild tale that it's almost unbelievable," I say. "Except, there's something foggy in my brain that tells me what you're saying is true."

"The worst part," Lexi continues as we step into class, "is that Nadia forced Mara and I to clean up the entire mess and do all the dishes."

"That's awful!" I exclaim, sitting at a desk. "I'm sorry you had to do all of that."

"The longer I'm at the home," Lexi says, settling into the desk next to me, "the more I'm thinking she's the wicked witch from the fairytales come to life. But oh my gosh, I thought I was going to die from shock when Dion came to pick you up."

"Right? Now I just need to figure out how to go on that

date with Dion without her locking me up and throwing away the key."

"Just don't have Dion pick you up after school today because it's painting-the-set-day. We could use someone there who's good at art."

I laugh at her ploy to get me involved. She's probably still worried about me after she saw my room this morning. "Good at painting a canvas black, you mean. I'm sure you'll find better artists in this school."

"Don't say such nonsense." She waves her hand. "I'm sure we could use some black chairs or something."

"Fine." I giggle, but then my mind goes to the words on my chair in my room. *Remember. Escape.* And my insides chill. "I'll come, but don't expect much."

Mr. Terring starts off class, but my eyes won't leave the door. Dion still hasn't come back. Is he with Chandra right now?

But then the door opens, and he strolls into class. Right away, the room seems to awaken. It's like his presence brightens everything. His gaze roves across the room until it lands on me. A slow smile works its way across his features. I'm absolutely riveted. There's just something absolutely compelling about him and I can't quite explain why.

And the frustration of not knowing is driving me crazy.

He moves through the room with ease, coming to stand at the desk just behind me. A guy is already sitting there but one glance at Dion sends him rising from his seat and scrambling to settle in the back row.

I lift my eyebrows at Dion. "Not nice," I whisper.

He smirks but settles at the desk without a flicker of guilt.

I expect Mr. Terring to stop his lecture or comment on the desk exchange, but he just continues droning on with his lecture.

Now that Dion is here, a grasp away from me, I can't concentrate on anything that Mr. Terring has to say. All I can focus on is what it would be like to kiss him.

Would sparks fly?

My whole body aches to wrap my arms around him and feel his body pressed against mine. I pull out a sheet of paper and write.

Where are you taking me on a date?

And then lowering the note below me, I hold it behind me without looking, pretending to be captivated with the lesson and not the hot boy behind me.

The note slips out of my fingers.

Then moments later, the paper slides back onto my desk.

Dion: It's a secret.

Me: How am I supposed to know what to wear?

Dion: Wear whatever makes you happy.

Me: But if I'm wearing a fancy dress and we're going to a water park that might be a problem.

Dion: True. In that case, you may want to wear something fancy.

Me: So, that is a problem. I don't own anything fancy.

Dion: You deserve the fanciest of everything.

I stare at the stream of messages running down the page and smile.

"Are you going to kiss that paper?" Lexi whispers, eyebrows raised in laughter.

I glare at her but tuck the note into my pocket.

After class, Dion slides beside me as I'm packing up my books. "You have American History class next, right?" he asks.

"Yeah, what about you?"

"Calculus. I was thinking about changing my schedule so we had more of the same classes. What do you think?"

My heart stutters. *Pull yourself together and act cool, Estrella!* "Really? I'd like that."

"Great." He smiles like I've just made his day. "I'll see you soon then."

He exits the classroom, and Lexi nudges me on the arm. "If you don't start moving, we're going to be late for history."

"Oh." I hurry and slip the strap of my backpack over my shoulder and head out into the hall. "Did you hear what Dion said? He's going to change his schedule so we can be in more classes together."

"Sounds a little bit overboard if you ask me."

As we walk, I pull out the paper we passed back and forth. His handwriting is swooping and romantic.

"Did you even hear anything that Mr. Terring said today?" Lexi chuckles. "Or is Dion providing you his own curriculum?"

I roll my eyes at her. "Ha. Ha. This was just a sweet note, that's all."

She grabs it from me, reading it. "Huh. I guess it's sweet. But definitely cryptic."

"Now you're sounding all negative like Mara," I say as we enter history. But when I search to find my seat, my feet falter.

Because there, sitting in the back of the room, is Tristan.

29

YOU DROP A BOMB LIKE
THAT AND DISAPPEAR?

ESTRELLA

Florida

"Uh-oh," Lexi whispers. "That's the guy from art class. What's he doing here?"

"I'm guessing he's in this class, too." I shoot her a you're-overreacting look. But inside, my pulse is racing. All I can think about are the symbols scratched across my floor. How I've planned to find him and demand for answers.

How my chair warned me of danger.

"Whatever." Lexi sighs. "I'm going to talk to Mrs. Doering and try to convince her to give me an extension on my essay."

As I shuffle down the aisle toward my desk, Tristan glances up, his piercing blue eyes taking me in with urgency. My heartbeat kicks up like I'm racing for my life.

He's here for me. I can just feel it. My gaze slides down to the leather necklace hanging around his neck.

The endless knot.

I spent all night scratching that symbol into my floor. He must know something.

I *have* to talk to him.

Guilt tugs at me. I totally ditched the guy for Dion, and he watched me do it. But what do I tell him? That there's something about his presence that warns me to run away? That my best friend thinks he's dangerous?

Or that I feel guilty every time I think about him?

Yeah, not telling him any of those things.

I purposely sit down at the desk beside him, determined this time to get some answers.

"Hey," I say, shooting him an apologetic smile. "Sorry about missing you in the media center yesterday. I really do want to talk."

"Hello," he says in that heart-stopping accent of his. "No worries. I get it."

"I wanted to ask you about that knot you're wearing," I begin. "Does it have a significant meaning to you? And why can you and I see those Grim Reaper things and no one else at school sees them?"

"Grim Reapers things?" He chuckles. "Those are excellent questions. They're actually called Wraiths."

He leans in close enough that I can smell his scent; fresh soap and a hint of some kind of spice. Heat emanates from his body, warming the AC chill in the air. I should pull away, but I don't. Once again, my traitorous eyes drift to his neck where his corded endless knot hangs. And then it slides down to his chest. He's built. Like he must work out a lot.

Oh my gosh, stop looking at his chest!

"This symbol means immortality," he explains.

"Obviously." I give him an incredulous look and then start pulling my books out of my backpack and setting them on my desk. I don't want to look too desperate. "Listen. I was hoping you could explain some things that I don't already know."

"Do you have this mark on your back just below your shoulder?"

I freeze. How could he know about my tattoo? "That's a weird question to ask."

He grins, eyes flashing wickedly like he's enjoying himself way too much. "I have the mark, too. And I can't say much right now, but I will tell you that's not a tattoo. It's a birthmark. And everyone with that mark can see those Grim Reaper things as you call them."

I open my mouth, then close it without speaking. How does one respond to that?

"Which seeing as you can see them," he continues, "I'm guessing you have the mark, too."

"I do." I whisper the words as if saying them out loud might be dangerous.

He nods solemnly and takes a deep breath as if my confession is a big deal.

"So what does this mean?" I ask. "Is it bad to have the mark?"

He glances at the door and shifts in his chair as if he's worried about something.

"The guy who brought you to school," Tristan begins. "Is he your boyfriend?"

"No." My face burns. Somehow that feels like a lie. "I mean, it's not like it's not a possibility."

"There's more that I need to tell you, and it's not safe to tell you here. Not with your boyfriend about to come into the room."

"What's that supposed to mean?" Suddenly I'm feeling too hot, like fire is burning my skin.

He groans and rubs his head. "I know I'm being cryptic. I'm terribly sorry about that. It's just...I don't know how else to say this, but you're in danger."

"Danger?"

His eyes are back on the door again and he taps his desk impatiently. "Meet me in the media center as soon as possible and hear me out."

Suddenly, he slips from his seat and darts out of the room before I have a chance to form an answer.

So that's it. You drop a bomb like that and disappear?

I'm still staring at the doorway where he just vanished through, my breath hitched with newfound fear when Dion comes waltzing into the room.

I clutch the sides of my desk, the room spinning a little. Is Dion the one that's putting me in danger?

Or is it someone else?

Dion's eyes land on me and his face brightens. He beelines it to the desk where Tristan was sitting only moments ago, but Lexi beats him to it.

"What did Tristan want?" Lexi asks, settling down beside me oblivious that she just took the seat Dion wanted.

I should tell her the truth. Get her opinion. But something stops me from telling her. So instead, I say, "He got his second period mixed up. Wanted directions."

She sniffs. "Well, that's boring."

For the rest of class, I can't focus on anything the teacher is saying. All I can think about is Tristan's warning that I'm in danger.

And the fact that I believe him.

30
I NEED TO TALK TO TRISTAN. ALONE
ESTRELLA

Florida

Tristan's words haunt me for the rest of class. I'm half-terrified, half-desperate to find out what he has to say. By the time second period ends, I hurry to the media center to find the answers I'm desperate for.

The moment I slip through the doors, I'm embraced by the sounds of hushed conversations and whispering pages. I cast my gaze around the room until I spy Tristan sitting in one of the cushioned chairs in the reference section alcove.

His wild blonde head is bent down, focused on his phone, so he hasn't spotted me yet. I edge over to stand by the couch opposite him and set my book bag on the coffee table between us. His head pops up. I don't know what to expect. A smile or a hello perhaps? Instead, he frowns and taps his phone against his thigh as if he's been waiting for a while. There's an intense fire to him, a heat in the air I realize every time I'm near him.

I hate that I like it.

"I wasn't sure you'd come." He studies me with a hint of wariness, rubbing the side of his jaw.

I cross my arms. "What do you expect? You told me that I'm in danger and basically insinuated my boyfriend was the reason."

"So he is your boyfriend?"

"Listen," I snap. This boy sure knows how to get under my skin. "No more beating around the bush. Get to the point."

"Good idea." He glances over his shoulder as if he's expecting someone. "Listen, what I'm going to tell you is going to be rather shocking. You may want to sit down."

"More shocking than telling me that I'm in danger?" I bristle. There's no way I'm sitting down now. The room is fairly full of students so it's not like he will be able to try anything here. Still, Tristan has a rough, wildness about him that I definitely don't trust. "I don't know who you are, but whatever you have to say better be good."

"Actually, I don't even know where to begin." He runs his hands through his hair. "First off, I'm not actually a student at this school. I've been sent here to help you regain your memories."

A chill courses through me, seizing my heart so suddenly it feels like it's frozen. How could he possibly know about my memory loss? I haven't told anyone except Dion.

"Who told you I lost my memory?" I ask. "Was it Dion?"

"Dion?" His eyes widen and he snorts. "Hardly. The two

of us are, shall I say, not on good terms." He leans forward, his hair tumbling into his eyes. "I'm here to help you remember who you really are."

Remember. Escape.

I suck in a deep breath and sag into the chair across from him. "Did we meet before my accident?"

"No, we've never met before. But you need to know that black-cloaked hooded thing you saw outside of art class, that creature will kill you the second it thinks you've started remembering anything from your past. This is why if it knew what you painted, you'd be dead before you could blink. I'm guessing that's why your friend freaked out."

"What I painted?"

"You painted an Eternity Ring." He says this like I'd know what it is.

"A what?"

He sighs and leans back in his chair. "It's complicated, but it has to do with that birthmark on your back. But that's not the important thing."

"And what *is* the important thing?"

He leans forward, those piercing blue eyes studying me like I'm the most important person in his world.

"You're not like the other kids at this school," he begins slowly as if testing to see the impact his words have on me. "You're special. And Dion, he's not who he says he is either."

"How do you know all of these things?" Unless...

My heart hammers in my chest, screaming at me that his words have truth to them. The events from last night, fuzzy as they are, tumble back to me.

But if he's right, then Dion's been lying to me.

Suddenly, I have no idea who to trust or who to believe.

It's too confusing. The answers I've been wanting are far more complicated.

"I need to go." I jerk to stand and turn on my heels.

"Please." Tristan grabs my arm and pulls me to face him. "It's not safe here for you. Let me take you somewhere where we can talk about this. Because there's more. A lot more."

Waking up to the creepy designs on my floor, the horrifying visions, the strange behaviors of the girls at the home. These thoughts spike fear through my chest. They scream at me, warning me to tread very, very carefully.

"I don't have anything in my past worth remembering," I whisper.

"If you'll just come with me, I can show you things you can't possibly imagine.

"My parents were killed. My friends don't bother to find me. I have no other family. There isn't anyone who cares that I exist."

"Are you sure? What if I could bring back your memories? Expose the truth of your past? I can explain why it's so important for you to remember."

Before I can respond, Dion's voice cuts through the air. "A little close for studying, don't you think?"

I jerk away from Tristan like I'm playing with fire. Dion is leaning against the bookshelf, looking sleek in his black polo shirt and jeans. Tristan crosses his arms over his chest and his face transforms into one of pure fury. My eyes flit between the two.

"You both know each other, I see," I state.

"No," they both say simultaneously.

"*Okay*," I say.

"You should leave," Dion tells Tristan. "Your presence isn't welcome here."

"My *presence*?" Tristan scoffs. "I think you've forgotten something, mate. This is mortal territory. So back off before you start something you can't finish."

"Mortal territory?" I repeat. "What do you mean by that?"

But neither offer me a glance.

"You underestimate me." Dion pulls away from the bookshelf, standing tall. "Regardless, things won't go so well when *they* see you."

"We already had a get-together." Tristan shrugs. "Last I checked, they're licking their wounds."

Dion's eyebrows rise and he steps closer to Tristan. "Well, isn't that something?"

The room feels like it's heating up and sweat beads up on my skin. There's static electricity buzzing along my skin and the lights above flicker. The strangest part is my mind begins to clear. The fog I felt this morning finally floats away and the events from last night begin to clarify in my mind.

The two continue to glare at each other, bodies tense and fists clenched as if they're about to get into a fistfight.

"Stop it." I step between them, pressing my palms against either chest to keep them from tackling each other. And as I do, I feel it. A rush of power surges into my palms, racing up my arms so intensely, so startling that I gasp. I pull my hands away and back up. "What happened?" I gape at them. "Who are you?"

They stop talking to each other and they focus on me. It's a little unnerving to receive their undivided attention.

"Are you okay?" Dion asks.

"You felt something, didn't you?" Tristan says with a satisfied look. "Now do you believe me?"

"I did feel something," I say. "What did you do to me?"

Dion's face softens. "I think we should go. It's not safe for you to be around *him*. He's going to get you killed." And then he shoots an angry look at Tristan.

My head spins. I have a million questions. I look over at Tristan, but he's running his hands through his hair, grimacing like Dion is speaking the truth.

"I'm just trying to help you remember who you are," Tristan finally says. "We didn't do whatever you just felt. *You* made that happen."

"I don't understand," I say. "You're talking in riddles."

"Did you want to go grab lunch?" Dion asks softly, all the hardness vanished. "I can explain everything then."

There's a tug at me, urging me to say yes. But another part of me clings to Tristan's words; *I can bring back your memories.*

I search Tristan's eyes, wondering if he's telling the truth. Can I trust him? I rub my temples because my headache is back, burning across my head and making it impossible to concentrate.

"Lunch sounds good," I finally say. "I didn't get breakfast this morning."

Dion takes a deep breath and smiles like he's relieved. Then he shoots a parting, scathing look at Tristan. "Stay away if you know what's best for you," he whispers to Tristan, but I still hear him. Then wraps his arm around me.

As we head out of the media center, I peer over my shoulder. Tristan sags back into the chair, his hair more disheveled than before. As if sensing my gaze, he looks up and our eyes meet.

I did not imagine that rushing surge racing through my veins. Even now, I feel something different about myself after touching these two. Something wild inside of me, waiting to be released. Waiting to be used.

I nod once, because there's one thing I'm sure of. I need to talk to Tristan again.

Alone.

31
MORTAL LIFE IS PURE TORTURE
DION

Florida

It takes every fiber in my body to get my anger and fear under control as I wrap my arm protectively around Estrella and escort her to the cafeteria. When she never showed up to her third-period class, I knew something was wrong. Panic had me searching the entire school. At first, I thought Quadril had followed through with his threat to kill her. But finding her with that disgusting Sabian wasn't much better.

"How are you doing?" I ask her, slightly terrified that the filthy dog fed her a bunch of lies.

Or worse. Told her the truth.

She stops in the middle of the hall, slipping out from under my arm to face me. Her hair tumbles over her shoulders. A single strand hangs over those gorgeous eyes of hers and she tucks it neatly behind her ear. More than anything, I want to pull her to me.

Kiss those lips like I've been dreaming of for what feels like an eternity.

Run my hands over her body.

And feel her heartbeat against my own.

But I don't. I can't.

"What happened back there between you and Tristan?" she asks. "And I know you say you've never met the guy, but you sure seemed to recognize him."

So the dog's name is Tristan. I bet he's the brother of the last Sabian Conduit. Things are worse than I suspected. Once Quadril discovers who the Sabian is, things could escalate quickly to the point that Estrella might not survive the day. And I won't let that happen.

"Fortunately, there's nothing going on between me and that other guy. But if he's who I think he is, then yes, our families do know each other and..."

How do I explain centuries of feuds? That the Empress ordered Tristan's sister's murder? How desperate he must be for revenge?

"Well," I finally say. "We don't get along. At all."

To put it mildly.

"He said my life was in danger," she whispers, glancing over her shoulder. "That I'm different from the other kids here at school. Why would he tell me that?"

I stiffen. I hadn't expected the mutt to use that tactic to sway her to his side. Maybe he's smarter than I'd given him credit for. Except what exactly is he trying to do? Is he searching for information? Hoping she has her powers still?

I don't know, but it can't be good.

"Because he knows that I care about you," I tell her. "And his family will do whatever they can to hurt my family. So hurting you will hurt me and them."

Her sea-blue eyes that always take my breath away assess me, and I know she's searching for the truth in my words. Finally, she nods as if she's satisfied with my explanation.

And it is the truth, I assure myself. At least, as much of the truth as I dare tell her.

"Come on," I say. "Let's get some food. I'm starving. And I bet you are, too."

As we head into the cafeteria, her face is still scrunched up pensively as if she's trying to put the pieces together. My heart splinters a little as I offer her a tray and we get in line. My mind goes back to the days when we told each other everything.

Every secret. Every hope and dream.

But all that is lost now. All lost in one moment.

A moment that I can't even think about.

"Which do you think tastes better?" Estrella's eyes twinkle as she points to the menu choices. "Soggy fish or hard chicken?"

"Soggy fish?" I offer, trying to smile. I can't let her see how much I feel the loss of who we were. Because this is us now. Stinky cafeterias, swarms of frail mortals, and soggy food.

I'll take it all over my old life if I can have her.

"Do you want to sit with me and my friends?" she asks. "Unless you're sitting with Chandra."

She nods over to where Chandra is now sitting with a

group of boys who are practically drooling as she's talking and gesturing grandly with her arms.

"I think Chandra is quite happy without me," I say with relief that Chandra isn't watching me like a hawk right now.

"Great. Then follow me." Estrella starts weaving her way through the tables to where her friends are sitting by the window.

The three girls look up at me in surprise as Estrella and I settle at the table. Seeing how her friends have been able to transition so well to the mortal world gives me hope that Estrella will be able to as well. While searching for Estrella, I'd read too many studies on the failure of the mortalization process. The rate of success is staggeringly low.

"Hiya," the red-strand hair girl says. Lexi, I believe her name is. "Thanks again for the ride this morning."

"Not a problem." I smile, wishing there was a way I could just give Estrella a ride instead of the whole crew. But soon, I'll be able to take her away from Nadia's to someplace safe, and it will be just the two of us. "Do you ladies need a ride home as well? I'm sure the bus isn't comfortable."

"We're going to work on the play's set after school," Lexi says. "Gotta take advantage of Estrella's amazing painting skills."

Lexi laughs while Estrella rolls her eyes as if she just told an inside joke. But I nearly drop my fork over Lexi's words.

"You like to paint?" I ask Estrella, trying not to seem too excited. Art used to be her favorite hobby. And to think that she hasn't lost that love gives me hope that maybe she hasn't lost her love for me, too. That maybe deep inside her, she could feel something for me again.

"Carving apparently, too," the brown curly-haired girl

with pale white skin offers. Her dark brown eyes assess me warily.

"Mara!" Lexi admonishes. "That wasn't funny."

Estrella clears her throat and pushes her food around her plate. Something happened that they're not telling me about.

"Estrella told us you're taking her out on a date," the third girl pipes up. She girl has dark brown skin and hundreds of braids tumbling about her shoulders. "You'll have to tell us where you're taking her so we can make sure she's dressed appropriately."

"Tiffany." Estrella half-covers her face. "Stop embarrassing me. If you all keep this up, I'm not sitting at this table anymore."

"That's a great question," I say, eager to change the subject to safer ground. "I was going to take Estrella somewhere fancy. She deserves a break from cafeteria food, don't you think?" I lift the wilted carrot up with my fork, proving my point. The girls laugh.

"Fancy, huh?" Lexi says. "Sounds like we might need to go on a shopping trip to prepare."

"Oh." Tiffany claps her hands together. "That would be fun!"

"As if Nadia will ever let us," Mara grumbles. "When was the last time we were allowed to go shopping?"

"And with what money?" Lexi adds. "It would take a year of saving our allowance."

An awkward silence falls on the table. I take in the four girls, heads down, pushing their food around. This will not do. How are they supposed to transition to mortals when they're not allowed to be normal people?

"Maybe I could talk to Nadia," I offer. "I mean, what is life without shopping? Besides, money isn't an issue for me. I have plenty."

"You don't have to do that for us," Estrella says, touching my arm lightly.

Do not focus on her hand.

"That would be awesome!" Lexi sits straighter, and her whole body practically sparkles. I glance around the cafeteria, but thankfully no one else seems to have noticed Lexi's skin and hair.

The fact that Lexi is at Nadia's home worries me the most. I wonder if Nadia knows these girls' history.

The grating bell rings. Instantly, everyone springs to life like scurrying ants. It is no wonder mortals die so early, living in this environment. The girls gather up their trays and backpacks, but a shift in the air sends a shot of warning through me.

A burning scent clings to the back of my throat and my eyes narrow. Something is wrong but I'm not sure what, and I feel the sudden urge to go investigate. After missing the presence of the Sabian, I'm not taking any more risks when it comes to Estrella.

"I'll see you later," I tell Estrella. "I need to stop at the office before my next class. Be careful, will you?"

"You're as paranoid as—" she says, but her words choke in the back of her throat. I flinch because somehow I knew she was going to say Tristan's name. "Yeah, I'll be careful."

"Great," I say before turning to her girlfriends. "Keep a close eye on her, will you?"

Lexi tucks her arm through Estrella's. "Always. We watch her like a hawk."

I'm still not convinced Lexi is the best person for Estrella to hang out with after what happened before.

But if my senses are right, there are bigger issues that I need to deal with right now.

I take off through the cafeteria, trying to not move too fast as to alarm the mortals but fast enough to bring me to the source of my fears.

32
ARE YOU THE DANGEROUS ONE?
TRISTAN

Florida

So far my plan to get Estrella to come with me has been a complete fiasco. Maybe I should've told her more about who she is, or maybe I should've just captured her and hoped she'd forgive me later. This place is crawling with Nazco and Wraiths, and I'm not sure how much longer I can stick around without causing a full-out battle.

Or even a war.

My phone vibrates. *Great*, it's Katka. She's probably calling to gloat.

"So how's it going?" Katka asks. "Conrad is preparing to join you."

"What? No, you promised me three days." I slip out of

the media center, checking to make sure no teachers see me talking on the phone. Detention with Mr. Roberts and his policy of doing absolutely nothing made a Nazco prison cell seem like a holiday.

"Actually, your father asked for an update. He's not happy."

Fabulous. Here we go again.

"When is he ever happy?" I snap.

I'm back to being the incompetent son who needs others to come in and get the work finished. But this time, I'm not going to fail. There's too much at stake here.

And Ivana's blood still calls to me. Just the thought of my sister sends my pulse racing.

I duck into an alcove when two teachers pass by talking. "Tell my father things are completely under control," I lie.

Okay, so it's not a total lie. Estrella did give me a nod, so that has to mean something, right? "She's agreed to come with me tonight. We're just having trouble sneaking out. This place reeks of Nazco."

I rub my forehead, hating myself for lying, and yet also hating that my father might find out I'm failing. I mean, once I talk to her, I'm sure she'll agree to come.

"Really? Wow, you have made progress." Katka sounds shocked and slightly skeptical. Has she no confidence in me? "You'd better hurry because we got an alert that one of their big dogs just arrived in the area last night. Someone from their council. My guess is either she's not transitioning well, or they spotted your involvement so now they're going to kill her off."

I decide to not mention my run-in with the Wraith yesterday between classes. "Beats me." Suddenly, a crawling sensation runs over my skin and my heart stops. "Hey, got to go."

I hang up on her just as a tall man strolls down the hallway. He's dressed out of place for a high school. He's wearing a black shirt and baggy dress pants under a black trench coat that hangs down to his boots. His brown hair is styled differently than most mortals wear it these days, wavy and shoulder length. A foul burning scent emits off him in sharp waves. I don't need to see his birthmark. There's no doubt he's immortal.

Then it hits me. He's probably an assassin. *Great*, I think, frowning.

I need to find Estrella. Now.

My feet eat up the corridor as I try to remember her schedule. If I'm right, she has calculus next. Room 124. I slip into the classroom, scanning the desks until I spot her in the back corner rummaging through her backpack. My usual self would just barrel in and take control of the situation, but there's something about Estrella that has me hesitating.

As if sensing my presence, her eyes lift to meet mine. Is it me or do they look brighter? Her lips quirk into a smile, and she pats the seat next to her. My heart skips a beat.

Damn, she is beautiful.

I shake my head, needing to stay focused on the task. Get her onto Sabian land. And if I can fake her death, all the better. This has nothing to do with her looks.

I settle beside her, lounging back in my chair as if it's just a typical day in school and I'm not I'm terrified of a Nazco assassin running about the halls.

"You found me." She flips open a notepad and starts

doodling. "So, is now the time when you're going to tell me all the details?"

My muscles tense and I glance around the room. Could there be spies here? I'm not the only one with the ability to cloak my powers or create a glamour.

"You're really good." I point to her drawings, avoiding the subject. "You might find that a lot of your answers can be found there."

"Why do you always have to be so cryptic? When I confronted Dion, he told me that I'm in danger because he likes me, and since your family wants to hurt his, I'm a target."

"He likes you, huh?" A rock settles in my stomach. Sure I suspected as much, but this is news. And not good news *at all.* "How long have you two been going out?"

"Oh, we're not official or anything. I mean, we met a few days ago."

"Could have fooled me. He's pretty possessive of you."

"What goes on between Dion and me is none of your business," she huffs. "Can we just focus on you telling me what's going on?"

"Believe me, I'm trying." I sigh and run my hands through my hair. "I didn't know it was going to be this hard."

The teacher starts taking roll, but Estrella isn't distracted.

"Or is Dion right?" she pushes. "And you're the dangerous one?"

I stare at her, rubbing my chin while she meets my gaze with a fierceness that I've yet to see before. I need to choose my next words carefully.

"There are those who don't want you to remember your past," I say. "But I want to help you."

"Why? What does it matter to you?"

Bugger. There's no way I'm going to answer that right now. "There's an assassin in the school hallway right now who is here to kill you. But if you come with me, I'll explain everything."

"An assassin?" She scrunches her face skeptically. "I hate to break the news to you, but I'm not the President's daughter and I don't carry around secret codes."

"Can you keep your tone down? No need to yell it out." I shift uncomfortably, glancing about the room. "Listen, let's get out of here. Go someplace safe where no one is listening and I'll explain everything."

"See?" She throws her hands up. "This is the problem. You don't actually tell me anything. You beat around the bush."

That's because if I tell her she was once an immortal, she'll laugh in my face and think I've lost my mind. And then there's *no* way she'll ever come with me.

"Time's up!" she announces.

"Time's up?" I ask incredulously. "This isn't some game show. This is serious."

"You had to think too hard to come up with an answer, which means I'm not going anywhere with you." She lifts her chin and focuses back on her notebook. "Goodbye, Tristan."

Wow. I lean back in shock. I just got dismissed. Might be the first time ever. Even Katka always bends to my will eventually.

"Excuse me, young man." The teacher is standing in

front of my desk, frowning down at me. "You're not a student in my class. Either you find *your* class immediately or you get detention."

Man, I really hate high school.

I shoot Estrella a pleading look, which only makes her smirk widen.

"I hope you'll change your mind." Then I take her pencil and scribble my phone number onto her pad of paper. "Call me if something goes wrong, okay?"

She presses her lips together, eyeing my phone number. I wait for her to crumble it into a ball, but she just folds it up and slips it into her backpack.

Then, nodding to the teacher, I exit the room. But the moment I step into the hallway, a snap of electricity sizzles through the air and mixes with the strange burning scent from earlier.

My pulse quickens in fear.

Finding a way to get Estrella to come with me is going to have to wait. I've got bigger problems to deal with.

33

DID YOU HOLD A PARTY AND FORGET TO INVITE ME?

TRISTAN

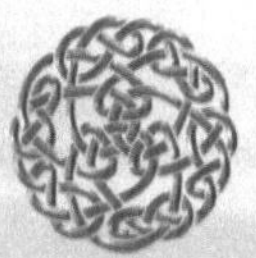

Florida

Forget pretending to be a well-behaved student. I take off down the hallway at a speed that made me glad all the students were tucked away in their classrooms. The scent draws me to a parking lot in the back of the school behind the gym.

A shimmer hovers about the air, warning me that immortals are cloaking the area in secrecy. Whatever is going down here can't be good.

Which is why I head directly to the source. The moment I step around the dumpsters, I halt in my tracks. Because there stands Dion faced off between two men. One is the Trench Coat dude I spied walking down the hallway earlier, this time holding a black ashen ring the size of a tire. The other is a pock-faced near-giant holding a metal spiked club.

All three of these immortals are Nazco, but it's obvious that Dion is about to fight the other two. Which means things are more complicated than I first thought. Dion must not be getting along with his people, or there are splinters within the Nazco ranks.

Interesting.

All three freeze as I stride closer, holding up my palms with a grin. "Did you decide to hold a party and forget to invite me?"

"Sabian!" The giant spits on the ground as if he tasted something disgusting. "What's he doing here?"

"Not just a Sabian." Trench Coat's eyebrows lift. "The prince."

"Tell me you brought drinks." I step closer, unbuttoning the top of my shirt while glancing over at Dion. His eyes are set, lips pressed into a grim line. He eyes me warily, his fingers twitching at his sides, but makes no move to attack me. "No? That's unfortunate. Snacks then?"

"You're after the girl." Trench Coat laughs maniacally. "That's got to be the only reason why you'd be here in this forsaken high school. Charming."

"Back off, Sabian dog," Giant says. "She's ours and we've been assigned this job. Your interference will just mess things up."

"Assassins, huh?" I cock my head to the side, assessing the two and their abilities. "Who hired you?"

"Don't you worry your pretty face about it," Trench Coat says. "Now run along before your daddy has two dead children."

"Well, for that comment," I roll up my sleeves, "now I have to stay for the good times."

"Truce for the next hour?" Dion asks me through gritted teeth. "I could use a hand here."

"Why not?" I shrug. "Got to keep the sides even, right?"

"She must be worth a pretty penny for her to have you both here," Giant says. "We just need her head and we'll be off."

Dion growls, and without hesitation holds out his palm. A bolt of electricity shoots out and hits Giant in the chest. His hulking body flies backward and thunders to the ground. Giant's body convulses from the intensity of the shock.

But Trench Coat is ready for the attack and whips out a ring the size of my hand. It sails through the air, heading directly for Dion. Ashes erupt from it, filling my lungs with choking smoke.

Poisonous ashes, I realize as my vision swims.

I snatch an iron pipe off the ground, wishing I hadn't left my sword in the car. I send a burst of my firepower across its surface so the pipe burns red-hot and flames lick its surface like dragon's teeth. With a swooping arc, I leap through the air and swipe the pipe against the ring. It knocks it from its trajectory milliseconds before slicing through Dion's neck.

And killing him.

The ring wobbles about in the air as if it can't quite regain its momentum.

"What kind of Sabian fool are you to save a Nazco?" Trench Coat cries out in frustration. He clenches his fist to regain control over the ring.

Dion nods a curt thanks to me. I shrug, not thrilled with the idea that I saved Dion's life, but it's a means to an end.

Then I aim my palm at the ring and propel fire through the air. The flames slam into the ring, exploding it into a plume of ashes. Upon seeing that his weapon is destroyed, Trench Coat's eyes widen, and he turns and starts racing away.

Dion flicks his hand again. Another stream of electricity jolts out from him, nailing Trench Coat in the back. The voltage sends Trench Coat stumbling to the ground. Undaunted, Dion slams another punch of electricity toward the sky, but this time he uses the bolt to carry him upward. He rides the bolt, flipping through the air. As he lands, he smashes his fist into Trench Coat's face, using the voltage to add to the blow.

"That is for even thinking of touching Estrella," he growls.

Trench Coat grunts, head lolling to the side.

"Dude," I say. "You've got it bad for her, don't you?"

"Don't get involved," Dion snaps.

"Think it's too late for that," I say. "You might want to duck."

Because Giant has risen from the ground, sparks still sputtering around him. He's hefting his club and is ready to smash Dion's skull.

But I'm already shooting off a ball of fire. Dion's eyes widen and he leaps out of the way just as the fire blasts against Giant's chest. The hulking man screams in pain, nearly dropping his club. I sprint at Giant as he tries to regain his footing. His eyes widen as I swoop my flaming pipe through the air. He doesn't even have a moment to cry out before I've sliced his head off in one smooth arc. His snarling face bounces across the pavement, severed from his body. Beheading is brutal, but it's the only sure way to kill an immortal.

"Remind me to never get in a fight with you," Dion tells me.

I smirk. "Right back at you."

I torch Giant's body. Flames hungrily eat at his flesh. I glance up to see that Dion is watching me, looking mildly impressed.

"Bonfire?" Dion points to Trench Guy sprawled at his feet.

"Not a bad way to get rid of the evidence," I agree, and set fire to Trench Coat's body as well.

"Touché." Dion cracks his neck and shakes out his hands. "Once the bodies are incinerated, we never speak of this moment again."

"Works for me." There's no way I'm telling anyone back home that I fought alongside a Nazco.

"And we are not friends or allies. This remains a secret between the two of us."

I resist smiling. So, this Nazco has an agenda his people don't know about. I can respect that. Besides, the dude obviously has high powers. Not something I want to face on my own.

"I couldn't agree more." I grip the iron tightly because despite the fact we literally saved each other's lives, I still don't trust Dion.

I start heading back to the school, hoping I'm not going to find any more assassins lurking about the hallways, when Dion calls to my back. "You can't have her."

I stop in my tracks and take a deep breath. Now that I understand the full magnitude of the situation, I realize everything with Estrella is a lot more complicated than I thought.

Nearly impossible.

"She should know the truth," I tell him.

The sleeve of his shirt is singed. His hair sticks up like it's been electrocuted. His shoulders sag as if his insides are being shredded.

He shakes his head, jaw tight. "If she is to live," he says, "she can't know."

"In my kingdom," I say, "we have a saying that truth sets one free and a lie binds one to enslavement."

His chin lifts in defiance and a flash cuts through his dark eyes.

I toss aside the pipe. It clatters to the ground. All the fight has left both of us for today. I stride away, the shadow of defeat chasing at my heels. Because we also have another saying.

There's nothing more powerful than love.

34
WHEN REAL LIFE IS MORE DRAMATIC THAN PLAY PRACTICE
ESTRELLA

Florida

I searched for both Dion and Tristan for the rest of the school day, but I couldn't find either of them anywhere.

Worry snakes up my spine as I head to the school auditorium where play practice is held after school. Are they okay? Tristan was talking about being in danger. Did something happen to him?

There's no doubt that Dion was really distracted today during lunch. Does he know something that I don't?

As I head into the auditorium, I glance over my shoulder, worried one of those Wraiths as Tristan called them is going to pop out and attack me.

But all I find are students milling about or heading out to the buses.

Involuntarily, a shiver curdles through me. My fingers reach for the infinity mark on my shoulder blade and my mind frantically tries to make sense of Tristan's words and warning. I need to figure out what is going on so I know what to do next.

"Hey, Lexi," I say as I work my way down the aisle of the auditorium toward the stage. She's standing in the center directing a group of students who are already at work, dragging out set pieces and covering the stage with tarps. "I'm ready to paint."

"Estrella!" Lexi dances as she says my name. "You made it. I was getting worried there for a moment. You know, we need to convince Nadia to get you a phone."

"I wish." I climb the steps and join her. "But she says not until my first month is up. So where do you want me to start."

"I'm feeling like the cityscape is calling your name." She drags me across the stage to a large wooden board cut into silhouette outlines of buildings. "What do you think?"

"I could give it a try," I say. "But I have a feeling that I've never done anything like this before."

"You'll be fine." She bends down and starts rummaging through a folder lying on the stage until she procures a picture of someone else's rendition of a cityscape. "For inspiration."

I take the drawing and stare at the way the yellow lights dot the dark buildings. Have I ever seen a big city like this at night?

Lexi pushes a paintbrush into my hand. "Also, I've got an idea for a nickname for Dion. How about Dionysus?"

"Isn't that like an ancient god's name?" I shake my head, wondering how I can come up with random things like that but not remember my old life. It's almost like someone took a scalpel and picked out specific things from my mind.

"Yes! I think it's perfect."

"Are you two talking about Dion?" Mara strolls over to where we're standing. She's changed into faded jeans and a tank top. Her hair has slightly fallen out of its tie, strands falling around her face, giving her a softer look. It's the first time I've seen her where she hasn't looked so uptight. "Because today I saw him running down the hall, which was bizarre."

"Running?" My heart stutters. "Was it like a running-to-class thing or running-from-something?"

"No clue. But don't you think there's something off about him? To be honest, I'm worried. Like you just met him, Estrella, and now you two are like life-long lovers?"

"We're not life-long lovers!" I snap, except something twinges on my inside. All those strange memories or dreams of the two of us.

Like we have had a past.

Like there's something inside me screaming to tell me the truth except it's stuffed down deep inside of me.

"There is something about him though, isn't there?" Lexi muses. "Like the other day at lunch, I got this weird feeling like I've known him from... you know...before."

"Oh, man." Mara rolls her eyes. "Not you, too. This is getting weird."

Our memory loss is one of the things that none of us talk

about. It's the ever-present elephant in the room. Actually, it's more like a fierce monster, threatening to consume us should we make one wrong move.

"Why didn't you tell me?" I ask. After today's chat with Tristan, first in the library and then in calculus, he has me questioning everything. I take her hand and whisper, "Do you think it's a memory?"

She shrugs and pops open a can of paint. "It's just a feeling."

"What kind of feeling?" I push. "Good or bad?"

Mara snorts. "You really need to chill. Going on feelings can really mess with your head."

My chest tightens so hard that I feel like it might snap. It's time to tell them what I've been thinking about ever since I left Nadia's this morning.

"I think we need to escape," I say.

Their heads snap up to stare at me.

"Nope." Mara shakes her head. "Not going to do this again. I hate to break the news to you, Estrella, but you're kind of growing on me. And I don't want to lose you, too."

"There's something wrong about Nadia's Home for Girls," I press on. "I have this horrible feeling in my gut that we're not safe there. Besides, it's obvious that Nadia is purposely serving us that tea to keep us from remembering. She's keeping us under her control."

Lexi frowns. "I'm not going to lie. I've thought about leaving a million times. But where would we go? We have no money, no friends or family, not even a high school degree."

"And think about what happened to Carla." Mara dips a brush into orange paint and starts brushing a wooden fence.

"She was talking crazy like you are right now. And where did that get her?"

"But she was working alone, right?" I point out. When they don't answer, I barrel on, "If we worked together, it would up our chances. We can't keep living like this. I'm going to find a way out for us, so start brainstorming ideas."

Someone clears their throat from below the stage. I spin to find Dion standing there, forehead creased, and for the first time since I've known him, looking slightly disheveled.

My eyes run over him. A few buttons are missing and the edge of his shirt appears to have been singed. His hair, normally neatly combed, hangs wildly over his forehead.

"Dion." I scramble off the stage. "Are you okay? You look—"

"I got in a little skirmish with some guys, but it's all good now."

"You got in a fight?" My heart kicks up a beat as Tristan's warning rattles my core once again. "Why? What's going on? Who did this to you?"

I step closer and press my hand on his arm. He flinches, almost like he's scared of me touching him.

This is not like Dion. Something happened.

"What are you not telling me?" I ask.

"Everything is under control." He rubs his forehead, indicating everything is definitely *not* under control. "I have some good news and bad news."

"Okay." I lick my lips. "Give me the bad news first."

He gently cups his hand over my elbow and leads me to the auditorium seats where we settle onto the chair's worn fabric. Over on the stage, my friends are all pretending to work, but I catch them peeking at us every once in a while.

"My father called," Dion begins, tugging me back to the conversation. "He wants to talk to me. In person."

"But isn't your family in Brazil?" I ask.

"Yes. Apparently whatever he wants to tell me can't be done on the phone. He doesn't trust it."

"That's a little extreme, but that's not really bad news. You'll just be gone for a little while, right?"

He sucks in a deep breath and scans the room, eyeing each of the students.

"Something's wrong. Let me help." I lean forward and touch his hand to ease his worries.

Static electricity skitters across my skin.

"Ouch." I jerk my hand back, rubbing my skin. "That was weird."

An image flashes through my mind. Jamie wielding forks like weapons at the dinner table. Sharp vines flowing out of Flora's hands. Nadia's words snapping my body to attention in a vice grip.

I blink and grip the sides of the chair. Memories. Those were memories from dinner last night. I'm sure of it.

"What was weird?" he asks. "Touching me? Did you feel something?"

I shake my head to clear my thoughts. Except everything is muddled and confusing.

"It's nothing." I swallow hard and try to smile. "So you said you had good news, too."

"The good news is I've asked my father to delay my trip to Brazil for a few days. We've got our date to go on after all."

His face softens as he says this and my muscles relax. Maybe I'm the one being paranoid here. This is all Tristan's fault. He's got me thinking that people are out to kill me and my life is in danger.

Except, what about the chair in my room?

Remember. Escape.

What about my lost memories that scream to be remembered?

"After drama practice," Dion continues and pulls out a credit card, handing it to me, "I thought you might want to go shopping with your girlfriends."

"Shopping?" I stare at the card.

"You said you didn't have anything to wear for our date. Thought you and your friends might want to get something nice. Buy whatever you want. It's on me. I wish I could go, but I need to deal with a few things."

"This is too generous. I mean, we're not even dating."

"Then maybe we should change that." He reaches out and his fingers skim across my cheek. My skin ignites under his touch and I lean into him, wanting more.

A crash erupts from the stage, pulling our attention away. It's Chandra, standing by a fallen set piece, hands on her hips, glaring at us. My heart sinks.

"What's she doing here?" I ask. "Please don't tell me she joined the play."

Dion grimaces. "If it's any consolation, she's a great actress."

"She hates me."

"She's going through some things, but don't let her get to you. She won't hurt you."

"Are you sure? Because if looks could kill…"

"Positive. So about the shopping, I got Nadia to send you all a van so you won't have to worry about anything."

"The warden is letting us out of our prison?"

Dion pales at my words. "Is that how you think about your home?"

"I wouldn't exactly call Nadia's place *home*."

His phone pings and he peeks at it. "I'm so sorry, but I've got to go. An emergency. Have fun at the mall. And be sure to stick close to your friends."

He rises from his seat and hurries down the aisle.

From the stage, I hear Lexi squeal.

I hurry over to join my friends. "Is everything okay?"

"I just got off the phone with Nadia," Lexi says breathlessly. "She gave us permission to stop by the mall on our way home. And wait for it...she's sending a van to take us there!"

Lexi starts bouncing around. I turn to watch Dion slip out the front doors of the auditorium. He did this. Got us to go and have fun.

"What's going on?" Tiffany peeks out from the wings where she'd been reciting her lines. When we tell her, Tiffany joins Lexi in dancing.

"Since when is Nadia so nice to us?" Mara asks, paint dripping onto the tarp. "Something's up."

Lexi huffs. "Why can't you just be happy about things for once?"

"I couldn't agree more." I flip the credit card in my hand, staring at it as an idea blooms in my mind. "In fact, I think this shopping trip might be the beginning of our escape plan."

35
COMMERCIALISM AT ITS FINEST
ESTRELLA

Florida

Nadia's van pulls up to the sidewalk outside of school right on time. There are paint stains on my jean shorts and shirt, but I don't care. Because today I have a plan. It's only the start of one, but every plan starts with a beginning, right?

The four of us clamber into the van, thanking Val for picking us up. He grunts in response as we snap on our seat belts.

Val is the home's groundskeeper and basically fixes anything around the place that needs fixing. The guy is over six feet tall with broad shoulders. He's got a harsh, square jaw and his head is bald except for a single tuft of hair in the back that Lexi claims he has to not know exists.

And he wears his sunglasses all the time. Like in the house. Even at night.

"Are you ready to experience commercialism at its finest?" Lexi rolls the window down as Val drives out of the parking lot and sticks her head out, yelling, "We're going shopping!"

Mara yanks Lexi inside. "Stop making a scene. It's embarrassing."

"If Lexi wants to express her feelings," Tiffany adjusts the butterfly clips in her dark curls, "she should. I mean, when was the last time Nadia let us go shopping without her?"

"An eternity." Lexi sighs, letting her head hit the back of the seat.

"By which you mean never." Mara pulls out a makeup compact and dusts her nose with a brush. "Still. It won't be that much fun. We hardly have any money in our accounts. I have like twenty-five dollars saved up from my allowance."

"I have a confession. Dion gave me his credit card." I wave it back and forth, grinning. "And said we could buy whatever we wanted."

Tiffany gasps. Lexi squeals.

"He what?" Mara asks. "What is he, rich?"

"Maybe," I shrug.

"Why?" Mara's eyes narrow. "No guy gives a girl his credit card without ulterior motives."

I shoot her a glare. "Dion is not that kind of guy."

"She's kind of right," Tiffany admits. "I mean, other than a fancy car, what do we really know about him?"

"Forget about Dion," I say, holding back my frustration

because I need them to focus on the point. "What matters is this is the beginning."

"The beginning of what?" Tiffany asks.

I'm about to explain my diabolical plan when I notice Val's sunglasses eyes lift to stare at me through the rearview mirror.

He's listening.

Of course, he's listening. I could smack myself on the head. What had I been thinking? That he was just some driver and gardener? Nadia's smarter than that. And now I need to be, too.

"The beginning of looking our finest," I lie. "No longer are the girls from Nadia's Home going to be wearing hand-me-downs and other people's cast-off clothes. We're going to be dressed in style."

Tiffany squeals in excitement but Lexi gives me a forced smile and Mara grimaces at the card like it's evil.

"Can I trust you all?" I ask with meaning.

"Trust us?" Tiffany asks. "Of course."

Lexi presses her lips together and Mara lifts her eyebrows in shock. They might not know exactly what I've got planned, but after our talk at the play set, these two have an idea of what I'm talking about.

"You can trust me." Lexi reaches over and squeezes my hand. "Always."

Mara rubs her head and groans. "Fine. I'm in. But if I get killed, I'm going to haunt you in the afterlife."

Tiffany giggles. "Killed from shopping? You're so dramatic, Mara."

The van trundles through the streets while I dig the slip

of paper Tristan gave me from my pocket. There's nothing on it except his phone number.

I don't know why I let him give this to me. I mean, I don't even have a phone. Where can I get one? A sliver of a memory hugs my mind. Something about Zayla. But it slips away from me like an ice cube skidding across the floor.

But it is an option, isn't it? And right now, I need to keep all my options open.

The van parks in a lot full of more cars than I've ever seen in my life. Excitement and a hint of fear bubble through me as we climb out of the van. This is the first place I have visited other than the hospital, Nadia's Home, and school. But when the four of us stroll into the air-conditioned mall, I freeze, overwhelmed by the amount of space and noise.

Sunlight streams through glass ceiling panels, casting rays against the marble floor and glass-walled shops.

A security guard barks on his walkie-talkie.

Music blares.

Two kids pull on their mom's pants, screaming.

There's so much to take in so quickly, I don't know what to look at first.

The girls, oblivious to my discomfort, take off down the wide corridor and I scurry to keep up with them, trying to take deep breaths like Lexi taught me at the beach. Val trails after us like he's gone from being our driver to our security guard. It's hard to decide if I should be comforted by his presence or worried.

"We'll start with Macy's," Lexi announces. "It's a *great* store with *great* deals. You're going to love it, Estrella."

"Let Estrella decide what she loves or doesn't love," Mara says. "Seriously."

You can do this, I tell myself as we enter the store. But all my plans to prepare to escape slip through my fingers like sand as reality hits me. What had I been thinking? I can barely manage to walk through the mall without freaking out. How will I be able to manage a whole escape?

I suck in deep breaths. *You can do this. You're strong enough.*

Tiffany leads us to the dress section and pulls one off the rack, holding it up to her body.

"What do you think?" she asks. "It feels like forever since I've bought something."

"Our allowance is pitiful," Mara says.

"Someday I'm going to get a job and make heaps of money," Lexi announces, holding up a sequin dress and spinning around. "Then we won't have to rely on Nadia or mysterious boys who drive fancy cars."

"You won't be getting a job if you run away from Nadia's," Mara points out. "Think about how hard it will be to survive without a high school degree. Or a brain that works properly." She adds that last part with a mumble.

"Run away?" Tiffany squeaks. "What are you talking about?"

Lexi and Mara look away, unable to meet Tiffany's eyes.

"I mentioned it while we were painting the set," I admit, glancing over at Val to make sure he's far enough away. "I was going to tell you, but I didn't want to do it in the van with Val there."

"We can't run away," Tiffany whisper-yells. "There's no way we'd make it on our own. We can barely function for one day, much less take care of ourselves. Besides, every girl who has tried to leave never made it."

"She has a point," Mara finally says. "No offense, Estrella, but you didn't look so hot this morning. What were all those drawings on the floor anyway?"

I knead my temples, my headache coming on. "I'm still working on that."

"Maybe a better plan," Mara continues, "is to graduate and try to make it on our own then."

"But don't you all feel it?" I ask, my voice pinched in desperation. "Things are not right at Nadia's. Doesn't it worry you that every girl who tried to leave has disappeared?"

"Of course it does." Lexi's eyes are wide with fear. "Why do you think we pretend to drink the tea and ignore those horrible creatures that lurk about the home?"

"You see horrible creatures?" Tiffany asks.

Lexi's shoulders stiffen. "It was a joke. Obviously."

"It's more than even that," I say, trying to recover from Lexi's slip. "There's something strange about all of us. The infinity marks on our bodies and the memory loss are a start, but you've got to admit it. We're not like the other kids at the school. We're different."

"Or we just have memory issues," Mara says and starts piling clothes into her arms. "Maybe we should start spending your boyfriend's money and just have fun like Tiffany said."

"Listen," Lexi says. "Today we go shopping and get ourselves a new wardrobe. We keep out of trouble, and once we graduate in a few months, we'll get out of here. Go some-place far away and start a new life. Okay?"

Mara shrugs while Tiffany nods vigorously and then starts biting her nails.

I shrug, crossing my arms, but inside I'm screaming for them to believe me. That we don't have until we graduate. Because by then, we'll all have lost our minds or be dead.

The girls immediately begin combing through the racks, gathering up armfuls of clothes. My hand reaches for the first garment beside me and I grab it, determination raging through me.

Maybe they don't see the danger, but that's okay. Because when the time comes, I'll be ready for all of us.

36
SECRET PLANS
DION

Florida

I park off a side street and slip out of my car, glancing about the area for anyone who might be following me. Once I'm sure I'm alone, I take off in long, quick strides. The warehouse lies in abandoned silence as I push open the outside door.

It groans in resistance, and I stiffen at the sound. I hold out my palms, ready to strike at the first movement. Once I'm satisfied all is safe, I slip through the narrow corridor and into a wide open space, cluttered with forgotten junk.

The air smells of rust, and it's choked with dust. Abandoned cars and tractors along with machinery make my trek to the meeting point a bit of a minefield. One misstep and I'll be sliced to shreds.

Finally, I reach the side office where the meeting is to

take place. It takes a moment for my eyes to adjust to the thick darkness.

"You made it right on time," a voice says from the desk across the office.

A flash of light from a car's headlight outside the grime-caked window slices the darkness, revealing BJ lounging in a faded leather chair, shiny boots propped up on the dust-coated desk.

Instantly, my body relaxes and I grin. In a few strides, I eat up the space between us and give my best friend a hug.

He's got dark hair like me, but it's a little longer and always looks like it could use a nice trimming. A scruff of a beard shadows his face and the eagle tattoo on his neck seems to glow. His real name is Bardn Jasper. BJ is the nickname I gave him while we were kids, and it stuck.

"You made it." I release the breath I was holding. "Thank you for coming."

"You kidding?" BJ scoffs and waves for me to sit in one of the dusty metal chairs. "This is the first time you've ever asked for a favor. How could I say no?"

"Still haven't shaved the facial hair yet, huh?" I joke.

He rubs his jaw, smiling. "The girls love it. It's gotta stay."

"Okay, man." I shake my head. "Whatever you say."

I perch on the edge of the chair and then leap back to my feet, needing to release my pent-up energy. Sparks flutter across my palms, my fear for Estrella's life taking over my ability to control myself.

"Did you find anything?" I ask, cutting right to the point. As much as I'm happy to see BJ again and want to catch up on life back home, I don't have time to waste, and every second I'm away from Estrella puts me on edge.

"Maybe." BJ shrugs. The light from my hands reflects in his eyes.

My chest tightens. "I don't have time for maybes."

He sighs, shaking his head, and I know right away he's not happy about what I've asked him to do. "I found two possibilities. A cabin in Alaska. Very remote, very cold, but then again you spent some time in the Midnight Kingdom so perhaps the cold doesn't bother you."

Remote is good, but I'm not a fan of being shuttered in a cabin for the rest of our lives. That's not the life I was hoping for.

"And the other?" I press.

"Jakarta, Indonesia."

"That's Ion territory. Won't work."

He swings his feet to the floor and leans forward. "They don't monitor that city, which makes it the perfect place to blend in and be forgotten. If you keep it cool for a while, over time you might even be able to go to the movies."

He chuckles, but I merely glower back at him.

"I'll take it," I say.

"Seriously, bruh." BJ leans over the desk, hands pressed together. "What's going on? What have you gotten yourself into that you need to hide out?"

"Just give me the name of the place and don't worry about it. It's safer for you that way."

"This is about the girl you met in the Midnight King-dom, isn't it? What was her name?"

"This is none of your concern."

"Estrella." BJ groans. "I told you to stay away from her.

She's trouble, man. Any immortal with that much power is sure to bring disaster with them. Besides, she betrayed our people."

"She never betrayed us. That's what the Empress and Quadril want everyone to believe. Besides, Estrella lost her powers. So that's not a problem anymore."

"Are you sure she completely lost her powers? Because if she hasn't finished the mortalization process then you're not out of the weeds."

He has a point and is touching too close to the truth, but there's no way I'm going to tell him that. I'm running out of time, and if that means that she can't finish her mortalization at Nadia's, then she can finish it with me in a safe location.

"If you truly care about me," I say, "you'll hand the information over."

"Fine." He holds out a slip of paper to me. "It will only be a matter of time before they find you. You might be powerful, but you're not *that* powerful."

A flicker of a memory flashes through my mind. Estrella and I were in that New York City apartment during her school field trip, the two of us battling for our lives. My power was amplified by her.

No. I squeeze my eyes shut. *That is done. Over.*

Right now, her safety and life come first.

A quick scan of the paper tells me he's given me an address and a contact name. Satisfied, I pull out the envelope from my jacket and drop it in front of BJ. Dust plumes in the envelope's wake.

BJ kicks it back across the desk with the edge of his boot. "Dude, no way."

"Take it," I say. "I know how much money this information cost you and it's the least I can do."

"Listen." BJ picks up the envelope and places it in my hand. "You're going to need all the cash you can muster to bribe and swindle your way out of the Empress's clutches. There's a third number at the bottom of that paper. It's my emergency number that no one knows I have. Call me if things get bad."

"I won't, but thank you." I pocket the money because he might be right. "From now on we're no longer friends. We got into a huge fight and we're not speaking to each other anymore."

"That's the story? That's the most boring, lamest story out there."

"Yeah. And shave the scruff, will you?"

"You survive the year and I'll shave it."

"Deal."

Just as I reach the doorway, BJ clears his throat, saying, "There's something else you might want to know."

I pause, hand on the doorknob.

37
SHOP TIL YOU DIE—I MEAN DROP
ESTRELLA

Florida

If I weren't planning my escape, I could see how shopping might be a fun pastime. While the girls gossip about different people in the play, I duck behind a row of jeans and pull out my sketching notebook. Ever since I started drawing in it, it's helped soothe my headaches and gives my mind an outlet. But today I'm using it to write down notes and ideas.

I can't allow another incident to happen like this morning where I woke up having forgotten everything that happened the previous night. If I can keep a journal of my thoughts, plans, and snippets of memories, then I'll always be moving forward instead of backward.

The important thing is to make sure no one finds the

journal. Still, it's hard to concentrate with Val lurking about and Tristan's warning ringing through my head.

Lexi skips my way. "Have you found a dress to wear on your date yet?"

Quickly, I tuck my journal into my jeans under my shirt and start sifting through a dress rack. Polka dot, sundress, spaghetti straps.

"Not yet." But then my fingers skim along a deep-blue dress that glitters like a starry night. I unhook it from the bar and hold it up. "Or maybe I have."

"Oh!" Lexi bounces on her toes. "Try it on!"

Once in the changing room, I slip the spaghetti straps over my shoulders and then head outside to stand in front of the mirrors, the chiffon train trailing in my wake. I spin around in a circle and the sequins sparkle under the fluorescent lights.

"I think it fits," I tell Lexi as she steps in beside me.

She squeals. "It's the perfect dress to wear on your date with Dion."

"You know," I say. "You're right. I'm going to get it."

Once I pay for our new wardrobes with Dion's card, we detour for lattes because according to Mara, it helps with the headache. Already that familiar pain throbs in my head like it knows it's close to teatime.

But as I'm grabbing my latte, the hair on my back pricks with the feeling that someone is watching us. I glance over my shoulder, scanning the mall outside of the coffee shop. For a brief moment, I think I see Chandra standing outside of one of the stores.

Is she spying on us? A group of ladies passes by, interrupting my view. I duck around them, but once I get past, there's no sign of her or anything out of the ordinary.

Either I'm completely paranoid or whoever is watching us knows what they're doing.

Still, the thought of not being able to defend myself doesn't sit well with me. I think about Jamie and her love for weapons. When I first came to the home, I thought she was a little extreme. Now, not so much.

At the far end of the long hallway, I spot a HomeGoods store. Something tells me there's a good chance they would have knives there. It's not much, but at least it's some sort of protection. Far better than the spoon Zayla gave me from her eclectic collection.

"What are you looking at?" Lexi asks.

A place that might have weapons, I think. But considering I don't think she'd like that too much, I say, "I'm going to run to the bathroom real quick."

"Meet us at the jewelry store just over there." Tiffany points to a bright pink sign that reads Jewels Rules.

The moment Val turns around, I dart away and slip into the crowds. My legs hurry me along down to the end of the mall, except the closer I get to the HomeGoods store, the more nervous I get. This is the first time I've been alone in an unfamiliar place. In fact, it's one of the first times I've been alone at all.

I clench my Macy's bag and try to take a sip of my coffee to calm myself.

Get in the store. Buy a knife. Find the girls.

Simple.

Until my eyes land on a man with tattoos running up his neck and across his cheeks standing in front of the store. His feet are planted firmly apart with his hands clasped in front of him, and his eyes are focused on me.

I jerk to a stop, causing a woman to bump into me, nearly knocking my coffee out of my hand. The guy by the store smiles as if he's playing some sort of mousetrap game. And today, I'm the mouse.

My heart slams against my chest.

Maybe I don't need to go to HomeGoods after all. Dion's words to stick close to my friends tumble back to me along with Tristan's warning that I'm in danger. And to call him if I needed his help.

To my left is a girl about my age sitting on a bench, tapping on her phone. I run over to her.

"Excuse me." I pull out Tristan's number. "Would you mind texting this number? Tell the person that Estrella is here at the mall and needs help."

The girl blows out a large bubble and then lets it pop. "Sure." She shrugs but squints at the number. "I guess."

"Thank you so much."

My feet shuffle back and forth as she types in the number and then the message. But a quick glance over my shoulder warns me that the tattoo guy is moving in my direction.

Abandoning the girl, I spin on my heels. I retrace my steps when my eyes land on a woman with streaked black and white hair and a tight bodice and skirt. It's not her outfit that catches my attention, but the fact that her eyes have a strange milky quality to them. They're lasered right on me.

Quickly, I switch directions. My feet hurry me toward another section of the mall. This hall is smaller than the rest and emptier with only a few forgotten stores. Some are gated off like they've been shut down.

That's when I realize this section leads to an exit.

I go to turn around, only to be met by a man wearing a black leather coat and matching pants. He steps in front of me and blocks my way, spreading his spurred boots apart and crossing his arms. There's determination in his eyes. He's not going to let me pass him.

My heart hammers against my chest.

The lights above us sputter out and a shiver snakes down my back. Smells of baking pretzels and the sound of kids laughing beckon me out of the corridor, but I'm frozen in terror.

A debate forms in my mind. Do I go around this guy or run for the exit?

As if to answer my question, a voice inside me screams, *Run!*

My heart stops, suspended as if I'm on the crest of a rollercoaster, ready to dive. I drop my bag and spin around, plunging into motion. I race for the exit. Behind, the man's footsteps slap the marble floor. I pump my arms, praying for help. In moments, he'll reach me.

Almost there. My hand wraps around the exit handle.

Gloved hands clutch hold of my wrist, wrenching me backward and into steel arms.

I scream, fighting against my captor's hold.

Coffee, I think. With my teeth, I rip off the lid and hurl the hot liquid into the man's face. He screams, clawing his hands across his skin. I burst into a run in the other direction only to slam into the black-and-white streaked woman.

She lifts out her arms and her skirts flare out. Mist curls outward from her body.

I blink in confusion as she leers at me with a curled smile. Those milky eyes.

"Go to sleep," she coos. "Don't make a peep."

A heaviness settles over my body and suddenly all I want to do is rest. My knees buckle and I sag to the floor.

The exit door behind me opens. Golden light as bright as the noon sun floods the corridor. Blinded, I duck my head into my armpit. Leather Guy grunts as if something hit him while Black-and-White Lady screeches in horror. The sleep lifts off me and I shake my head to clear it.

When I stand up, the leather man is running out the exit, holding a bleeding arm, and Black-and-White Lady is nowhere to be seen.

I'm left alone with my apparent savior.

Who is...

"Tristan?" I whisper. "You came."

I suck in a breath, taking in him. Broad shoulders. Wild curls. Sharp jaw. There's no doubt about it. Every line and curve of him warns me that he's beautiful and dangerous all mixed into one. My eyes drift down to a glowing sword in his hand and a body half-crouched like he's about to go into battle.

"Why are you holding a sword?" I ask, backtracking. "Did you just stab that man with it? Not that I'm upset or anything. That guy was creepy. It's just, you're kind of freaking me out, too."

"You need to come with me." His face is twisted in worry, and he slips his sword into what must be a sheath strapped to his back. "You're in danger. Those two were assassins. They might not have been successful, but there will be more."

I bristle. "Obviously. I'm not a complete idiot to know they were trying to either kill or kidnap me. But that doesn't mean I should trust you. How do I not know that you're just as dangerous? Or more so?"

He rubs his hand over his face and rolls his neck as if he's slightly annoyed. "Listen," he finally says. "If I wanted to hurt you, I could've done it already. It would be nothing for me to take you right now. But this needs to be your choice, not mine."

I back up even further, swallowing. He's right. There's no way I could stop him from hurting me if he wanted to. Besides, I am the one who asked him to come. It doesn't change the fact that my insides are still warning me that he can't be trusted.

"Where would you take me?" I ask.

"Far away from here. Somewhere safe where you could have time to recover and regain your memories."

"I'm not going to lie. That's tempting. I mean, I do want to regain my memories, but I don't know you and I definitely don't trust you. I mean, what's in this for you? It's not like you're hanging around me just for fun."

"You're right." He grins sheepishly. "Let's just say, you're important to my people, too."

"Now that definitely makes me to go with you," I snap sarcastically, marching over and picking up my Macy's bag.

"What if I were to tell you that you're only experiencing a part of you? That I know people who could help you regain some of your memories?"

I scuff my shoe on the marble floor. He just hit a nerve. Not that I'm going to tell him. "I can't leave my friends."

And Dion. I frown at that thought. Why do I feel like Dion is such an important part of who I am?

A wind kicks up, yanking at my clothes and hair. Did someone turn on the AC at full blast?

"What's happening?" I look around.

"Right. Appears that's my notice to leave." He flashes me a sad, lopsided smile as he pushes his sun-streaked hair out of his eyes. "You should get back. Your friends are worried about you."

I eye him warily, rubbing my arms and trying to stop my whole body from shaking. "How did you know my friends were here?"

He nods behind me, and I turn to find them walking around the corner.

"Estrella!" Lexi calls, breaking into a run. "There you are!"

And just behind them, I spy Chandra strolling up to a display by one of the stores. She's waving her hand in the air. I shake my head. That girl is a strange one. But what about this night hasn't been strange?

Assassins? A woman telling me to sleep? Flaming swords?

Tristan backs up, rubbing his side and grimacing. His clothes snap in the wind.

"Wait," I say. "Did that guy hurt you?"

"Nah. We met a few years back. He knew better than to stick around. This is a wound from the other day."

"Okay..."

"Be careful, will you?" Tristan's brow furrows. "And

don't go off alone like that again. Not everyone is nice like me." That brings back the mischievous grin of his.

"Right." I lick my dry lips. I'm about to thank him, but he's already spinning on his heels and vanishing out the door.

38
DON'T ASK 'CAUSE YOU DON'T WANT TO KNOW
DION

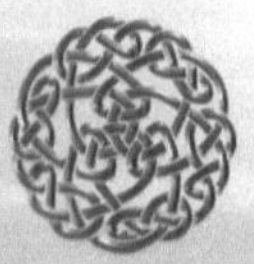

Florida

I pause, muscles tensing, and turn back to face my best friend. "What do you mean there's something else I might want to know?"

"It could be nothing," BJ begins, but he's rubbing the back of his neck, which he only does when he's worried.

"Except you wouldn't have mentioned it if it were nothing."

"It's the Empress."

Now my whole body is as stiff as a board. "What about her?"

"She's looking for something. It's top secret, but you know me, I have my ways. She's sent a special crew out looking for some sort of lost artifact."

My whole body freezes because I know exactly what she's after. "Interesting. Any idea of what this artifact might be?"

"No clue. Just that it was last seen at an art exhibit at The Met."

My phone pings. A text from Chandra pops up.

Chandra: Two assassins showed up.

My heart dives and I stab at the phone.

Is she okay?

Chandra: That Sabian saved her before I could reach them.

I glower at this news.

Did he try to take her?

Chandra: No. They talked and then he left.

I rub my forehead. What does Tristan want? Whatever he's doing doesn't add up.

"Everything cool?" BJ asks, dragging me back to the dusty office.

"If you hear anything else about that search," I say, "let me know."

"Get your story straight, man." He huffs and stares at the ceiling. "I thought we weere now enemies and didn't talk."

"We are unless you hear something."

"I'm making up a better story. One where I beat you up and win."

"No one will believe it," I call over my shoulder.

I hurry out of the warehouse and jump into my car. I should have never left her. It was foolish of me to think Chandra would keep Estrella safe. My foot slams on the gas.

I reach Nadia's Home for Girls in record time, but when I skid up to the entrance, the gates are closed. The Wraiths leer down at me, clearly not planning on opening them. Frustration rushes through my body. I need to see her. Make sure she's okay. She must be terrified after what happened.

Then a new thought hits me. What if she tells Nadia about the attack? If that happens, Nadia might not allow Estrella to leave the home. My mind whips through all the possible scenarios and none are good enough.

She's running out of time.

Suddenly, lights from a van flood the darkened street and illuminate the sharp iron gates. Another text pings on my phone.

Chandra: Estrella and her friends should be returning to Nadia's soon.

Hope fills me. This must be her van.

The gates moan open and the van rumbles through them. I slam on the gas and dart my car through it before the Wraiths have time to shut it. It's a risky move to get them upset, but at the same time, they are fickle creatures. They might not care as long as I don't get in their way.

Or they might try to kill me.

It's a toss-up, but I'm willing to take the risk.

I pull my car alongside the van and leap out just as the girls start tumbling out.

"Oh, Dion!" Lexi squeals, holding up packages. "Thank

you so much for the shopping spree! We had a blast, didn't we, girls?"

Lexi gives the other three meaningful looks.

"It was great," Mara says in a tone that I can't quite read.

"Absolutely amazing," Tiffany adds.

But my eyes are only on Estrella. She steps out of the van and comes over to me. Her long blonde hair tumbles over her shoulders and her eyes shine in the fading light. She's so beautiful and strong, and yet, there's an uncertainty haunting her eyes. I want to swoop her into my arms and hold her close, promising to keep her safe always.

Except that would be a lie. How can I keep her safe if she hasn't completely transitioned into a mortal? With Quadril being so determined to hunt her down and kill her without giving her a chance to make the transition, it makes everything impossible.

"Hey," Estrella says, her lips curving into a smile. "Thanks for the shopping spree. It was so...fun. But you're here. I thought you were busy tonight."

"I was." I pocket my hands, afraid my electricity will spark since I'm all worked up. "But then Chandra called. Said she saw you at the mall. Is everything okay? Are you okay?"

Estrella clears her throat and looks pointedly at their driver. Val, I think his name is. I lift my eyebrows in surprise. Whatever happened at the mall, it's clear the girls are not telling anyone.

Which is good. And yet, it makes me wonder how much she knows.

"Yeah, we saw her," she says. "She didn't really stick around to say hi. Think she was busy shopping."

She didn't completely answer my question. I want to ask her for all the details, but where do I begin? And if I start talking about something, will that trigger her memories? At this point, I don't even know what I'm doing anymore.

"I'm glad you had a good time." I reach out and skim my fingers along the side of her face. She smells of blossoms and the sea. Every inch of me wants to lean down and kiss her, but it's too dangerous.

As a former Channeler, she could pull some of my powers out of me, which could spark her memories and stop the mortalization process.

"Time to go inside," Val barks at Estrella. "It's already past dinner time."

Estrella nods and turns back to me. "So I'll see you tomorrow night?"

"Tomorrow night." I nod. "We'll talk then."

I smile and wave to her friends as the four head inside. But even after the door shuts, I can't seem to move. My mind races, desperate to find a solution to this impossible situation.

Moonbeams illuminate the house in an eerie glow; the chimes of forgetting clinking against each other, swaying in the sea breeze. The light from the lighthouse flashes as if to warn all who come near to flee.

Finally, I force my feet to move. I've got work to do.

I'm running out of time.

39
A STARRY NIGHT FLIGHT
ESTRELLA

Florida

It takes forever to get ready for my date with Dion. Which is silly since I was planning on just slipping on my dress, brushing my hair, and heading out. But Lexi won't have any of that. She's determined to straighten my hair and paint my face with makeup.

"I'm now late for my date," I pout as Lexi swipes red lipstick on my lips.

"Good," she says. "It's important for a guy to wait for their date. It builds tension and heightens the whole experience."

"What if I don't want any tension?"

"You do." She swivels me to face the mirror. "Trust me."

I stare at my reflection. My curls have been straightened

and glisten in the lamplight. Thanks to Lexi's lotion, my bare shoulders sparkle just a little under my deep blue spaghetti-strapped dress that we named Starry Night. It even has a small trail of chiffon material that makes me feel like a princess.

And with the effects of the makeup, my eyes look wider and brighter than ever.

Lexi sighs. "You look fabulous. I'm just glad you're going to be able to get out and have some fun. I don't want you to worry about anything tonight. Especially after those people tried to mug you. I can't even believe it."

I smile, but inside my nerves kick up again. When the girls found me in the mall, they questioned me about why I looked so freaked out. I told them some people tried to steal my dress. They were shocked and horrified, but we decided to not tell anyone what happened. If Nadia found out I'd been in danger, there's no way she'd let us take any more trips.

So standing here now, it feels like our secrets are swirling around us, bonding Lexi and I, and yet they threaten our lives, too.

I go to grab my backpack when Lexi stops me. "Don't tell me you're taking that with you to dinner." she says.

"I need something to put my stuff in."

"That's not going to work at all." She shakes her head and then leaves before returning with a black purse. "It is not a perfect match to your dress, but it's superior to that ugly thing you call a backpack."

"Thanks, Lexi. For everything." I squeeze her hand, her touch warming my soul. I stuff in my lipstick, hairbrush, pencil, and mini notebook I've been using to draw on and write my notes in. I can't risk leaving it here in the house. "You did great. Now let's just hope Dion recognizes me."

The two of us laugh and I head downstairs. I'm actually feeling really nervous by the time I step into the living room where Dion is waiting for me. What if I mess things up for us tonight? What if he realizes what a brainless wit I am?

But the moment he turns to face me, all those fears fade away. His eyes drink me in like I'm the most beautiful person he's ever seen.

"You're stunning," Dion chokes, and my stomach flutters.

Thank you, Lexi!

"You don't look so bad yourself," I say.

Okay, so that's a lie. He looks incredibly sexy in black pants, a black jacket that hugs his toned body, and a crisp white shirt that contrasts with his tanned skin and dark hair.

He clears his throat, and I can feel the air sizzle around us. I'm about to reach for his hand, but he quickly pockets it as if to purposely keep us from touching.

"This is not how I usually run things," Nadia says from where she's sitting primly on the couch. "If anything goes wrong, I'm putting the blame on you."

I hadn't realized she was in the room. I mean, how could I when Dion is here? His presence seems to rule even the air.

"You worry too much," Dion tells her. Then he opens the front door, letting in a rush of sea air. "Besides, the safest place for her is with me."

Before I step outside, I peer over my shoulder. My

friends are all gathered at the top of the stairs landing. When they see I've spotted them, Lexi and Tiffany burst into giggles.

"Have fun!" Lexi waves.

"You look gorgeous," Tiffany adds.

"Don't do anything I wouldn't do," Mara warns, but then gives me a wink.

I blow them a kiss and then head into the cool twilight. Once I slip into the car, I allow myself to relax, happy to be free from Nadia's clutches.

But more than that, tonight I'm determined to get to the bottom of what is going on between Tristan and Dion. Plus, I still can't get over how Dion came racing over here the moment Chandra told him I was talking to Tristan. Is there something going on with him that he's not telling me?

The sun is setting as we pull through the gates of Nadia's Home. I glance over at Dion, taking in his profile; the smooth nose and his curved jaw. The car holds his spicy scent. His body is relaxed, maybe the most relaxed since I met him. As if he senses me watching him, he looks over and flashes me a smile. My breath catches. There's something so familiar about him.

"This is pretty exciting," I say once we take the highway. I stare out at the stretch of endless marsh bordering the road. "It's the furthest I've been away from Nadia's since I arrived. Where are we going?"

"Under the Sea. It's a popular seafood restaurant. I think you'll like it."

Soon he pulls into a parking lot that looks nothing like a restaurant. Across the way rises a large building that reads Palm Coast Helicopter and beyond that are five helicopters lined up on a landing pad.

"This doesn't look like a restaurant," I say. "Unless I'm missing something here."

Dion parks and his lips quirk into a smile. "The restaurant is located in downtown Orlando. Thought a helicopter might be a faster method of transportation."

My heart skips. "Is it safe?" And then all the fears that kept me up last night race back to me. "After what happened in the mall, I'm a little hesitant about everything."

"I'm sorry about last night. Chandra told me that some people tried to mug you. I'm glad you're okay. But if this," he waves to the helicopters outside, "is too much, we'll do something else."

I bite my lip, thinking about yesterday. That had not been a mere mugging. Unless Chandra overheard me telling my friends. If that's the case, she's starting to sound like a stalker. Those people had strange powers and then Tristan was there with a sword. I stayed up all night trying to make sense of what happened.

But if Dion thinks that was two people trying to mug me, then that's the story I need to go with until I can figure things out and make my plan of escape.

"What happened last night isn't your fault." I glance over at our method of transportation. "Does Nadia know about the helicopter? Because I don't think it would be on her approved activity list."

Dion laughs, shaking his head. "She definitely doesn't. And if it's okay with you, I'd rather keep it that way."

"Then you've just talked me into it. Let's go have some fun."

The wind whips at my dress as I step out of the car and the last trickles of sunlight hug the horizon as if begging to stay. Dion leads me inside the building where he talks to the pilot and then after signing off on some forms, we head outside to the helicopter pad.

My nerves zing around my chest in excitement along with a trickle of fear at the thought of flying. I'm pretty sure I've never flown before but knowing I'm with Dion makes me feel like I could do anything.

My dress tangles around my legs but Dion helps me climb inside, an electric shock tingling across my hand. He's electrifying. I feel a little dizzy just being here with him. Once we're settled inside with our headsets on and snapped into our safety belts, I allow myself to relax.

"It is pretty amazing." I flash him a smile. "I'm not going to want to go back home after this."

"I wish you didn't have to," Dion says.

The chopper lifts into the air and my stomach flips. Through the window, I can see for miles; long stretches of wide-open fields, houses, and condos clutter along the beach, and then the dark midnight-blue ocean yawning out beyond.

"Nadia would flip out if she knew I was doing this," I say, giggling. "She seemed pretty worried about us just going out to a restaurant."

He chuckles and his hand goes to reach for mine, but then suddenly, he pulls it away and clenches his hands together, his knuckles whitening.

"Great view, isn't it?" he asks, looking out the window.

Okay, so this is a bit awkward. Something is going on here that I don't really understand. He wasn't acting like himself in the auditorium either. I need to say something to break the strained silence. It's thick and suffocating, as if we're holding back unspoken words.

"So tell me a little about yourself," I begin. "Do you have any brothers or sisters?"

"Only child," he says.

I wait for him to give me some more information, but he's silent. What is up with this boy not talking?

"What about your parents?" I ask. "It must be hard with them being so far away."

He presses his lips together and rubs his jaw with one hand. "My father isn't pleased I'm here in Florida. He'd rather I come work for him."

"I'm sorry to hear that. Why did you decide to come here? Not that I'm upset or anything. I'm glad you did, but if your family wants you to be closer to home, that must make things difficult."

"My boss has some work for me to look over in this area and it was a great opportunity that I couldn't say no to. It also gave me the chance to get out on my own. Stretch my wings a little."

"Right now just going out on a date with you feels like I'm stretching my wings. Like I'm literally flying." I grin and point out the window. Below, dotted lights pop up as street-lights and houses turn on their lights. "So what do you do for work? I'm surprised your boss asked you to come here since you're still in high school."

"I'm in charge of some of her assets, and it's a line of work that takes a lot of dedication." He rubs his forehead like something is bothering him. "I just hope I can do the job and not mess up. Lately, I worry I'm messing everything up."

"I'm sorry you feel that way," I say. "Ever since the accident, I've been getting these really bad headaches. The pain is so intense that sometimes I pass out. That's actually what happened when I first saw you at school."

His face darkens. I'm not sure if it's from anger or sadness. "I'm sorry you're dealing with this." His voice is softer and deeper, as if just saying those words took so much out of him.

"It's not your fault. But the pain isn't the worst part. It's the dreams. They're..."

I hesitate and glance shyly over at him, unsure if I should even be telling him all this. Will he run away from me the moment we land? Dismiss me? But when I look at him, I find him studying me, his eyes as dark as endless pools. The pain stretches across his features, pulling his forehead into a frown and tightening his lips.

"They're intense," I finally say. "But the wildest part? Sometimes they're so real that they don't feel like dreams, but memories. That sounds crazy, doesn't it? Do you think I'm crazy?"

"I think you're the farthest thing from crazy." His voice is thick with emotion. "You're perfect. Headaches, dreams, passing out. Makes no difference to me. I'm so sorry you're going through all of this. But we're here. Together. That's all that matters. And I'm going to be here with you through all of it."

"Thank you," I whisper.

Something deep inside of me flares up. Like his words hold truth to them and that truth sparks to a part of me that has been buried.

40

DINER DEALS

TRISTAN

Florida

The neon lights of the diner combined with the smells of grease and cracked vinyl seats make for the perfect dining location. I stare morbidly at the menu.

French fries, onion rings, and a whole page devoted to greasy hamburgers. The healthiest thing on the menu would be the garden salad, which based on the picture appears more like a bunch of white lettuce with a slice of radish and cucumber.

I've got to say, I'm completely unimpressed with these mortals' food. It's absolutely revolting that any of them even manage to survive as long as they do by eating this rubbish.

But there are only two restaurants in this whole area I'd qualify as food passable to consume and that's exactly where the Wraiths and Nazco will be looking for me to show up. It doesn't help that every assassin within a sixty-kilometer radius seems desperate to slice Estrella's pretty head off her neck.

I toss the menu aside and rub my side, grimacing. The Wraith knife's wound still burns from our encounter outside of Estrella's art class. It's been slow to heal and I certainly don't have time for injuries.

The bell to the diner's door dings. There's a shift in the air, and for a brief moment, the room brightens as if the lights have been given extra life. The waitress's slumped shoulders lift like she's been given a boost, and even the music seems peppier.

Brilliant. I roll my eyes, knowing exactly who unfortunately entered.

"I'm going to kill Katka," I mutter.

"Interesting choice of cuisine." A brown-haired man even taller than me heaves himself into the booth. His golden eyes sparkle with mischief as he drums his fingers on the table, clearly excited to see me.

Between the two of us, we practically overpower the tiny space.

"Conrad." I glare at my best friend and pick up my artery-clog-inducing menu as if it's far more interesting than him. "I told Katka you shouldn't come."

"You do know, mate." Conrad gives me The Look. The one that is supposed to remind me of all the times we fought side by side and he saved my butt. "There are very few I travel the portals for."

"I'm so fortunate," I say dryly. "You're wasting your time coming here."

"It's the soggy knickers and wet socks," he continues. "A real downer."

"I'm so glad you came all the way from England to complain about your soggy knickers. Or perhaps you're here for the cuisine?"

"Hello, gentlemen." The waitress slides up to our table, coffee pot in hand. Dark circles ring her eyes and her hair hangs limp around her face. "What can I get you tonight?"

"Tough night?" Conrad asks her.

"More like a tough year," she says with a sigh. "Two people called in so I'm running this dining room all by myself. If people actually tipped, it might be worth my time."

"Tough times to be sure," Conrad says and touches her wrist briefly. "We'll take whatever is the most popular dish and with much thanks."

"You've got it."

"Two waters as well." I pass her the sticky menu and once she leaves, I say. "I told Katka to give me three days. Which means I still have until tomorrow."

"Actually, it was your father. And you know how he is with time. So subjective. But it was Katka who recommended I go."

"I knew it!" I slam my fist on the table. A slight splinter cracks where my fist hit.

Conrad's eyebrows lift. "You going to pay for that?"

"Sure. Whatever." Sighing, I lean back against the seat, thinking through everything. If my father sent him, it means I'm running out of time.

The waitress plops two glasses of water on our table and scurries off.

"So what's the problem, mate?" Conrad asks. "Other than it appears as if you're injured, so now I understand why Katka sent me."

I pick up the saltshaker and bat it between my palms. "She won't come with me."

"The Nazco girl?" At my nod, he frowns and leans back in his booth, arms crossed. "So just take her. What's the issue?"

"I can't. Well, I can. Obviously." I smirk and he rolls his eyes. "But there's something different about her. I can't explain it."

"Aw, mate, don't tell me you're smitten with the girl."

"Absolutely not!" I practically yell, shifting so the table lifts and makes the waters slosh over their rims. "Honestly, I can't explain it. But my gut tells me there's more going on than we initially expected. The fact that she's even willing to talk to me tells me her subconscious is at work. The other girls from the rehabilitation center instinctively know I'm to be avoided at all costs. But Estrella, she *wants* to talk to me."

"No offense, but when have you ever been the expert at someone's subconsciousness?"

"Trust me. For her to work with us, she's going to have to choose to. Forcing her will only complicate things."

The waitress bustles up to the table. Her skin looks a little brighter and the dark circles under her eyes have vanished. Now it's my turn to lift my eyebrows at Conrad. He shrugs, saying, "Everyone needs a little help once in a while."

She slides a large plate in front of each of us. It's piled with soggy mashed potatoes and some sort of fried meat slathered in gravy.

I point to it. "This is what you ordered us? I'm starving. As in literally starving because I haven't had a decent meal since I left Slovakia. And now I'm going to have to eat this or I'll pass out and die."

"Quite the tragic life you lead." But even Conrad doesn't look too pleased with our food options. "Why did you even choose this dive?"

"What snobby Nazco would even come within thirty meters of this place?"

"Point taken. But back to the girl. What do you mean that there's more to her?"

I take a bite of—chicken?—and glower at my plate. "First off, I think she's recovering. Not fully, but she's asking questions she would only ask if she were remembering things."

"She won't fully recover even with a Master Healer," Conrad says. "I don't have the skills to even touch the damage that's been done to her. She may recover pieces and fragments, but an immortal never fully recovers from the mortalization process."

"This is why I first thought this whole idea of my father's was outrageous." My thoughts wander to the way she looked at me. Like she wanted to trust me. Like she was willing to risk it all to find herself again.

"But there's more to the situation," I say. "Things just got a whole lot more complicated."

Conrad leans back, letting out a long breath. "Why?"

"Wraiths are hovering about the school like prison guards. And on top of that, Dion Cabral is lurking about pretending to be a student just to be with her."

"Cabral, as in from the House of Cabral?" Conrad leans forward, and I know I've gotten his attention.

"Yup. And just like every member in his family, he's got high powers."

Conrad blows out a long breath. "That is peculiar. But how do you know he's got these powers?"

"Just trust me on this." I'm definitely not going to tell him that I fought alongside this Nazco. "Things got worse when two assassins showed up at school, hunting Estrella and trying to kill her."

"Are you sure the assassins were trying to kill her and not you?"

"One hundred percent sure." I attempt the potatoes and spit them out. "What is this? Pig slop?"

The waitress comes running over. "Is everything okay? You look like there's something wrong with your food."

I cringe. Maybe I did yell out those words a little too loud. She has a hard enough life as it is; she doesn't need me worrying her more. "Everything is excellent. Send our compliments to the chef."

Her eyebrows lift as if she doesn't believe a word I said, but she nods and smiles shyly at me.

"Great," Conrad says. "Now you've gotten the waitress to fall in love with you."

"I just didn't want her to worry. Listen, I'll leave a generous tip." I wave my hand. "But here's the thing. Two more assassins showed up at the mall when Estrella was shopping with her friends. If she hadn't called me, it would've gone well for her."

"She called you? That's a start."

"She was a bit desperate."

"Something isn't tracking. It's like there are two factions among the Nazco and they're not in agreement with Estrella being kept alive."

"Exactly. Which makes me wonder if her powers are greater than we first suspected. Maybe even greater than the Nazco even knows."

"So what's your plan?" Conrad asks.

"I've no plan." I rub my eyes. "That's the problem."

"Why didn't you report this to your father?"

"If I reported my suspicions, Father would send a whole army here in a split second. If we swept in and kidnapped her, there's no way she'll trust us, much less work with us. And if I'm wrong, I'll officially be sent as an outcast to oversee some remote city in Siberia. I've screwed up one time too many times for my father's patience. You know we never, ever see eye to eye on things."

Conrad takes a sip of water and shakes his head. "This is tricky. But my biggest question is, why are you sitting in this dive and not watching over her right now?"

"She's with the Cabral Nazco." I rearrange my food around my plate. My stomach twists just thinking about her being with him.

Conrad stares at me hard. "Right."

"She'll be safe as long as she's with him. And the home she's at is high security. Makes me wonder who else they're transitioning there."

"This is complicated." He rubs the side of his face. "But you said she'll talk to you?"

"At first I thought I was getting through to her, but then Dion Cabral showed up and she completely blocked me out."

"So this is what you do." Conrad pushes his plate away and leans over the table. "First, you let me heal that wound of yours. Then get the girl far enough away from that Nazco or any of the assassins. And you tell her the truth."

"The truth?"

"Yeah. If you want her to trust you, mate, you've got to lay it all out there and let the pieces fall as they will."

"Won't that make things worse? She won't believe me. It could drive her further away. Or worse, it might trigger safeguards the Nazco implanted in her. The headaches are an indicator that they've done something to her mind."

"Maybe. Or maybe she'll identify the truth deep down inside herself."

41

A FAIRYTALE DATE TO RIVAL ALL OTHERS

ESTRELLA

Florida

Once we land and step out of the helicopter, Dion escorts me to a car waiting for us on the landing strip. I feel like a princess as I slip inside the passenger seat, and I'm a little dizzy from all the attention.

Or maybe it's just that my headache is starting to ramp up.

Dion settles into the driver's seat and his eyes dance with excitement.

The car buzzes out of the lot and I stare out the window as we whizz down the highway, heading into the city. Skyscrapers sparkle like rectangular prisms, cutting against the black night. It's all so...different. An overwhelming sense floods me that this is not home. None of it. The buildings, the wide, brightly-lit highways, and cars zipping along at top speeds.

A nagging sensation tugs at me that I'm living in a foreign place. My mind drifts to the dream I had with Dion and me holding hands in the snowy world. What was that?

A fantasy? But then why did it feel so real? And what were all those pictures of my burned home that Ms. Blaire showed me? My headache worsens, so I press my eyes closed and lean against the seat rest.

"You sure you're okay?" Dion asks, his voice soft.

I try to smile, but I'm sure it looks fake. "Headache. I get them sometimes after the accident."

"Just relax," he says. "You can rest if you need to. Or maybe some food will help."

I'm about to tell him about the dream when I realize we've already left the highway and are pulling into a parking lot.

"I hope you like this place," he says as he parks at the restaurant. "I'm excited to take you here."

He hops out to open my door and I step out.

Palm trees stand at attention around the parking lot, their trunks wrapped in white lights as if cloaked in stars. We stroll under a midnight awning. Music mixed with a recording of waves reaches my ears and smells of grilled fish waft over me. My heart speeds up as we draw closer. I'm hardly an expert on restaurants, but from the looks of it, this place is way fancier than anything I saw at the mall.

My fingers skim over my dress's smooth sequins and suddenly I'm glad I went shopping.

A maître d' bows as we enter. His tuxedo is so crisp and sharp on him that I wonder how he's even able to bend in it.

My fingers twitch at my side. I wish Dion would take my hand, but every time I've tried to touch him, it's like he's retreated into himself and avoided me. Maybe he's just shy.

But when I glance over at him, that theory is dashed. He's standing confident as ever, doling out his name and reservation number with the ease of a pro. When he catches me staring at him, he smiles warmly and gives me a wink.

I can't resist it anymore. I reach out and take his hand in mine.

A spark rushes through me, and it's like I'm drinking cold, electrifying water. Invigorating. Intoxicating.

And I'm desperate for more of him.

My heart stutters and suddenly my whole body craves to wrap my arms around him and press my lips to his. A flash of images rattles through my mind.

The two of us together.

Books surround us.

I'm holding a red rose.

The maître d' clears his throat. "If you'll follow me."

I startle, dropping my hand from his. What is wrong with me? I'm becoming a daydreaming idiot. A stab of pain rushes through me and I press my fingers to my forehead as if that could stop its source. Bile rises up in my throat.

Oh, no. Please don't let me throw up in front of all these people!

Dion's hand supports me. I'm jerked upright because it's like I've been shocked with static electricity. The room spins a little and I find myself swaying, but the headache starts to relax.

"You okay?" Dion asks, worry filling his face. "We can leave if you need to."

I clench my fists, determined to not let this headache ruin my night. This is supposed to be my night out having fun, not lying on the bed recovering from a stupid migraine.

"I'm fine." I take a shaky breath as the pain calms. "Just had a moment there."

"We can sit down and rest if you need," he offers.

"Nope." I turn to face the maître d'. "I'm good."

The man nods graciously and leads us into a glass tunnel that spears through a massive aquarium. A shark glides by to our right, staring at us with unblinking eyes while a manta ray swooshes above our heads. A school of fish swims past in perfect formation.

My feet falter and my mouth falls open as I take it all in. We are literally walking through an aquarium.

"Do you like this place?" Dion whispers in my ear. His breath tingles against my skin, sparking my body to life.

"It's incredible." I lean closer to him. "It's like we've entered some fairy-tale world."

"I thought of you when I saw the advertisement. I know you've always been curious about the ocean."

I frown. "Did I tell you that?" Because honestly, the thought never occurred to me.

"Maybe I'm mistaken." He rubs the back of his neck, grimacing. "Let's find our table."

We stroll the rest of the way through the tunnel, taking in the sights while my heart swims like the fish around me. The end of the passageway yawns open to a cozy dining room lit by the aqua glow of the aquarium and candlelight. The maître d' sits us next to the wall of the aquarium and hands us menus.

I peek over my menu at Dion. He makes a cursory read of

his and sets it down, smiling that melt-worthy smile when he catches me staring at him. Mortified, I duck behind my menu before he can see the five shades of red my face must have turned.

I'm acting like some silly schoolgirl. But, hello? I didn't pass out. This is progress, I decide. But right now, I need to focus on what I want to order before our server comes back.

In the end, I point to a random item on the menu when the server returns and munch on a breadstick to keep my hands occupied. While we wait for our food, Dion teaches me the names of the fish that swim past us. Inspired, I withdraw the mini-notebook I stuffed in my purse, careful to open it to a page that doesn't show my escape plans.

My cartoons of the fish make Dion laugh and I relax, drawing with bigger strokes and crazier caricatures. As I draw, the motion soothes me. I have no memory of learning how to do this, but it's obvious that my brain connects to it and that connection seems to help my brain process whatever trauma I had from the accident.

"Ah, yes." Dion points to my version of the pufferfish as our food arrived. "We could call him Porky the Pufferfish."

I giggle and then sketch one of the sea anemones. "And this is Spike, from my world history class."

"Of course! But where is his girlfriend? Aren't they always together?"

I roll my eyes. "Yes, poor Spike." I add some seaweed around his neck and next to him, I draw a nose-ringed clownfish pulling the seaweed like a chain.

Dion leans back, laughing. "Now *that* is classic." He pulls the caricature closer to him. "Don't they remind you of Tanix and Silvia?"

I fork an asparagus bite. "Who?"

"You know—" He stops himself. His forehead knits up as he shakes his head. "Never mind. I was uh, confused."

But those names do sound familiar, I think as I chew. "Are they in our lit class?"

"No." He slides the sketch back to me and clears his throat, his composure obviously ruffled. "Like I said, I was just confused. How about dessert?"

A niggling sensation runs down the back of my spine. Is he lying? Or am I making something out of nothing?

I stab the fork in the air at him. "You're changing the subject, aren't you? Very suave."

"It's what I do best." He grins. "That's what I love about you, Estrella. You're perceptive."

My face must be redder than the coral next to me. Did he mean flippantly or was it something more? Would he still like me if he knew the horrible things I dreamed of? "You hardly know me."

"And you're talented." He points to my drawings. "I'm glad you're helping out with the school play."

"Yeah, I'm really liking it." But I pull my hand away as I think about the plans of escape that began to form while painting the set. "I'm trying to fit in and figure everything out, but sometimes I wish I knew what my previous life was like. You know?"

He swallows hard and nods slowly. Just seeing his empathy and understanding lets me unravel so many of my emotions.

"Like when did I learn to draw and paint?" I continue, and suddenly my questions start tumbling out of me like water rushing over a waterfall. "What were my parents like?

I keep thinking I must have some other relatives some-where. Mrs. Blaire didn't think I had anyone, but there must be some lost aunt or uncle."

I stop talking and shake my head. "I'm sorry. I'm a mess. I don't know why I just unloaded on you. But it shows that as much as I love tonight and everything you've done to make this evening absolutely amazing, you need to know that I still need some time to get my life in order."

"Estrella." He leans closer. "I'm just glad for any moment I get with you. Every second we have together is a gift."

I stare at him, wondering if all guys are this nice. Or is there something more here that I'm not understanding? My thoughts flit to all the doubts I've been having about him. The questions and worries that have stirred up over things that have happened.

My eyes drift to the knife perched on the edge of my plate and my heartbeat kicks up. It's small, but it's serrated. It could come in handy. I just need to distract Dion long enough to swipe it. If he knew I was stealing knives, he would definitely think I'm paranoid.

A shark swoops by and I point it out to him. Just as his attention is pulled away, I slip the knife off the table and tuck it into my purse.

The knife might not have a bite as sharp as the sharks, but its cold metal reassures me. A tool for my plan in the making.

With the knife securely tucked away in my purse, my muscles relax and I lean back in my chair. The candle on the table flickers and the fish swim lazily past in the giant aquarium. This date with Dion is the one night where I can be free of everything I've been dealing with. A night to have fun and escape Nadia and her rules and the creepy Wraiths lurking about. I need to enjoy myself and not let everything that has happened ruin this night.

"You know," I tell Dion, sitting across the table from me. "I think we should live it up and order dessert."

When the chocolate clamshells arrive, I eagerly dig into mine. They're filled with vanilla pudding and drizzled with caramel and chocolate, making them sinful. The smooth sweetness explodes in my mouth. I might have lost my memories, but I don't think I've ever experienced anything so delicious.

"Not that I remember what most desserts taste like," I say as I scoop up a bite and let the hot pudding slide down my throat. "But this sure beats the cafeteria pudding. It's the perfect ending to a perfect night."

"It can always be this way, Estrella," Dion says with sudden intensity, setting his spoon down.

I swirl my spoon in my dish. "What do you mean?"

He gazes into the tank beside us, not answering. He could be a lifetime away for all I know. "Dion? You okay?"

"Yes—I am." He runs a hand over his eyes as if he's in pain. Then his face smooths out and he reaches for my hand, but suddenly pulls back as if my touch might hurt him. "Hang in there, my little star. Not much longer and then everything will be fine. You'll see."

The nickname he just gave me somehow feels right. My chest aches and I can't explain why. Suddenly, I decide I can't take any more of his cryptic words. Is he keeping secrets from me? Tristan said that his family and Dion's family don't get along. Could that mean Dion has strange powers like Tristan?

"Is this about Tristan and those people who attacked me in the mall?"

He sucks in a deep breath. "Yes, but I promise I won't let them hurt you."

Except Dion couldn't be with me everywhere at every second. And how can Dion protect me from people who are anything but ordinary?

I think about Tristan's words: "What if I were to tell you that you're only experiencing a part of you. That I know people who could help you regain some of your memories."

What would it be like to be my full self? There's no doubt I feel like I'm missing a part of me. An important part.

I mull over those thoughts as we finish our date. When we arrive back at Nadia's, Dion walks me up to the porch.

"Good night," I say.

As if in desperation, he grasps my hand and twists me to face him. His touch is electric, enticing me to him, and I step closer until there's only a breath keeping us apart. There's a dreamy look in his eyes. I breathe in his minty breath and spicy scent.

"*Buenas noches*, Estrella," he whispers, his eyes sparkling in the moonlight. His fingertips graze the strap of my dress, a shiver zings down my spine. "I know I shouldn't but—"

He tilts my chin up with his fingers and kisses me. My world spins and it's like fireworks are exploding through my body. His lips are soft and gentle, and as I press my body against his, our kiss intensifies.

His lips move down to my neck, and it's like a trail of electricity is zipping across my skin, igniting every cell in my body. My hands grasp hold of his shirt because I need to hold him close and never let him go.

An image flashes through my mind. It's the two of us kissing, just like this, but in a wintery-white garden beneath a tree drenched in snow. A shiver slices through me, cold and icy like a touch of death. I break away and push him back, startled by what I saw.

Was that a memory? It felt like one. But it couldn't be. It makes no sense!

"I'm sorry." His breathing is ragged. "I went too fast. I won't do that again."

"It's not you. You didn't do anything wrong. It's me."

My pulse is racing. I have to take deep breaths just to calm myself. I don't understand what is happening and the memory only made my heart sink with foreboding. There's a bitter taste in my mouth and something in my gut sours this moment.

"What can I do?" His voice sounds pained, broken.

"Nothing." What I really need is time and space to get all the madness in my head worked out.

"Good night, Dion." I open the door, unable to meet his gaze. "Thank you. It was a wonderful night."

Guilt cuts into me for ruining a perfect date, but this is my life. Broken. Confusing.

Which is why I need to get answers to what is happening to me. There's only one person who I know can help me.

And apparently, he's Dion's greatest enemy.

42
I'LL KEEP YOUR LITTLE PET SAFE
DION

Florida

Of all the idiotic, stupid things I could've done, I chose the absolute worst thing.

I kissed her.

I slam my fist on the steering wheel and career out of the gates of Nadia's Home for Girls. My feet push on the gas pedal, and the car accelerates to speeds above the human-approved limits. But right now, I don't care.

My car zooms through the sleepy seaside town until I've reached the villa that I rented with—unfortunately—Chandra. She's probably still in a foul mood because I ditched her by taking the helicopter. She followed us to the airport but remained in her car until we took off. Thankfully, Estrella didn't notice. The last thing I need is for her to feel like Chandra is stalking her.

Even if it's true.

Darkness drapes the town like a wool blanket as I drag myself out of the car. Father will be angry I'm late meeting him, but I wasn't about to miss my date with Estrella for anything. My heart wishes I could bypass the villa and beeline it straight to the pond outside, but for Estrella's sake, I need to give Chandra instructions before I leave. So gritting my teeth, I stalk inside.

"A helicopter?" Chandra greets me. "A little over the top, don't you think?"

She's perched on the kitchen counter, drinking a smoothie. In front of her are strawberries, blueberries, a banana peel, and—yikes—knives swirling through the air. They spin round and round in a dance she's creating with her wind.

"I wanted to impress her." I approach warily.

Chandra holds a grudge like a treasure, and Estrella has given her enough reasons to be lugging around a chest full of them. She lifts her dark brown eyes, assessing me. The knives twitch in the whirlwind. I stiffen, my muscles tense, ready to flee.

"You kissed her, didn't you?" She flicks her hand, causing the knives to swish through the air and stab the wooden cabinet behind her. They're like sentries, lined up in a straight row, ready to serve their master. "When the Empress ordered us to watch over her, she didn't mean to exchange saliva."

"Hardly," I say, trying to act nonchalant. Chandra is hitting too close to home. My insides churn in fear. "I was merely taking her out to see how far her transition to mortality had progressed."

Did she see me kiss Estrella? No, I would've heard Nadia's gates open. Besides, there hadn't been time for her to watch and then get back here before me, right? She's got to be bluffing.

But if word got back to the Empress about what I'd done, she'd have me replaced so quickly, I wouldn't even have time to execute my escape plan for Estella.

I need to be very careful. This is not the time to mess things up.

Estrella's words, "Nadia's Home is more like a prison," still vibrate through my mind. I can't live knowing she's suffering like this. I need to find a better, safer place for her to transition. And once she has, no one will care if she's alive or dead.

They'll forget about her.

And then the two of us can live peacefully. Even if she won't be immortal, at least she'll have a full human life. That's more than she's going to get with the way things are progressing right now.

"My father has summoned me," I say, changing the subject. "I'll be back before the end of the school day tomorrow if all goes well."

Chandra sets down her glass. "Does the Empress know you're leaving town?"

"If she asks, feel free to tell her. With Quadril sending out a kill order on Estrella, you'll need to be extra vigilant."

"It's not the assassins I'm worried about." She slips off the counter and sashays closer to me. "It's Estrella. I'm worried the mortalization process isn't latching on properly.

Nadia's supposed to be one of the most successful wardens but she's doing a pretty crappy job if you ask me. I think it's because she still has some of her Channeler abilities. She's sapping people's powers from them and slowly healing herself."

"That's the stupidest idea ever." Except it's probably true. And I can't have Chandra realizing that.

I think about our kiss. How her eyes looked brighter afterward. And in the restaurant, her headache faded after I touched her. I'm an idiot.

She skims her razor-sharp nails along the buttons of my shirt, her full lips curling into a smile. "I remember the first time you kissed me. You seemed to like it."

I grind my teeth. I have no time for her games. "Keep her alive and safe until I return."

"You're no fun." She pushes her lips into a pout. "Fine. I'll keep your little pet safe. Just don't forget. She'll never be the same girl you fell in love with."

"You don't know what you're talking about," I half-growl, sparks fluttering across my palms.

"Oh, I know her well enough." Then she leans closer and whispers into my ear, "Especially how she'll feel if she ever finds out you've been lying to her. She'll never forgive you."

My head jerks as if she stabbed me with her knives. A cut that rips at my gut and twists so hard, I want to throw up. I backpedal away from Chandra and storm across the room toward the back entrance. Her words burn against my chest because they're too close to the truth. No, they are the truth. But I can't worry about those things right now.

Soon, very soon, I'll have whisked Estrella away, and

we'll leave behind all of this madness. And everything will have been forgotten.

We'll start fresh.

She'll be safe.

The thick, muggy night welcomes me as I slip out the sliding glass doors and cross the lawn. Cicadas chirp and palms wave in the breeze as if trying to soothe my tortured thoughts.

I should've changed clothes and brought my travel bag, but I've already wasted enough time talking. The sooner I get to Brazil to talk to my father, the sooner I can get back to Estrella and start our new forever.

43
PRISON BREAK 101
ESTRELLA

Florida

Nadia is waiting for me when I step inside. She's sitting on the couch, her needle puncturing the material of her embroidery. The crystals from the colored chandeliers glitter over her, spilling fractured light across her skin. I'm half-hoping my friends are here waiting for me, too, but it's late and well past everyone's curfew.

"You're five minutes late for curfew," she snaps with a sour frown.

"I'm so sorry." I scramble for some sort of excuse. "I don't have a watch or phone so it was hard to judge the time."

Nadia rolls her eyes, evidently not pleased I put the blame back on her. I wait for her to execute her punishment, but then her attention focuses hard on me, assessing my body from head to toe as if she's searching for something.

I stiffen under her scrutiny and tuck my purse firmly against the side of my dress, hoping her gaze skips over it. What if she asks to check my bag and finds the knife?

Or worse, reads my journal?

My heartbeat quickens, pattering against my ribcage like a trapped bird. There's no way I can think of a good excuse for that. My words would sentence me.

A memory shivers back to me, cold and unwanted. Her locking up my body like a board as if she had some sort of magic power. Could that really have happened? Is that even possible?

Her eyes bore deeper into mine in assessment. Slowly, she rises from her seat and comes to me. Her hand pats my cheek as if she's petting a dog.

"Don't worry, Estrella," she whispers, her words snaking across my skin. "I'm going to fix you. I just need a little more time and then my work will be done."

A cold sensation like hard wire twists out of her palm, biting my skin as she pets me. I swallow the whimper threatening to escape my lips. I step back, breaking contact with her. What did she just do? What did I feel?

A chilling horror slices through me as I'm hit with a new realization. She's not normal.

My thoughts ricochet back to the people in the mall. They had some sort of weird powers too, didn't they? Could she be one of them?

Is she even human?

Fear forces a fake smile across my face. I try to laugh, but it comes out more like a choking gasp.

"Um," I say. "Such an exhausting day. I can't wait to have some tea and go to sleep."

Her eyebrows flick up and she nods thoughtfully.

"Tomorrow night." She waves me off. "You have kitchen duty and floor duty for being five minutes late."

"Yes, ma'am," I quickly say, backing away.

"Your tea is sitting by your bed."

"Wonderful! That's great. I can't wait to drink it. Goodnight."

I pick up the sides of my long dress and scurry out of the room, willing my feet to flee. It's not easy to climb the three flights of stairs in heels and a gown, but soon I hit the top floor. When I stumble breathlessly into my hallway, I spy Zayla sneaking out of Mara's bedroom, holding one of the new shoes Mara got at the mall when we went shopping. Just seeing her sneaking about and stealing things somehow calms my frazzled nerves. At least someone has control of something here.

"Mara is going to be mad when she finds her shoe is missing," I say, unable to hide my smile.

"Shh." Zayla presses a finger to her lips. "Secrets."

I clutch my purse tighter. I have some secrets of my own.

"You do know she'll assume you took it." Anytime something goes missing, everyone puts the blame on her. "You should make a decoy or something."

Zayla steps closer to me. "Where is your Christmas secret?"

"Christmas secret?" I frown in confusion. "What are you talking about?"

Zayla takes my hand and pulls me down the hall toward my room. My palm tingles from her touch. She darts a quick glance over her shoulder, making sure no one is watching, and then pushes me inside. The moment the door is shut, she starts moving about my space, eyes roving over my dresser piled with the new clothes I bought and the books stacked in the corner.

"Um...what are you doing?" I rub my palm. It's still tingling. So weird.

Her hand skims over the back of the chair where the carving, *Remember. Escape* is located. A smile quirks across her face as if by touching the words, she could read them.

"Don't move that," I say.

I can't let her see the back of my chair. What would she think of me?

Her eyes snap to my purse, and she grins, eyes twinkling. "Secrets."

I bite my lip. It's strange, but I get the feeling she knows I'm hiding a knife inside it. But how would that be possible?

She crosses the room with quick and measured steps and picks up my mattress. I step closer. "What are you doing?"

After digging around, she turns and holds up a chain from her fingertips. A locket sways from its silver strand. A moment tugs at my mind. Me hiding it under the mattress the night I'd drank the tea and forgotten.

The locket has my name on it.

And two people who may have been my parents.

"You gave that to me, didn't you?" At her nod, I ask, "How did you know that was there?"

Her only answer is to slip it over my head. It lands against my chest, cold and hard. I don't know how to explain the feeling other than it feels like the necklace is supposed to be pressed close to my heart. My fingers trace the engraving of my name across the surface.

Maybe I can trust her after all.

"Thank you," I say. "I would never have found it if it weren't for you. I must have hidden it and forgotten."

She nods with a knowing smile and moves to leave, but I hold her back.

"Zayla. Have you ever been in Nadia's office?"

Her brow knits and lips purse, but she nods.

"Do you think you can get me in there?" I dare ask.

She twists her hands, and her eyes flicker from the door to the floor as if she can't decide what to do. Slowly, she backs away.

Crap, I'm losing my opportunity.

"I don't think it's safe living here," I quickly add. "I want to find a way to get us all out of here before..." The words stick on my tongue but I press on. "I could be wrong, but I think Nadia's office has the answers we need. Maybe if I could go through our records, I could find names of family members who could help us."

Zayla has backed up all the way to the door and her hand clutches the doorknob so tightly her knuckles are white. Her eyes stare hard on the floor, but I think she's listening. Then she opens the door and slips out into the corridor without a sound.

I sigh. "So much for that idea."

I change out of my beautiful dress and hang it in my closet. Will I ever have such a magical night again? Did I ruin my chances with Dion? And why do I keep imagining moments where we've kissed before? It's strange, and after everything that has happened in the last few days, pretty unsettling.

My brain races a million miles a minute as I try to put together pieces of everything that's happened since my accident. I drag my chair back in front of the door just in case Nadia decides to come in. The words, *Remember. Escape* haunt me.

Warn me.

A long, tortured breath heaves out of my core and I turn to a task that screams for my attention. Because deep down I know I don't have much time left. Nadia has grown suspicious. I've got a sick feeling that whatever plans she has to "fix" me are going to happen sooner than later.

Days? Hours?

I lay out my escape tools on my bedspread.

A locket.

My notebook.

A knife.

Tristan's phone number.

A spoon.

Dion's credit card.

I bite my lip as I assess my collection. It's not enough. But it has to be. Because tonight, I'm putting my plan into action.

Tonight, I'm escaping.

44

IT'S SO ON

ESTRELLA

Florida

The black shirt and jeans hug my body like a shadow. The last thing I need to deal with is my bright, blonde hair. I twist it into a bun at the nape of my neck, deciding it will have to be enough.

I shrug my backpack on and then slowly open the door. It creaks as if warning me to stop, but my will is set. Tonight I'm going to get answers, and if all goes well, I'm leaving this place forever.

My sneakers tiptoe down the wooden floors, moonlight sneaking in from the windows and the occasional flash of the lighthouse illuminating the sleepy darkness. Lexi's room is first. It's unlocked and I dart inside. I creep to her bed and lightly touch her arm.

Her skin is hot to the touch, and for a moment, I wonder

if she's got a fever. But her eyes blink open, and she jerks around, swinging her pillow and knocking me backward.

I catch myself on the bedpost just before I smash onto the floor.

"Lexi!" I whisper-yell. "It's me. Estrella."

"You scared the living ghosts out of me." She plops back onto her pillow and tucks her blanket to her chin. "Why are you sneaking about like a criminal?"

"I'm going to break into Nadia's office."

"Bad, bad idea." She bolts to sitting, her red hair jutting out like electric sparks are spitting out of it. I rub my eyes, wondering if I'm seeing things. "Have you not listened to a single thing I've told you from day one? Stay low, don't get noticed, and you might get out of this place."

"How many girls do you know have gotten out?"

"Like you want a number?"

"Yes."

She tosses her covers off and slips to the edge of the bed, assessing my black outfit. "You look like an amateur thief."

"You don't know of any girls, do you?"

"No." She rolls her eyes. "But I haven't been here that long. I'm hardly an expert."

"We're getting out of here."

"Or what? We'll die trying."

"You think Nadia will kill us?" I ask, skeptically. "She wouldn't stoop that low, would she?"

"Those things outside," Lexi's voice is low, a deathly whisper. "They got her last time. Carla."

I suck in a shuddered breath. "So that's what happened to her," I say, finally understanding.

Lexi massages her temples, grimacing as if in pain. "And

I don't know how to explain it, but it's like I know what that feels like, and it scares me. Does that even make sense?"

An ache pulls on my chest as if deep down in the darkest, forgotten places of my mind there's something…something important I used to know.

"Yes," I say, and suddenly I don't want her to have any part of my escape plan. I want her to stay here tucked under her covers. Safe. "It makes complete sense."

The door clicks open, and I jolt to standing. It's Jamie. She slips inside, moonlight slicing across the top of her face and making her dark blonde curls shine. She doesn't say a single word as she closes the door behind her.

"Jamie," I say. "What are you doing here?"

Her only answer is to flip a spoon through her fingers and stare at the two of us. She may be tiny with a round face and large eyes, but there's something dangerous about her. And yet, there's also something inside of me that tells me I could trust her with my life.

I dig into my backpack and pull out the knife I stole from the restaurant. "Somehow I have the feeling this will get better use in your hands."

Her eyes widen, and a smile breaks across her face as she takes it. The door scrapes open once again, and Mara steps into the room.

"Why is everyone up and about tonight?" I ask.

"I went to your room to ask about your date, but you weren't there," Mara says. "Figured you'd be here. Why are you dressed like a burglar?"

"I'm going to break into Nadia's office," I say. "If either of you wants to come, I could use someone to watch the door."

Jamie nods firmly, sliding her finger along the knife's smooth surface. "I will come."

"She speaks," Lexi says. "Now we know what will loosen her up. Knives."

"Thank you, Jamie." Just knowing she'll be at my side boosts my confidence.

"You really want a death sentence, don't you?" Mara crosses her arms.

"We need answers," I say. "Nadia's office has to have them."

Lexi slips into a shirt and pants. I press my hand on her arm.

"No, you stay," I say. "Someone needs to be here to take care of the girls if something should happen to us."

She hesitates, and I know my words have hit a nerve. She does care about all the girls here. Without her, what would they do? Her hands slow as she pulls her hair free from beneath the shirt.

"I can't let you go in there alone," she says.

"Jamie's coming with me," I say, but then another idea hits me. "Or you could help us by providing a distraction. Can you do that?"

"What kind of distraction?"

45
THE BOOKSHELF THAT PLAYED HIDE-AND-SEEK
ESTRELLA

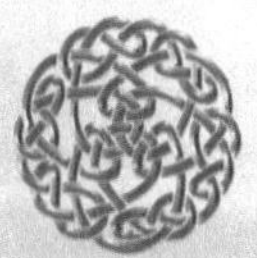

Florida

The wind moans, blowing against the sea house as if it's sending a warning to turn and run. The door of Nadia's office stands before me. My hand shakes as I grasp hold of the doorknob.

"It's locked," I whisper to the girls.

"Of course it's locked," Mara snorts. "Let's go back upstairs and forget about this."

"If you're going to be so negative," Lexi says, "go back to bed."

Mara huffs but doesn't move. Honestly, I kept waiting for her to turn around and go back to her room, but for some reason, she's still here. Jamie leans against the wall, twirling the knife happily through her fingers and blowing out a large, pink bubble of gum as if breaking into the headmistress's room is something we do every day before breakfast.

"We can't leave." I grind my teeth in frustration. "We're so close."

A silhouette slithering down the hall catches my attention, and I stiffen. But then a flash from the lighthouse zips past the window, illuminating the corridor. It's Zayla, hiding behind her curtain of light brown hair, her frail frame shadowing the wall. She looks like a ghostly nightmare. She presses her finger to her lips and holds up a paperclip to me.

I frown, confused. "Um… that's nice."

Then she slips it into the lock, and after a few wiggles and a click, the door swings open.

I gape at her in shock. "Impressive."

She grins triumphantly while Jamie pops her bubble.

"Clever trick," Mara mumbles.

I duck into Nadia's office, my nerves zinging about me, warning me that every second I waste is valuable. The room smells like a mix of old wood and the sharp scent of antiseptic. Nadia's desk sits across the room, papers neatly stacked and pens lined up like soldiers ready for war. I don't turn on the light. Instead, I rely on the moonlight spilling across the place, outlining the bookshelves, couch, and two worn leather chairs.

"Where do you think she holds our files?" I ask.

"Her computer?" Lexi suggests.

"One, two, find the shoe," Zayla sings happily as she starts running her hands along the bookshelves. "Three, four, behind the door."

"Shhh," Mara snaps. "Now's not the time for singing."

"Okay," I say. "Lexi, you go to the tearoom and hide there. If you hear someone coming down the stairs, sit at the piano and start playing."

"But I don't play the piano."

"Nadia doesn't know that. Just pretend you're remembering something or you don't talk like Min. This is a great time to use those acting skills."

"Huh, that might be fun," Lexi says and hurries off.

I turn to Zayla. "We're looking for Nadia's secrets. You think you could find those?"

"Secrets." Zayla's eyes glint mischievously.

"Jamie, you watch the door, and Mara, um..."

"I'll look for secrets." She makes quotation marks as she says secrets and rolls her eyes.

We all get to work, scouring the office. Branches hit the windowpane with a *bam, bam, bam*. I jerk from the sound and my heart clatters. Thunder cracks against the night. The wind continues its howl, and a flash of lightning bolts across the room, strengthening the shadows and skittering goosebumps across my skin.

I swallow hard, desperate to quiet the hammering of my pulse as I search through the bookshelves for any records of the home's occupants. At the desk, Zayla is gathering up a full collection of objects, including a tape dispenser and pencil sharpener. She stretches out her shirt to create a basket with it and begins dropping the items inside it.

"Zayla!" I whisper-yell. "We're only looking for secrets. Not office supplies. Okay?"

She bites her lip and nods, reluctantly setting everything back on the counter. Jamie crosses the room, and after rummaging through the desk, gathers up a pair of scissors and a letter opener, tucking them into the waist of her jeans next to the butter knife I gave her. I open my mouth to stop her but clamp it shut as she heads back to the doorway to keep watch.

If we do run into trouble, some sort of weapon is better than none.

"This is why everyone at school thinks we're freaks," Mara mutters to me. "We think office supplies are treasures."

"Or we're so desperate to find something that gives us a sense of who we are," I offer.

The minutes tick down, and I'm nowhere closer to finding any clues as to who I am or who my friends are. I release a frustrated huff, spinning in a circle in the center of the room. Disappointment settles over me.

"This is like looking for a penny in a lake," I mutter. "An impossible task."

Zayla settles on the floor and starts running her hands across the floorboards.

"One, two, find the shoe," she sings. "Three, four, behind the door."

The flash of the lighthouse beams across a bookshelf. A frown pulls at my face.

"Those books in that section look different from the others in the room, almost as if..." I hurry to the shelf.

The spines feel too stiff under my fingers as if they aren't spines at all, but wood painted to look like books.

"They're fake," I announce. "This has to mean something."

One book gives in a little to my touch. I push on it. Something inside clicks. A section of the shelf pushes open and I gasp.

"It's a door," I say. "You were right, Zayla."

46

THE DAGGER'S GUIDE TO SELF-DEFENSE

ESTRELLA

Florida

I dare slip through the fake bookshelf opening. Cool air wafts over my face, and my eyes blink against the darkness. I scrape my hand across the wall, eagerly searching for a light switch. It's a risk, but we don't have time to stumble about in the dark.

The moment I flick it on, my breath leaves me.

Sconce lights flicker to life around a circular room. Not just any room. This is the base of the lighthouse. Curved stone walls painted in a shell-white span the perimeter. A wrought-iron staircase spirals up through its center before stopping at a small hatch door at the top.

A roaring fills my ears as I step inside. There's something

powerful about this room. Something deeper and stronger is here, calling for me.

"We found it," I say, breathlessly.

"Secrets!" Zayla squeaks.

"I never...I just...wow," Mara says.

Objects are piled up on shelves and I step closer to inspect them. Clocks, backpacks, books, and even dolls. A filing cabinet is pressed against one wall, and I'm about to go to it when something tugs at my core, pulling for my attention. I turn to find an illuminated glass case showcasing weapons on pedestals. They glitter like they're infused with magic.

Swords with the sharpest steel shimmer, reminding me of the one clenched in Tristan's hand. Knives are tucked in a belt like they're ready to be plucked and tossed at an incoming enemy.

My fingers touch the cool glass. As I do, one dagger flashes. Its pommel glimmers a fiery blue as if begging for me to free it. The center has a face like an ancient god, and its ends are flanked by strange guardian-like creatures. My fingers tingle. The dagger shudders from where it sits on its pedestal.

Jamie rushes inside, and when her eyes land on the case, she gasps. She squats in front of the knife belt. Her eyes take on a brightness that wasn't there before.

"How I've missed you," she says, trailing her fingers over the glass.

"Are those yours?" I ask.

"Yes." She paws at the glass. Her hands shake as if she's desperate to touch them.

I frown, my head spinning. Who are these friends of mine?

Who am I?

Zayla grabs a piece of clothing on one shelf and is about to load objects into it, but I stop her.

"Not yet," I say. "If we take anything on these shelves, it will be too obvious. Nadia will know what we've been up to. We're here to get information and then we'll come back for the rest of it once we have a plan."

Zayla sticks her lip out in a pout and stares at the shelf forlornly. Jamie growls something under her breath. A searing pain stabs at my temple and I close my eyes, struggling to remain standing.

Moaning, I try to push away the pain. I need to stay focused. This is not the time for me to have an episode and pass out. But despite my determination, my knees start to buckle. A hand takes mine and squeezes it, causing a shudder to rush into my palm.

My eyes flutter open, and I jerk straight. It's like I sucked in a breath of fresh air, and the world is now clearer. Jamie is holding my hand, her face pulled into a worried frown.

"Stay strong," she whispers.

"Yes." I nod. "Strong."

Oddly invigorated, I march over to the filing cabinet, yanking the drawer open. Folders with all of our names labeled on them are crammed into the middle drawer.

"This is it," I say.

The pound of the piano startles the silence.

Lexi!

"Someone is coming!" I whisper. "We need to get out of here!"

I heft a stack of folders out of the cabinet and tuck them protectively against my chest. We rush through Nadia's office and into the hallway, only to pause like frightened rabbits. Voices echo through the corridor from the tearoom.

"What in earth's name are you doing up in the middle of the night playing the piano?" Nadia half-screams.

"Miss Nadia!" Lexi's voice is overly loud. "I had this dream that I was a master pianist. I couldn't wait until morning to see if the dream was telling me the truth."

"You insolent girl!"

"Please. Let me play for you, and you can tell me if I truly am talented."

Bells ring.

"That's the alarm," Mara whispers, fear lacing her voice. "Someone must have turned it on. This is bad."

"The orderlies are coming." Jamie whips out the scissors and butter knife, crouching as if she is going to attack whoever comes our way.

"If we're lucky," Mara says. "It's those creepy things that worry me."

"Quick," I order. "Back inside."

Once we've returned to the office, I shut the door and lock it.

"Yay," Mara mutters. "Now we're stuck in here until they think to look in this room and find us."

A creak whips my attention to the door. The hallway door knob is turning! A ripple of fear bubbles over me and I back away, pulling the girls with me with one hand while pressing the files against my chest with the other. The lock holds, and for a moment, I let my muscles relax. That is until the sound of a piece of metal slides into the lock.

"They've got a key!" I choke. "Hurry, back to the secret room."

We rush through the pretend bookshelf door, but as Jamie and I try to close it, claws sharp as nails wrap around the doorframe. Grunting, I fight to shove it closed. I slam my body against the door, heart racing. I look at Jamie.

"Wraith," I whisper.

"Weapons," she says.

I nod. "It's the only way to get out of here if we want to survive." Then I call out, "Mara, take over for Jamie. Zayla, see if you can open that weapons cabinet."

Mara rushes to take Jamie's place by pushing against the door while Jamie and Zayla run to work the glass cabinet.

"I should never have left my room," Mara says.

We continue to press our bodies against the door, groaning. A beak slips through the space, sharp and bone-white. The claws clack against the edge. My pulse pounds against my temples as I imagine them raking across my skin, sweat dripping down my face.

With a sudden jerk, the door slams open, sending Mara and I tumbling backward to the ground. The folders fly out of my hands and scatter across the floor. The creature bounds across the space and looms over us like it's death itself preparing to devour us.

Shreds of its cloak flutter about as it spreads its wings and lifts above us.

My whole body shudders. I crawl backward, trying to escape. Mara whimpers beside me. Fear has captured our voices and frozen our muscles.

Suddenly knives fly through the air, stabbing at the creature. It turns its beady red eyes to glare at Jamie, who's standing with her feet spread apart, knives clenched at her hands. Her blonde hair sticks up on end, mimicking the knives she's holding.

Behind her, the cabinet hangs open. Zayla is touching each object like she's desperate to take them all, but they're too hot to touch. The sound of crashing waves hits my ears, waking me from my terror. The dagger flashes blue as if it's calling to me.

Jamie deftly twirls her knives through her hands before twisting her body and flinging out the knives in rapid succession. They spin through the air like they're creating a dance of their own.

One stabs the creature in the eye. Two hit its neck. The Wraith shrieks in pain.

I use the distraction to duck away, but I'm not fast enough. The Wraith snatches me up and lifts me into the air like I'm feather-light. Black blood drips from its eyeball. The stench of the creature overwhelms my senses, and I gag. I kick and twist to escape, but its claws sink into my skin. I scream in agony.

"Zayla," I say. "Dagger."

"Die," the Wraith croaks.

It lifts its other arm and the claws gleam in the pale light, prepping to plunge into me.

My heart seizes. "Now, Zayla!"

Zayla tosses the dagger to Jamie, who flings it at the creature. Gold and steel flash through the air as it drives toward the Wraith's heart. But the creature must have also been aware of our intentions, because it ducks just in time.

But I'm ready. I twist my body, crying out against the

pain, and reach for the dagger. It's too far away from me as the Wraith sidesteps and jerks me away from the blade.

Come, I call it with my mind.

It shouldn't be possible, but it's like it hears my plea. Its trajectory alters so the hilt slams into my palm. I wrap my fingers around the grip. A flash of a memory—or is it a message?— washes over me.

A woman, eyes as blue as the ocean.

A whisper, "Wield my power."

There isn't time to understand what this means or how this is even happening. Claws move to rake across my chest but I swipe the dagger across the Wraith's arm, slicing it off.

The creature cries out in pain and drops me.

I slam to the ground, but my thoughts are drawn to the dagger.

A surge of energy is rushing from the dagger's hilt into my palm. The power of it is like waves crashing against the shore, the scent of the sea filling my nostrils. Instantly, I feel so alive.

So powerful.

Like I have been breathing stale air, and now I'm drinking in the ocean breeze.

I leap to my feet and with a forceful thrust, slam the dagger into the Wraith's chest. It stabs through the ribcage, cutting straight to its heart. The creature chokes and its wings sag.

Before I can blink, it dissolves into a pile of dust on the cold floor. A whoosh of wind swirls around the remains until every last particle vanishes before our eyes.

47
RUN, HIDE, REPEAT
ESTRELLA

Florida

"You killed it," Mara gasps. "You really, actually killed it."

"They die, die, die," Zayla sings.

"Yeah." I hold up the dagger. The blade swirls with a frothy blue and then returns to its normal state. "This is no ordinary weapon."

The girls stare at me wide-eyed and pale, but they're alive, and that sends a wave of relief through me.

The sound of people yelling in the hall drags our attention back through the bookshelf doorway and into Nadia's office.

"Orderlies," Maria says.

"Nadia," Zayla adds.

"We're going to get in a lot of trouble when she finds out what we've done," Mara says.

"We keep it a secret for as long as we can." I tuck the dagger into the waist of my pants.

"Secret." Zayla's eyes brighten.

"Yeah." Mara nods, eying the knife warily. "If we get out of here alive, this secret stays between us."

"Nadia doesn't know we're here," I say. "Or she'd be standing in front of us right now. Jamie, shut and lock the office door. We'll go out the window."

"That's how Carla escaped," Mara says darkly. "And she died."

I turn to Zayla. "Are there any other ways out of this place?"

Her eyes lift to the spiral staircase and she points to the hatch door at the top.

"So you want to trap us even more?" Mara asks.

"I trust Zayla," I say. Then when Jamie comes running back in, I add, "Lock up the cabinet and the secret entrance. We're going to hide all evidence that we were here. Jamie, you've got to leave the knives behind."

She shakes her head no.

"You have to. They're obviously yours. She'll know you took them."

"You returning that dagger?" Mara lifts her eyebrows.

"No," I say guiltily. "But something tells me that this wasn't mine in the first place, which means she won't connect its loss to me right away. Besides, it's obvious we need it in case we face those Wraiths again. Hurry. We're out of time."

Mara and I frantically gather up the folders while Jamie

closes us inside the room and Zayla locks the cabinet. My hands shake as I tuck the files against my chest.

"Turn off the lights," I tell Jamie. "We have to make it look like we weren't here."

Darkness envelops the room. Disorientation nearly cripples me until I notice the pale blue light emanating from the dagger's blade. I pull it out and lift it so it can guide us.

"That weapon scares me," Mara says. "You sure it's safe?"

"Safer than the Wraiths," I say. "Zayla, lead the way."

She takes off up the wrought-iron stairs. We stumble awkwardly into the shadowy light after her.

Our feet clamor against the metal, mimicking the pounding of my heart. Higher and higher we climb. All I can think about is if we will be able to get through that trap door. And if we do, how long will we be able to hide out at the top of the lighthouse before someone finds us?

By the time we reach the top level, we're breathless, gasping for air. Zayla reaches up and works the paperclip into the lock. As we wait, voices leak through the bookshelf door.

"Do you think they came in here?" It's Val's voice, deep and hard.

"Crap," Mara says. "They're in Nadia's office."

"Cross your fingers they don't check this room," I say.

The lock snaps above us. Zayla pushes open the hatch door, and I let out a relieved breath.

She scrambles up the rest of the ladder and disappears through the hole. Jamie climbs up next, and Mara and I pass up the folders to her to free our hands.

Once Mara is through, I scale up the ladder, but as I'm

about to push my way through the hatch, the sound of the hidden book door unlatching echoes through the room. Light spills into the darkness.

My whole body freezes. I can't move, terror holding me in place. But then the girls hoist me the rest of the way up. Zayla quietly closes the hatch and twists the lock.

As soon as my belly hits the floor, I'm greeted by white twinkle lights hanging from the walls of the small space. It's a warm welcome to a safe haven. Above, a smaller ladder leads to another door that looks like it opens to the top of the lighthouse. Knickknacks clutter the walls and boxes overflow with collected treasures. I know this place. I've been here before, but I had forgotten.

"This is your secret room," I tell Zayla.

She presses her finger to her lips and says, "Shhh."

That's when I realize we can actually hear the sounds from below still. Which means they can hear us, too. We freeze, crouched in the tiny space. I hardly dare breathe.

Zayla presses a Band-Aid over my arm where it's bleeding and I mouth a thank you.

"It doesn't look like anyone came in here," Val's voice echoes up to us.

"Perhaps," Nadia says. "I'll do a more thorough check in the morning. Right now I need a thorough sweep of the premises. Send the Wraiths out on the grounds and have your orderlies check each girl's room and make sure everyone is accounted for."

"Yes, madam."

"Something is off," she says. "I can feel it."

"Go." Zayla points to the narrow stairs behind her. "Hurry."

None of us wait a second. We tiptoe down the steps and as we enter the top floor of the house, I rush down the hall. I'm opening the door to my room when the scuffle of footsteps pound the stairs.

"I better find everyone tucked safely in their bed," Nadia's voice calls out. "Anyone not in their room will suffer greatly."

48

WHEN THE TRUTH JUST RAISES MORE QUESTIONS

ESTRELLA

Florida

I duck inside my room and ease my door shut so Nadia won't hear it click. With swift steps, I dart to my bed and stuff the files and dagger under the mattress. Then I rip off my black clothes like one possessed.

I'm wrestling myself into my nightshirt when the doorknob twists. Desperate, I throw myself onto my bed, recoiling under the covers as the door slams open and Nadia flicks on the light.

My eyes blink against the brightness. I sit up, squinting, making sure to keep my bandaged arm hidden.

"What's going on?" I ask, pretending she's woken me.

She grunts, taking me in with sharp, measured scrutiny before she slams the door shut.

Darkness sweeps across the room and I lie there, waiting. My body is as still as stone. Hardly breathing, hardly believing that I'm still alive.

Rain splashes against my window and the winds wail.

I clutch my covers, finally allowing my mind to process what just happened. What my friends and I found. What those files might reveal. More doors slam shut and the thump of footsteps rattle the floors. But soon all is silent within the house once again.

I peek at my arm where the Wraith's claw dug into my skin. Dried blood is crusted over the skin, and the cut burns an angry red, but the bleeding has stopped. I just hope I don't get an infection.

Finally, I dare creep out of bed and lift up the mattress. I pull out the dagger, brushing my fingers over it. The blade flashes an ocean blue. A wash of cool breeze swiftly floods my senses, and it's almost like I can taste the salt of the sea on the tip of my tongue.

The image of a powerful wave crashing against the shoreline fills my vision. It's that same feeling as when I plunged the blade into the heart of that horrible Wraith creature and it crumbled to dust.

Fear curdles my veins, causing me to nearly drop the dagger. This weapon is powerful. I don't know what it is or how it works, but it's terrifying. I slip the blade back under the mattress, safe from prying eyes.

Safe from me.

I focus my attention on the files. One by one, I line them up in neat, even rows. Names are printed on each folder.

Lexi, Mara, Tiffany, Jamie, Zayla, Min...

An ache pulls at me because deep down I know that

once I open the folders, everything will change. My body numbs when I find the file labeled Estrella Cortez. My hand shakes as I crack it open.

A birth certificate and past school records lie inside. They're the same ones I remember my school had on file for me. Next are the pictures of my burned trailer home that Mrs. Blaire, my caseworker, showed me.

The pages flip through my fingers as I frantically search for something I don't already know.

It's the fifth page that freezes me in place. It looks different from the others. It has a fancy, ribbon edging. The top reads my full name and beneath is a list of information that sucks the air from my lungs.

Name: Estrella Cortez
    Age: 18
    Birth location: Midnight Kingdom, Antarctica
    Family: Deceased
    Schooling: The Midnight Academy
    Ability: Channeler, high powers
    History: Talented but excommunicated due to foreseen betrayal.
    Procedure: Sent to Nadia's Rehabilitation Home for memory treatment. If treatment is unsuccessful, terminate.
    Treatment period: Six months

The papers drop from my fingers and flutter to the floor. Their truth hits me harder than the storm raging outside.

The buzzing in my ears keeps me from hearing the door

opening. A hand presses on my shoulder, and I jerk, instinctively reaching under my mattress for the dagger. But as I look over my shoulder, I find it's Lexi, her green eyes dark with concern. Her hand on my shoulder is warm and comforting against the chill of the rainstorm.

"You okay?" Lexi asks.

I nod. "You?"

"Dish duty until the end of my days."

"Does she know what we did?"

"She suspects something is off, but she can't prove anything. Good job on covering your tracks." She plops down at my side, staring at folders, her forehead scrunched up. "What is all of this?"

"The truth." I take the one with her name on it and pass it to her. "I grabbed what I could, but we don't have much time until Nadia realizes her files are missing."

And her dagger, I think.

Lexi opens her file, and as she flips from page to page, tears stream down her face. "It says I'm from the Midnight Kingdom, Antarctica. This is so messed up."

"It's like we get answers that only lead to more questions. Maybe if we go through everyone's files, we can find some family members who are still alive. They might be willing to help us."

"Unless they're the ones who sent us here," she says.

"True." My fingers skim across the line in my file, *Family: Deceased.* An ache rushes over my chest.

"It says I'm a fire wielder. What does that even mean?"

"I don't know." My mind flashes back to those people in the mall and then to Tristan with his flaming sword. "But I'm going to get answers no matter what."

"I've always wondered... No, I've always *known* we were different."

"It's not safe for us here anymore," I say. "Which is why tomorrow we need to escape before it's too late."

"That's a tall order. How are we even going to do that?"

"I'll find a way." I squeeze her hand. "I promise."

~

Did you enjoy the story?
If you enjoyed this story, I'd appreciate your time and effort
if you'd leave a review and share
with other readers what you loved about the book.

Bonus fun!
Would you like a little more? Head over to my website and
find out how you can get a special bonus scene with Estrella
and Dion. Plus, check out the bonus art!
https://christinafarley.com/the-immortal-bound-series/

Don't want the story to end?
Don't worry, you can read the next book in the series, THE
IMMORTAL HEART. It's full
of *more* action, *more* romance, and *more* intrigue!

Continue the Series!

THE
IMMORTAL
HEART

CHRISTINA FARLEY

YOUR NEXT ADVENTURE

The Immortal Heart (Book 2): Continue Estrella's journey!

The Dreamscape Series: A thrilling near-future adventure where your dreams are no longer safe.

The Gilded Series: A bestselling contemporary fantasy set in Korea.

The Princess and the Page: Get enchanted in this magical, fairytale mash-up set in France.

The Thief of Time: A magical school for librarians.

Fairy Tale Road: Choose your fairy tale ending in this adult romance where revenge, romance, and the allure of the unknown beckon at every turn.

About the Author

CHRISTINA FARLEY writes romantic fantasy and thrilling adventures inspired by her travels. When not wandering the world or creating imaginary ones, she spends time with her family in Florida where they are busy preparing for the next World Cup, baking cheesecakes, and raising a pet dragon in disguise as a very furry cat.

Visit her online:
ChristinaFarley.com
Instagram: @ChristinaLFarley
Facebook: @ChristinaFarleyAuthor
YouTube: @ChristinaFarley
TikTok: @ChristinaFarleyAuthor

Join Christina's Newsletter, the Travelogue: Exclusive access to videos, book updates, giveaways:
https://tinyurl.com/ypb9pm9a

STAY IN TOUCH

I hope you'll stay in touch by joining my newsletter group, The Travelogue, or VIP Reader Group so we can continue to take more adventures together. If you sign up, you'll receive a free book as my way of saying you're awesome.

Christina's Newsletter: Reader news, writing tips, giveaways, and book updates: https://tinyurl.com/ypb9pm9a

Christina's VIP Reader Club: Weekly update with insider news, exclusive content, and exclusive giveaways: https://tinyurl.com/mryncvmf

ACKNOWLEDGMENTS

I truly believe that each of us is special and carries our own inner magic. But sometimes there are those who might try to take away your magic and steal the thing that makes you unique. They might say you're not good enough, belittle, or reject you. But I'm here to tell you that I believe in you, and I know that you make this world a brighter, better place. These thoughts were what inspired Estrella's story.

Writing this book was a collaborative effort with many of my readers. This story began as a Kindle Vella serial and many readers voted on the events and characters in the story. Without them, Estrella's story would not be what it is today. I'm so grateful for their input in the story.

A special thanks goes out to my VIP Reader Group: Christy S, Laura P, Mila C, Beth G, Andrea M, Ava M, Kendra P, Laziz T, Ana B, Amanda F, Jennifer A, Aziza E, Marisela Z, Eva M, Jenny H, Christina V, Amber J, Shana D, Kelli J, Bert B, Dianna B, Tez M, Bri L, Candi M, Julianne J, Amy P, Kris D, Sheree W, Jamie G, Jan W, Stephanie B, Ells, Heath W, Willa Z, Sarah W, Theresa L, Adalyn B, Kirstian S, Jami, Jerry N, Kate H, Joyce K, Tiffany L, Vivi B, Alison R, Callie T, Sunny B,

Finely T, Margaret T, Billy F, Jocelyn M, Laziza T, and Merry M. You all are the best!

A huge thanks to Paul at Trif Book Design for your vision for my series and for creating such a stunning cover. I'm in awe of your talent. The gorgeous map is all thanks to Veronika Wunder. She really saw how to capture my vision of the land of the Nazco!

Thank you to my copyeditor, Sarah Ward, for making this manuscript shine to perfection. To my MiG Writing group, you are ever faithful through highs and lows: Andrea Mack, Debbie Ridpath Ohi, and Carmella van Vleet. Always, always to Amy Christine Parker and Vivi Barnes.

I could not still be writing without the support of my parents, brother, David, and sister, Julianne. They are always there to encourage and support me. To my boys who are always willing to talk through plot holes and help me overcome mental blocks. Plus, they never say no when I tell them we need to take a family trip for inspiration!

To the love of my life, Doug. I love our brainstorming sessions and appreciate you taking the time to always be there for me when I need you. You show me your love in the most unexpected ways. Can we arrange our next brainstorming session in Bora Bora?

As always, I'm thankful to God for giving me the strength and words to write each day. Every word is a gift, and I keep pinching myself I'm able to be writing and sharing stories.

* 9 7 9 8 9 8 6 4 6 2 4 3 1 *